THE
Bayside
HEROES
EMERGENCY MEDICAL TECHNICIAN
Fired
UP
USA TODAY BESTSELLING AUTHOR
K.K. ALLEN

THE Bayside HEROES

Fired UP

USA TODAY BESTSELLING AUTHOR

K.K. ALLEN

This book is a work of fiction. Names, characters, places, and incidents either are products of the author's imagination or are used fictitiously. Any resemblance to actual events or locales or persons, living or dead, is coincidental.

Cover Design: Kandi Steiner
Cover Photography: Perrywinkle Photography
Editing / Proofreading: Red Adept Editing
Formatting: K.K. Allen

Contact SayHello@KK-Allen.com with questions.

To first responders everywhere who put their lives at risk every day to help others. Your heroism inspired Asher's character. Thank you for all that you do.

PROLOGUE
ASHER

My chest feels like it's going to explode. Heat ripples through me with each push as my shoulders and triceps take the brunt of the impact. Just a little higher. A little more. Beads of sweat slide down my neck as I grunt out the last few inches of my strain.

"This is what you get for skipping the gym for two weeks, Moore. Let's go."

I glare up at Aaron Jacobs, my best friend and co-worker, who is spotting my bench press reps at the fire station's in-house gym. He's the worst kind of motivator—a tough-love kind of guy—but he's also providing the kick in my ass I know I need right now.

After regaining my focus, I use my last bit of strength to finish the press.

"Atta boy."

I let the bar down, and he helps me rack it. All the muscle tension I've been holding releases in one big whoosh. The second I get my breath back, I tip my neck back to catch the smug look on Aaron's face. "You don't have to be such a condescending asshole."

He chuckles. "Can't help it. I never thought you of all people would let an ankle sprain take you out for two weeks."

I sit up and shake my head. "It wasn't just the sprain. It was the damn back spasms that killed me. Chief threatened probation if I so much as set foot back in a gym until the doc cleared me."

I frown at the memory of the blast that forced me to jump from a second-story window. Not only did I land wrong on my feet, but I fell backward into a stack of rotting plywood. Everyone was too focused on the four kids my team had just rescued from the fire to poke fun at me then. But ever since, it's been nonstop harassment from my crew.

"Heard you missed the ladder, Moore. Better luck next time."

"I thought pussies always landed on their feet."

They didn't go easy. They *never* go easy.

Aaron chuckles. "Probably because your stubborn ass would have tried to hop straight into a fire on your one good foot. He knows you too well."

I'm not going to argue there. Chief Boone has been in charge at Station 24 in Tampa, Florida, during the five years I've alternated duties as firefighter and EMT. A father-son type of bond exists between us, especially after my pops passed away last winter, but the man is never afraid to remind me that he's my boss. If anything, he's harder on me than on most of the other guys here.

I stretch out my right leg and rotate my ankle slowly, testing the motion as my foot makes several circles.

"Look at that," Aaron says. "Now, you're good as new."

I wink at him. "Just in time for your wedding this weekend."

"That's right. Wouldn't want my best man limping down the aisle."

I scrunch my face and wave away his comment. "Nah,

who cares about that? In fact, the ladies would probably dig it. A wounded firefighter in a suit, in need of *lots* of tending to." I wink and hop onto my feet. "I was thinking more about the after-party." I move my ass to the old Justin Bieber hit streaming through the gym speakers. Something about getting peaches out in Georgia. "Oh yeah. The ladies aren't going to be able to resist these moves."

Aaron tosses his workout towel at my face and takes a seat on the bench. "You sure it was the fall that gave you those back spasms?" He points at my ass, which I haven't stopped shaking. "Or was it the way you throw that thing around?"

I stop in mid-move, make a face, and shrug. "No complaints yet."

"No women either."

The topic sours me instantly. I'm well aware of the drought that is my sex life, but after Sheena and I separated two years ago, I closed off the part of me that I'd given away too freely before. Now, even though the chains are broken, I can't forget the hell I went through to get here. That's one fire I can't see myself ever jumping back into.

"I was still technically married. It didn't feel right."

Aaron wrinkles his forehead. "You have no excuses now."

I shrug. "I'm not going to argue. I finally feel ready to get back out there, but I'm in no hurry to jump into another marriage."

"You say that now, but you're a commitment kind of man. You won't be single for long. It will just take the right woman. Until then, there's nothing wrong with a little casual sex."

I cringe at the thought of sleeping around. I married Sheena straight out of high school. Casual sex is not a concept I grasp easily.

"You've been through a lot," Aaron continues, "but it's

definitely time to get back out there. Sheena isn't the only woman you're ever going to love, but you're going to have a hell of a time finding the next one if you don't start looking. What's it been, two years since you got laid?"

I open my mouth and then snap it shut as heat rushes up my neck. "Not exactly."

Aaron's eyes widen. "You just said you didn't feel right..." I remain silent until Aaron connects the dots. "No fucking way. You slept with Sheena after you separated?"

I shake my head. "It didn't mean anything. It was the night the divorce was finalized. Emotions were high, and she wanted closure."

"Closure?" Aaron's voice is high-pitched. It takes a lot to shock my best friend. "It's not closure if the woman is still in love with you."

"It doesn't change the reality of our situation. You know I tried. Even after I found out about the infidelity, I tried. But at the end of the day, we both deserve to have the things we want in a relationship, and the two of us just aren't right for each other anymore."

Aaron sighs. "I'm with you, Ash. I'm just saying, Sheena already spent the last two years putting you through hell by stalling the divorce and then trying to get you to change your mind at the last minute. What makes you think she'll stop now?"

"Because we're divorced. It's over. And I'm ready to move on."

He studies me with worried eyes, like he fears I'll get roped back into what turned into a toxic situation of lies, deceit, cheating, and manipulation. He's not wrong to think the way he does. He was there for me through it all. What he doesn't yet realize is that while I may not be eager to jump into another marriage, I'm eager to move forward. I learned a lot about love and relationships from what I had with Sheena. I know what I want, what I don't want, and I know there's no rush. This time, I'm going to do things right.

I plant myself behind him in an obvious attempt to change the subject. "Stop delaying, Jacobs. You have a wedding to get buff for."

He gives me a cocky wink. "Becca knows what she's getting herself into. Now, that stair climb in a few weeks is another matter." He points at me as if remembering something. "Speaking of, have you secured a photographer for the calendar yet? They'll need to be at the climb."

I close my eyes and groan as dread fills me. "Shit. No, not yet. It completely slipped my mind with everything going on. I'll get on it."

Aaron and I have been talking about starting a charity together for years. We want to raise funds for burn victims and their families. One of our first ideas is to put together a firefighter calendar that we can sell at the end of the year. Our plan is rock solid, filled with the support of local radio stations that will give us free promotion as well as local businesses that will help with things like catering and securing venues for special events. The only thing missing is a photographer.

Aaron shakes his head. "You better. We don't have much time left."

I wave him away and point at the bench to shut him up. "I'll take care of it. Don't worry."

He glares as if he doesn't know if I'll pull through and then flashes me a grin before lying down on the bench. "Fine. Let's do this."

We're just about to jump on the treadmills for some cardio when the tones drop, alerting our fire and medic teams of an emergency. Just like always, the alarm chiming through the speaker system fuels the first dose of adrenaline that pumps through my veins, and I'm hyper-focused on all that comes next.

Our attention turns to the scrolling screen. Just by the red text, we know immediately we're heading to a traffic accident. Of what caliber, we have no idea. That's how the job is 98 percent of the time. Completely unpredictable. Mental preparedness is everything.

Instinct has us jogging through the narrow hallway, down to the main bay, and to our assigned vehicles. I grab my shirt off the side mirror of the ambulance, where I'd left it before my workout, and slip it on.

My paramedic counterpart today, Pete, climbs into the driver's seat at the same time I hop into the passenger seat. We exchange a nod while listening to the communication coming from dispatch, which details the scene we're about to approach. The gist of it—a foggy morning pileup on I-4. A mass-casualty incident. And we're the fourth crew to be called out.

"Shit. This isn't going to be pretty." I mutter the words while I simmer with sympathy, nervousness, and passion in equal measure.

As proud as I felt serving in the army, this is where I'm meant to be. With this crew, at this station, jumping into an endless variety of situations to help those in need—it's an honor beyond belief that I wouldn't trade for the world.

Pete turns on the flashers and sirens then shifts into drive. A second later, we're pulling onto E. Davis Boulevard, which is just a block away from Bayside Regional Hospital on Tampa's Davis Islands. We're a good four miles from this particular accident, but thanks to our location, we have a unique advantage to get to the front of the scene.

Pete maneuvers the city streets like a pro, flying past lavish Mediterranean-style buildings, pastel-colored condos, outdoor shopping centers, luxury marinas, and more. It's a ritzy town— that's for sure—but it also houses some of the best medical care in the world.

By the time we arrive at the scene, it's clear why we were called. We're going to need everyone we can get out here. There's got to be countless injuries, with the most severe happening right where we'll pulling up to park.

Holy fuck, what a disaster.

The traffic backup stretches beyond my line of vision. While one crew is already working to clear a temporary path for traffic to start moving, another is tending to injuries, and a third is loading up a passenger on a stretcher to make a beeline for the hospital. And since we got called, two other stations got the alert too.

From what I can see at first glance, there are two rolled cars, several more totaled, and about a dozen fender benders. I hop out of the ambulance. Smoke is everywhere, the smell of burned rubber and oil overwhelming my senses. The sound of a saw comes from where the rescue squad is already sawing open the door of a car to retrieve an unconscious driver. Crying comes from near the car, loud sobs as a teenage girl waits to see if her mom is going to make it out of this alive.

"Moore! Jeffries!" Chief Boone calls. We look up to find him pointing at the rescue squad from about fifty feet away. "You'll need the basket for transport. They're ready for you now!"

And just like that, Chief moves his attention elsewhere. At a scene like this, amid so much chaos, he will be all over the place.

"You got this?" Pete calls to me, already jogging toward our mission.

"On it." I unload the yellow basket stretcher, tuck it under my arm, and jog after him. At this point, my vision is a tunnel of exactly where I need to be while determining my quickest path to get there.

I weave around a collision near the shoulder and halt as a dark-haired woman trips over a bumper lying in the road and stumbles backward. Just before she teeters over and falls on her ass, I lurch into action and curl an arm beneath her to catch her.

She gasps and turns to me, her big green eyes just wide enough that I spot a swirl of gold within them. In a single glance, I can read her every emotion—surprise, fear, confusion, embarrassment. It's just a split second, but I see it all. And that's not all I see.

I see a rare beauty with thick brows, long, fluttering eyelashes, a cute button nose, strong cheekbones, and two perfectly luscious lips.

"Are you okay, miss?"

"Yes. I'm so sorry," she says. "I was just..."

It's my natural instinct to give the woman cradled in my arm a once-over to make sure she's okay. That's a mistake. She looks fine—better than fine. Maybe a little shaken up, but that could have easily been caused by running into me. Either way, she's a distraction that I need to tear myself away from immediately.

An internal chastising jars me back into hyper-focus mode. *You have a job to do, Moore.*

I start to lift her, steadying her until I'm certain she can stand on her own. "It's best to leave this area clear so our emergency crews can get through."

Her face darkens in a shade of obvious embarrassment. "I-I didn't know I was in the way." She backs up, wobbling a bit, but she's able to steady herself just fine. "I was taking photos for—"

My hand rises to stop her as my gaze falls to the professional camera in her hands. Frustration rumbles through me. Taking in her pink-and-gray suit dress, I would bet money that she's some sort of journalist or blogger. It all makes sense now.

My eyes narrow and meet hers again. "I can't tell you to put your camera away, but you should know you're only a distraction out here. There are lives at stake."

Her face twists with more confusion. "But I—"

"Moore, get your ass over here!" Chief booms.

"Back to your car, miss." My words come out much harsher than I intended, but I've dealt with the media enough to know how it works. They'll do anything to get the money shot, even if that means standing in my way.

I level her with a stern look and a final message. "If you have to take your pictures, do it from the side of the road."

Without another word, I step away from the woman and head toward the vehicle currently being sawed in half in hopes of salvaging whatever lives we possibly can.

By the time we get to Bayside Regional, the bloodied man on my stretcher is in critical care. He's unconscious with a bone protruding from his lower leg, and it seems he's not the only one in dire need of help.

Looking around, it's clear that this accident has become an all-hands-on-deck situation. Code T is the alert currently being transmitted over the emergency room speakers as Pete and I burst through the automatic sliding doors.

The adrenaline pumping through my veins has me moving quickly until I look up to find Beck Munroe, an internist and one of my closest friends, ready and waiting for the handoff.

"Open fracture, left lower leg, good pulse," I call out from the head of the gurney. "I've administered two milligrams of Dilaudid," I tell Beck, conveying the urgency of the man's condition by my tone.

Beck tells me he understands with a nod, and that's all the signal I need to step back to clear the way amid a flurry of activity.

As I walk through the doors of the ER and head back to the ambulance, a sense of unease washes over me, as it always does after I transfer a patient. Unlike the doctors at Bayside, I don't get to see these people through their care. I don't get to know if they make it out alive in the end.

I may have been dealing with medical trauma for upward of ten years, both here and back when I was in the army, but it never gets easier. Not every case is the same. Not every life can be saved. But I'll keep coming back every single day if that means I can play a small part in somebody's second chance at life.

"You all right there, Moore?" Pete asks when I climb into the ambulance beside him.

I turn to face him, not sure how to answer. "Can we ever be okay after something like that?" I shake my head. "I hope everyone makes it out okay." I reach for my seat belt. "Why?"

Pete shrugs and puts the vehicle in drive. "You seemed a little off at the accident scene. The way you yelled at that woman like you were all fired up—"

"She was in the way." I cut him a look and roll my shoulders, feeling the tension mounting, even though the hard part of our call is over. "Photojournalists love to jump on this stuff with no regard for the safety of others."

Pete shakes his head and lets out a laugh. "Dude, didn't you see her SUV? She'd been hit. She was just taking pictures of her car."

Dread hits me, and just like that, I feel like the biggest asshole in the world. "You're fucking with me."

Pete hits the gas and starts to drive us away from

Bayside Regional and the one block back to the station. "Definitely not."

"I was such an asshole."

He nods. "Yup."

I groan and roll the back of my head against the headrest. "Well, fuck. This day couldn't get much worse, could it?"

"I don't know, man," Pete says with another chuckle that has me confident that he'll be talking about this at the station later.

I'm going to get so much shit for this.

"That chick was superhot. And the way you caught her, all heroic and shit. That could have been a storybook meet-cute right there. You blew it, bro."

I glare at Pete, wondering when in the hell he became so confident that he could talk to his superior like that. "What the hell is a meet-cute?"

"You know," he says. "When a couple in a romantic comedy meet for the first time in a super cute way. My girlfriend is totally into all that stuff."

I huff and turn to face the window, trying to pull up a mental image of the woman from earlier today. Apparently, I had been too in the zone to recognize what had really been going on with her. "Yeah, well, I guess this is what you would call a plot twist." I hold my hands up like I'm reading a movie poster. "Guy meets beautiful girl. Guy is an ass and loses beautiful girl before he ever had a chance. Guy ends up old and alone. The end." I shrug, bitterness from my last relationship creeping into my chest. "Sounds about right, considering my luck."

Pete pulls into the open bay, parks, then claps me on the shoulder and squeezes. "Or maybe just don't be an ass next time."

I reach over to punch his chest, but he's already jumping out of the vehicle, leaving laughter in his wake.

I'm left alone in the ambulance, kicking myself for handling a situation in such an uncharacteristic way.

While it's hard to drum up an image of the woman to confirm Pete's assessment about her looks, those wide green eyes of hers might just haunt me forever.

Maybe Pete had gotten one thing right. Maybe I'd blown my chance before I even had one.

CHAPTER ONE

ASHER

"Ahh, I can smell the polished wood already." I take a dramatic sniff as a show for my buddy Greg's benefit and jab him in the side with my elbow. "This is just what you need, dude. You'll see."

We're approaching Shipwrecked, our favorite sports pub and meetup spot. My goal is to snap my friend out of whatever daze he's been in lately. Greg Weston is an anesthesiologist at Bayside Regional, so he's naturally a busy guy, but there's definitely something on his mind lately that I haven't been able to pry from him.

Greg twists his lips in amusement. "After the week we've had... yeah, you might be right."

"It'll be fun," I promise him again. If there's anything I'm known for among my friends, it's cheering them up when they're in whatever funk work or life brought upon them. I expect tonight will be no different.

We open the door and are immediately blasted with classic rock music coming from the surrounding speakers. It's mid-October, and hockey and basketball games play on the large television screens mounted on the walls. Loud voices fill all the empty spaces of the room, but the sound of pool balls cracking together then sinking into their rightful pockets serve as the true music to my ears.

After a long twelve-hour shift, a pit stop at Shipwrecked is a must, but it's on rare nights like these that I'm able to round up my closest friends from the hospital. Beck is already waiting for us on the other side of the bar. He's standing with Larsen Belle, a good friend of ours who also works at Bayside Regional, his head bent close to hers.

"Uh-oh," I mutter, elbowing Greg in his side. "Looks serious."

Greg glances in the direction I'm referencing and nods. "It does indeed."

The two of us share an all-knowing grin, a secret message playing between us. Whatever static is in the air is about to change.

Greg tosses an arm around Beck's shoulders while I approach Lars. "What's this I see? Getting friendly with good ol' Becky boy over here? I thought you don't have time for relationships, Dr. Belle."

Lars shoots me a glare, causing my smile to grow.

"I hate to break it to you guys," Greg starts, "but we're at a bar, not the hospital morgue."

Lars tosses Greg a smile, seemingly appreciative of the change in mood. As one of the clinical psychiatrists at Bayside Regional, her work hours are already stretched to the max.

Beck nudges Greg, a dash of annoyance flickering across his expression. "Get off, kid."

"I'm older than you, asshole," Greg quips back with a shove. "And nowhere near as broody."

We all get a laugh out of that, and I jump in, hoping to keep the amusement rolling. "What did the bartender say to the horse?"

"What?" Beck asks deadpan.

"Why the long face?" I puff out my chest, proud of that

oldie but goodie I've been hearing around the fire station as of late. I lean into Lars, waiting for her to give me props, too, but she just wrinkles her nose. Then I look around, scoffing at my unamused group of friends. The bartender, Harry, mutters a "Cheers, mate," and slides a glass over to me containing my usual order—Irish whiskey, neat.

I don't have to order. He knows the routine. My twenty-four-hour shift ends at the station, and Shipwrecked is my first stop before I head home for a long winter's nap. And when I can, I get my buddies to come along too. Since we all work grueling shifts in and near the hospital, it's nice to let off some steam.

"What?" I ask defensively. "Is this about the pileup last week?"

I don't even know why I ask. Usually when we have an all-hands-on-deck sort of event, it really fucks with our heads. For different reasons, of course, given our varying professions. Of course that's what's got them all tied up in knots.

"Here we go," Beck says with a groan. "Asher's dick is so big—"

"It was an intense morning," Lars adds, giving Beck a look of understanding.

Clearly, these two are having their own conversation. I try not to pay too much attention to it, still eager to change the mood. I walk over to Beck and lean against the bar beside him. "You're getting soft, Becky. That pileup was just another Tuesday morning for me." Lies, but I'm trying.

My nickname for Beck finally brings an honest chuckle from somewhere deep in his chest. I've known Beck for a long time, and while he's always been a little hard on himself, whatever is going on with him seems to be hitting him deep.

Lars continues throwing jabs at me, per usual, but it's all in good fun. I think it's because she likes me the best.

She makes some quip about me hiding a deep sense of inadequacy, and I use the opportunity to flex my bicep. "Nothing inadequate here. You're looking at Mr. January, remember?" I wink. "Cover guy."

Lars can't keep her cool any longer. "Oh, great," she says with a laugh before taking another sip of her drink to finish it off.

I haven't let my group of friends forget who was voted to be Mr. January in the calendar our station put out last year. We'd done it as a joke, but it's not a joke anymore, considering we were able to raise a significant amount of money for charity. That was the seed that had given Aaron and I the idea for the organization we've been putting together. Hence, the calendar that still needs a photographer. I growl internally at the way I've procrastinated to find one.

"You know you loved it, Lars," I say. "Tell you what—I'll even get you a signed copy of this year's calendar. All the guys. Gals too."

"Now I have something to look forward to," Lars says as she grabs a twenty and slides it across the bar. "On that note, I'm calling it a night. I've got an early morning tomorrow."

"Hey, that's not fair," Greg protests. "I just got here. I was *dragged* here against my will. If I have to stay, you do too."

I scoff at Greg's jab at me. Too bad for him, he's already enjoying himself. Mission accomplished.

Lars just gives a little finger wave to Greg, causing Beck to chuckle and start after her. "I'll walk you out, Lars." He turns around and nods to Greg and me. "Don't get too wild without me."

"Lightweights," I call out, realizing he's not coming back.

"Like a resident nurse," Greg adds.

Beck flips us off over his shoulder, and then they're gone.

"You're lucky I invited Owens, or I'd be bailing on you too," Greg tells me like it's a warning.

Sheesh, it's a tough crowd tonight. "Maybe it's you and your buddy who are the lucky ones. You're hanging out with Mr. January, remember?" I start to flex again, but Greg punches me in the arm.

And that's when I see her. Something about the dark-haired woman walking into the bar looking like she doesn't belong gets me all fired up. My gaze scrolls over her features slowly, trying to figure out why she looks so familiar. Her hair is long, parted down the middle with one side reaching the top of her breast.

I don't mean to ogle the woman—or at least, what I can see of her from the other side of the bar—but she's like a fucking bright orb in the darkest room. She's all I see, and I study her like she's the only thing I'll ever see.

She takes a seat at a booth in the front corner of the room, so far away that whoever she joined is partially blocked by a wood pillar. I consider approaching her, even though she's with company, not that I'd know what to say when I got there. It's been a long time since I've tried to talk to a female who isn't Lars, a co-worker, or one of my patients. Do I tell her she looks familiar? Do I ask if she fell from heaven? What do I say?

I'm practically panicking when I remember that I'm here with Greg, who's currently lost in whatever hockey game is playing on television.

"Hey, I know I joked about it, but... are you doing okay? After the accident last week?" I ask him. Something twists in my gut at my own memory of the horrific pileup.

He shrugs. "I'm fine."

I raise a brow. "That's convincing."

"I don't know," Greg says. "I have the same attitude you

do about it." He frowns. "Which I'm not sure is a good thing, but it's true. It's just another day at the hospital. I specialized in trauma when I was in Chicago for this exact reason—so that when I'm called in, I can be calm and do my job."

"Hear, hear," I say, clinking his glass with mine. "Still… you seem a bit off this week."

He lifts his shoulders and drops them heavily. "Just some stuff on my mind."

A guy I don't recognize approaches, and I realize instantly it must be Greg's infamous friend Dane Owns, who Greg had mentioned was coming.

"Sorry I'm late." Dane claps Greg on the back. Then he gestures at Harry, who's standing at the bar, and orders a drink.

My eyes flicker back to the woman on the other side of the room while Harry grabs Dane his beer of choice. I feel like I should know her. Certainly, I would remember meeting her. Again, I think about walking over to introduce myself, but seeing as I begged Greg to come here and Dane just joined us, I don't want to be rude.

"I can't believe it's taken us this long to meet," I say to Dane. "West here talks about you like you're his lover."

"He wishes," Dane teases.

I gather that Dane and Greg were roommates as undergrads and have stayed close. And Dane seems cool enough. He's into fishing and football like me, and he's all ears when I talk about the renovations I'm doing on my home.

At some point, Greg gets on a phone call, Dane is transfixed by something on the screen, and my focus goes back to the woman. The reason she looks familiar finally hits me. *She's the woman from the accident.* How could I have forgotten?

Shit. I lean back in my seat as I recall the last time I'd seen her. I'd been a complete asshole, thinking she was a photojournalist when really, her car had just been rear-ended and she was taking photos for insurance purposes. The way I'd jumped to conclusions that day was very unlike me.

Then again, I'm still trying to figure out who *me* is. My separation from my ex-wife was one thing, but finalizing the divorce was an entirely new beast. Sure, I still have my same friends, and I was able to put a hefty down payment on a fixer-upper home, but I feel like a failure for the way my marriage ended.

No matter what, I shouldn't have taken it out on that beautiful woman, who is now infiltrating my mind and my bar. She'd come to Shipwrecked. If that isn't a sign that I need to talk to her, then I don't know what is.

CHAPTER TWO

MEADOW

Two hours earlier

W*hat a freaking week.*

The Davis Drive streetlights reflect an array of colors against the wet asphalt as I pull my rental into the parking lot of a local bar where I'm to meet a friend. After getting run off the road in a horrific highway pileup last week, my car is finally out of the shop. Since then, I've had to deal with police reports, insurance claims, and pissed-off clients whose appointments I've missed throughout the week because of the hassle. I deserve a drink. Or two. Maybe three.

"You made it!"

I look up to see my friend Becca waving at me from a booth against the side of the room.

I smile and quicken my steps toward her, happy to find a full drink on my side of the table. "Is that what I think it is?" I ask and gasp with delight.

"Whiskey sour on the rocks."

"You remembered," I gush, genuinely emotional over

the fact that my old friend remembered my drink order from our college days at UCF.

Becca jumps up from her seat with a little shriek. "It's so good to see you." She wraps her arms around me and pulls me in for her signature hug. It's just how I remember it from back in the day. Warm, strong, loving. She's like a soul whisperer, the way she tugs all the emotions to the surface with that one embrace.

"It's so good to see you, Bec. It's been too long."

She pulls away, still gripping my shoulders, her expression flooding with empathy. "What are the odds you'd get into a wreck the same week you move here?" She narrows her eyes at mine like she's trying to read them for clues. "You okay?"

I let out a small laugh and take a seat across from her. "I'm exhausted. I've had a lot of photo shoots to make up for because of that horrific accident. It's been one thing after the other ever since. Physically, I'm fine, though. I just hope everyone else is okay too." I shudder at the visual that just passed through my mind. "They had to use a saw to get a man out of a car. I don't even know if he's still alive. It was awful, Bec."

She frowns and reaches for her drink. "I'm glad it wasn't worse for you. I hear so many stories from Aaron. He's always warning me to avoid that turnoff on foggy mornings, like the one you got caught in. Those guys just know what to expect by this point. I would have warned you if I knew you were heading that way."

I give her a small smile. "You cannot control my fate, Becca Ann. You never could, and you never will."

She folds her arms while giving me a smug smile. "That's what you think. You're in my territory now, which means you need me. I'll show you around, introduce you to people..." She grins. "And you have a sitter for little Tate whenever you need one. Just ask."

I tilt my head, wondering how I had ever managed without my friend all these years. Our distance has been entirely my fault. After Milton and I married, he graduated from the police academy, and we moved around from city to city, to wherever a new opportunity took him. So while Becca and I spoke often and had seen each other a handful of times, she's never even met my little boy.

"Shouldn't you be focusing on your wedding first? We can talk about babysitting later." I take a sip of my drink and sigh as I feel my entire body relax. "Oh God, I needed this."

"Good. Drink up." Becca leans forward and smiles. "Speaking of my wedding. I have a job opportunity for you."

I perk up and lean forward. "You need a photographer?"

She laughs and shakes her head. "No, you're a guest at my wedding. I will not let you work. Besides, we already signed a contract with someone long before I knew you were moving here. I have a different job opportunity. Kind of. This is with someone who will be at my wedding."

I lean back, ready to hear it. "Considering I blew it with two of my new clients today, I'm listening."

"Well, Aaron and his buddy have been working on this fundraising venture to help burn victims and their families. They got this crazy idea to put together a firefighter calendar that they'll sell to raise money for their charity. But they still need a photographer." Becca searches my eyes, and I know she's assessing my reaction. "It wouldn't require too much of your time, and they would be so grateful. They'll pay for all your supplies, your food, any lodging required, and your gas. It wouldn't put you out of pocket at all."

As soon as I get the gist of what she's asking and realize the job would require me to volunteer my time, my gut churns. I set my drink down, my eyes lingering on the amber liquid, before I pull in a deep breath and let it out slowly. "Becca," I start then flip my lids up to look back at her. "I'm so flattered that you thought of me, and it sounds like such a great idea, but I don't think I'm the right fit."

She looks visibly dejected. "What? No. You're the perfect fit. I was just looking through your website again, and I've never been so stunned over photographs before. The way you use lighting to capture your subjects is just awe-inspiring. They're strangers to me, but it's like I can see their souls. As soon as Aaron told me they still need a photographer for the calendar, I immediately thought of you."

Guilt and embarrassment swarm through me. "That's so sweet of you to say, but I still don't think I'm the right person for the job."

She presses her shoulders back and regards me with a challenge. "Why not?" This is the Becca I remember. Adamant, persistent, yet supportive in every way. Which is why I should just come out with the real reason.

"It's just—money has been tight ever since Milton died. He didn't tell me about the kind of debt he was in before we married. It was a sore subject, especially with a baby on the way. My photography business did okay, but it didn't cover what I had to pay to the credit companies and what-not. The only way out of it was to sell the house, use the equity to pay off what he owed, and move in with my mom for a bit. Anyway,"—I shake my head, not wanting to sour our happy reunion—"that's the main reason we moved back home. Between finding new clients and caring for Tate, I can't even imagine taking on something so important."

Becca sinks back, looking dejected. "Oh, Meadow, I'm so sorry. I had no idea." She looks over my shoulder for a bit like she's in deep thought and then looks back at me. "I hate what you've been through. I wish there was a way I could help."

I shake my head. "You are too sweet, but it's not your responsibility. I think moving here was the right thing to do. Tate is young enough that he can make new friends easily, and the area is so beautiful I'm sure I'll find clients in no time."

Becca nods. "I'm certain you will too." She opens her mouth and then snaps it shut again.

"What?" I ask with a laugh.

She sighs. "I mean, the calendar is totally Aaron's thing, but I can't help but think it's a great opportunity to get your name out there. He knows a lot of people, most of whom have families. And they'd only need you for a few hours here and there. I really don't think it would take away from your normal schedule too much. And I'm sure they'd let you bring Tate if you wanted to." She tilts her head, her eyes wide with hope. "Are you sure you don't want to at least think about this?"

The possibility that an opportunity like this could help me find paying clients carries some weight. "I don't know, Bec."

She holds up her hands, her eyes lighting up. "Say no more. I'm going to give Aaron your information so he can tell you all the details. It's not like you have to make a decision today. And if you still think it's a bad idea, no hard feelings."

It won't hurt to hear more. Besides, it will be much easier to reject Aaron than it is to refuse Becca, so I drop the resistance—for now. "I really appreciate it. Thank you for thinking of me."

She covers my hand with hers. "Always. Now, tell me about Tate. Where is the little guy, anyway?"

"With my mom. She took him on a cruise for the week so I could get settled. They're having a blast. Look." I pull out my phone to the last message my mom sent me. She'd attached a picture of Tate staring into the camera, his smile as big as the sun. He's wearing arm floaties, and his face is smeared with sunblock. My mother can never be too cautious.

"They look like they're having so much fun," Becca says, "and I'm sure she's thrilled you two are here to stay."

"That, she is." I smile, grateful to have such a supportive mom who is crazy about her grandson. "I should have accepted her help years ago, but I was too stubborn. I thought I could make it on my own."

Becca's jaw drops. "You have been making it on your own. Give yourself some credit, Meadow. You run an incredibly successful photography business. That's more than I can say for myself. There's no shame in wanting to be somewhere you have support. And Tate needs his grandma in his life now more than ever. You made the right decision."

"I know, I know." I sigh and tilt my empty glass. "Another one? This one's on me."

The conversation moves fluidly from one topic to the next, but we mostly focus on her wedding and all the events leading up to it. It sounds like it's going to be a classy affair, with all the bells and whistles intact. I love hearing about how she selected the venue and the elaborate effort put into choosing the food, cake, and flowers. Milton and I had none of that at our quick elopement after finding out I was six weeks pregnant. At the time, all I cared about was marrying before I gave birth, but I would have loved to have the big, fancy wedding with all my friends and relatives in attendance.

"I cannot wait to see you in your dress," I tell Becca when we're parting ways at the table. "I'll be the girl in the back row without a date."

Becca laughs. "Good. That means I can set you up with

someone. In fact..." She studies me with narrowed eyes. "Aaron's buddy is superhot, divorced, and ridiculously nice. In fact..." She pauses and looks around the room, but we can't see much of the bar from where we're sitting. "He frequents this place. Maybe he's here."

"Hmm, let me guess. Firefighter?"

She peers back at me with innocent ideas. "Yes, but—"

I laugh. "I'm going to pass."

Becca groans. "Oh, Meadow. Really? You have a thing against all public service men now?"

"I don't have a thing against them." I smile. "I just don't need that anxiety again. The waiting up all night for them to come home when their shift finally ends. The watching the news and worrying that every incident might involve them." I look up and realize how insensitive I just was to get lost in my feelings when Becca is about to marry a firefighter. "Oh God, Bec, I'm sorry."

She dismisses my worry with a wave of her hand. "What have I told you? You don't pick 'em. The universe does." She looks down at her buzzing phone. "That's Aaron. We're taking our last dance class tonight." She giggles, stands up, and gives me one last hug. "Gotta go."

"See you Saturday," I call out. "At your wedding," I add for extra effect.

She's practically at the exit when she hears me, turns around, and covers her mouth like she can't even believe the sound of my words. "I'm getting married," she says, her excitement radiating from her.

Laughing, I walk up to the bar and wait for the bartender to notice me. After all that talking, I forgot to order a single thing to eat. When he finally takes my order, I ask for a drink to go with it. I might as well have one more while I wait.

I'm opening my wallet when a tall figure slides up beside me to talk to the bartender. "This one's on me,

Harry," the man says, his voice thick and smooth like honey.

I look up to find an incredibly handsome man with light, wavy brown hair and mild scruff covering his strong jaw up to his cheeks. He's dressed in a plain white T-shirt and jeans, but the man is anything but casual. He peers down at me with a familiar, heart-stopping gaze, and it's in that moment when our eyes meet that I realize I've seen him before.

Instantly, my mood turns sour as I recall the harsh words he'd said to me last week, turning a terrible morning into something much worse. Not only had I almost gotten leveled by the guy after that car accident, but he'd made me feel guilty for being there to begin with. Like I could have helped it.

I lean over the bar to catch Harry's attention at the register and wave my hand until he looks at me. "Do not let this man pay for me."

Harry shrugs and slides me a fresh drink. "Sorry, love. Too late. It's already been put it on this lad's tab."

When I look back over at the man, I regret it. He flashes me a smile. A sweet, innocent, and friendly smile that makes me want to do the opposite of hate him.

"Please," he says. "It's the least I can do after how I spoke to you last week."

I fold my arms and narrow my eyes. "I was just taking photos of my mutilated car, thank you very much. I'm a photographer, but I wasn't working at the accident."

He cringes and nods. "I realized that too late, and I'm an ass for that."

"But you wouldn't let me explain."

"When I saw the professional camera, I jumped to the wrong conclusion. I'm sorry."

"It didn't occur to you that maybe that professional camera was for my *profession*?"

He holds up his hands. "It didn't. I get pretty intense when I'm working." His gaze flickers over me the way it did last week when he was cradling me in his arms. "Are you okay? You weren't injured or anything?"

I shake my head. "I'm one of the lucky ones." I watch his eyes flicker like he's picturing the same scene I am. "How did everyone else make out?"

He lets out a heavy breath. "Surprisingly okay. No deaths, thank goodness. I'm glad you escaped unharmed." He shifts his weight, his eyebrows bunching together in the middle. "You should know that I don't normally speak to people like that, especially beautiful women."

My cheeks heat as my eyes search his, trying to figure out if he's hitting on me or just being sweet because he feels bad. I accept the latter explanation and relax some. "Well, thank you for the apology. I wasn't expecting to ever see you again."

He looks around. "You must be new around here. My buddies and I frequent this joint." He nods to a booth in the back of the room occupied by a well-built man with dark hair and a thick beard, then he turns back to me and narrows his eyes. "I definitely would have noticed you."

"You caught me. I grew up around here, but I just moved back from California."

"Ah," he says while leaning his side against the bar. "What for? Work? Family?"

I let out an uncomfortable laugh. Not because I'm uncomfortable with this beautiful man but because I'm not used to talking at length with strangers. Especially ridiculously good-looking ones. "Both, I guess."

"So, you're a photographer, huh?"

"I am."

"Do you have a card or something? I'd love to check out your work."

"Not on me at the moment. Sorry."

He tilts his head. "What kind of photography?"

Something about his curiosity and flirtatious demeanor spark something deep in my chest. Excitement, maybe. It's been a long time since I felt open to bantering with a member of the opposite sex. I'd almost forgotten about the bubbly feeling that goes hand in hand with my racing pulse. But then I remember that he only came over because he felt guilty for his earlier behavior. That's all it takes to talk myself out of entertaining his prolonged apology.

"You don't have to do this, you know?"

He looks genuinely confused. "Do what?"

I gesture between him and me. "This. Make nice because you feel bad for earlier. You apologized. You bought me dinner." I smile to let him know I mean it wholeheartedly. "You're forgiven."

"What if I don't want to be forgiven so soon?"

I'm a little afraid to take the bait on that one. "Then I'd say that you're doomed to a lifetime of disappointment."

His smile almost blinds me, and I'm not the only one who notices it. A gaggle of girls on the other side of the bar gaze at him like he's some sort of rock god. I tear my eyes away from them and look back at him as he runs his fingers through his thick hair. The movement shouldn't drive me to press my thighs together from the warmth that builds between them, but it absolutely does. But that's not all. I catch a whiff of his scent, too—even that is perfection. It's like he just showered in some rich spa filled with tropical fruits and the ocean breeze.

I've been around this man for less than ten minutes, and all my senses are coming alive as if for the first time, and everything about that is terrifying.

I swallow, hoping that when I speak again, I don't sound as flustered as I feel. "Okay then, well..." I lift my glass in a toast. "Here's to you and your guilty conscience, I guess."

His eyebrows bend together. "That's not fair. I didn't bring my drink over."

Just then, Harry sets a bag of food on the counter. I eye it then take a swig of my drink. "Hate to break it to you..." I snatch the bag while setting my drink down. "But life is anything but fair."

With a final glance at the gorgeous specimen of a man I hope to never see again, I give him a tilted smile and a nod. "Thanks for dinner."

CHAPTER THREE

ASHER

Not a second after the woman walks away, I realize I never even asked for her name. I twist my neck to stare at the doorway she's walking through and have a long debate with myself about whether I should go after her. Instinct has my muscles twitching, but experience freezes me on the spot.

There's no question she's beautiful, with dark hair that frames her heart-shaped face and lashes so long they pull me straight into her big green eyes. To top it off, she was nice enough to accept my apology without too much grief. But my inexperience with dating has done more harm than good in the confidence department.

I turn back around to find Harry setting down a glass of whiskey I'd never ordered.

"Thought you could use that." He winks, clearly referencing the woman I just totally blew it with.

"Thanks, Harry. You're a mind reader."

He nods and whips a towel from his back pocket to begin wiping down a glass.

Back at the high-top, I sit down in my stool across from Dane and hand him a new drink. I can't believe I just met the guy tonight. He fits right in. Apparently, he's been pretty unhappy in his job and might end up as a security guard at Bayside Regional, which would be cool.

"Thanks, dude."

"No problem." I hold up my whiskey, and he meets me halfway to clank glasses. "Thanks for sticking around. I saw someone I recognized at the bar and wanted to say hi."

Dane quirks a brow. "Saw that. You get her number?"

My glass is pressed to my lips when I chuckle and shake my head. I take a quick swig and set it back down. "Didn't even get her name."

He widens his eyes and whistles. "That's a shame. What if you never see her again?"

"What makes you think I want her number?"

Dane sits up straight, a sly smile tipping his cheeks. "Maybe it was the way you fucked her with your eyes. You weren't hiding it well."

My phone buzzes before I can give him a smart retort. "Shoot. I need to check this. One second."

Ignoring the lingering thoughts I have for the mystery woman, I pull out my phone and tap to read a new message from Aaron.

Becca knows a photographer. She says to call her.

Okay, I type back quickly. *Send me her info.*

I will.

Wish me luck.

You need more than luck. The stair climb is in less than a month.

Annoyance shakes through me at yet another reminder of the ball that I dropped.

Don't you have a dance class to skip off to?

You're just jealous my moves will be better than those back-breaking ones of yours.

I chuckle and shake my head.

Oh, it's on.

Call her, he types again. *From what Becca says, you'll need to talk her into working with a bunch of sweaty Tampa firefighters.*

My lip tips up on one side in a half smile. *Is that how you want me to word it? What if she says no?*

Then I guess you have less time to find someone else. Let me know how it goes.

The next message is a contact card. *Meadow Matthews* is the woman's name. There's also a website address, so I click it and open up a gallery of photos featuring a variety of studio and outdoor shots, most of which feature families, newborns, or newly engaged couples. But when I tap on a link for *fantasy*, I immediately understand what makes this woman stand out from the rest. Each photo in this gallery is enhanced with some type of supernatural element, whether it's butterfly wings on a baby or an engagement photo set on the moon. My imagination goes wild when I think about all the possibilities that having a talent like Meadow would open up for our calendar shoot.

I look up to find Dane's eyes on the television.

"Sorry," I say. "I'm organizing a fundraising event, and I dropped the ball recently. I'm trying to secure a photographer, and my buddy just gave me her information."

"Oh yeah?" Dane asks, appearing interested. "What's the event?"

I let out a laugh. "A firefighter calendar." Before Dane can react, I launch into my brief rundown. "Our station put together a calendar as a joke last year. Super low-budget because we didn't expect much to come from it. And man, those babies sold like hotcakes all over the area. The local radio station even picked up the story. So we took all that money and donated it. This year, my buddy Aaron and I are organizing the event for real. Bigger budget, and we're donating the proceeds to the Burn Foundation to help burn victims and their families."

Dane looks impressed. "That's some hero shit right there. Anything I can do to help?"

I knew I liked the guy the moment we started chatting. "If you're free at the end of the month, we're having a stair climb at Raymond James Stadium. There's an entry fee, and then each squad has a landing page where donations can be made. Dollar a step."

Dane nods. "I need to check my schedule. If I get this job at the hospital, I'm not sure what my hours will be."

We exchange numbers, and I shoot him a message with all the details.

When Dane heads to the bathroom, my thoughts immediately return to the photographer I'm supposed to contact. I take another sip of my whiskey and contemplate what I'll even say. Text messaging is probably not the most professional method of communication, but neither would be calling her from a loud bar. I could wait until tomorrow to call, but I've already put this off long enough. Ending my internal debate, I start tapping out a message.

Hi, Meadow. This is Becca's friend Asher. I just looked through your impressive photo gallery on your website. You have a new fan.

I cringe at the corniness of my own message but send it anyway. Icebreakers are always so awkward. I'm nearly done with my drink when I finally get a response.

Hi, Asher. Thank you. I'm flattered :)

A whoosh of relief flows through me as I start tapping out another message.

Did Becca tell you about the calendar project Aaron and I are working on?

She did. I think what you're doing for burn victims is incredible.

I don't know why I sense a *but* coming, so I jump in before she can add it.

I'd be happy to give you more information. I'm on the

hunt for the right photographer, and your skills are unmatched.

That is so sweet of you to say, but I'll tell you what I told Becca. I'm not sure I'm the right fit.

My heart sinks for purely selfish reasons. I'd procrastinated on my task of securing a photographer, and now my one and only lead is a dud. We're cutting it way too close.

Can I ask why?

The silence that follows feels more awkward than the icebreaker, and by the time Dane and I settle the bill and walk out of Shipwrecked, I still haven't heard back from Meadow. As soon as I'm in my car and heading north on I-275, away from Davis Islands, I call Aaron. He should be done with his dance lesson by now.

"What's up?"

"Hey," I start. "You sure this Meadow woman is interested in the gig? She seems pretty hesitant, and I haven't even told her what it entails."

Aaron sounds like he's talking to someone else, probably Becca. "Yeah, sorry, man. Becca says Meadow was sorta hesitant when they talked about it earlier. I guess with her just moving here, it will be hard for her to volunteer when she needs the time to start up her business."

I frown. "But this gig would be the best thing for that. Think about how many of these guys have families or are getting married soon."

"Yeah—oh, hold on. Becca wants me to put you on speaker."

I hear shuffling before Becca's voice comes on the line. "Hey, Ash."

"Hey, Bec. Okay, so give me the lowdown about your girl. We're running out of time here. How do I convince her?"

Becca chuckles. "Oh no, don't put all the pressure on me because you procrastinated."

"You had one job, Moore!" yells Aaron, who sounds far off in the background, probably because he's grabbing a beer from the fridge.

I cringe. "Look. I was injured and on painkillers for two weeks. Give me a pass on this one."

"Didn't you start back to work last week?"

Becca's question causes a frustrated growl to rumble through me. "Yes, and I've been searching high and low ever since."

"Fine," Becca says, still laughing. "You get a pass, but that doesn't change Meadow's answer. She's open to hearing more, but don't push, okay? She's been through a lot lately, and this move is a pretty big deal for her. Your best bet is to stress how you can work with her schedule and how the gig would only help her grow her business, but maybe you should consider finding someone else."

Feeling dejected, I take Becca's words seriously. "You got it, Bec. Thanks for the lead, anyway. She really is talented."

"She's incredible. The thing is she doesn't even realize just how incredible. She's always been that way. Modest to a fault."

"I'll keep that in mind."

The three of us hang up, and I drive the rest of the way home in silence. I pull up to my home in Ybor City. The porch lights are still on from when I left for my shift yesterday, illuminating the half columns along the front of the wide porch and the fully grown royal poinciana tree with its bright-green, furry leaves and red flowers on the side of the drive. The house itself is a total work in progress, but that was why I bought it. When I'm not working, there's sure to be a project to keep me busy.

When I check my phone again, I realize Meadow still hasn't responded, and then I read what I wrote last and feel like an ass for asking her reason for not wanting the job. I lie down on my couch and try to think of a way to redeem myself.

Sorry, I text. *Your reasons are none of my business. I only asked because if it's your availability, that's something we can work with.*

I'm surprised to see bubbles immediately pop up, indicating that she's already responding.

I was on the phone. Not ignoring you. I guess I would feel awful if I was the cause for any delays. My life is sort of a disaster at the moment.

Something about her response tugs at my chest. It's like I can relate to this woman, even though I don't even know her. For reasons beyond me, I type the next message.

Well, you couldn't be in safer hands. My profession requires me to handle disasters well.

I smile when the bubbles pop up again.

You might handle fires just fine, but my life is more the rubble that comes after the fire. I'm still figuring out how to sort through the debris.

I can tell she's making a joke, but again, I feel that tug in my chest. Instinct has me wanting to push her harder, to call her and convince her somehow to just take the job, and we'll figure out the details later. But then I remember Becca's words. "*Don't push, okay? She's been through a lot lately, and this move is a pretty big deal for her.*"

With a heavy sigh, I know I need to back off.

I'll tell you what. Take a few days to think about it. If you want more information, you have my number. I can't start looking for a new photographer until next week, anyway. But no pressure if you can't commit right now.

A few minutes go by while I wait for the message bubbles to turn into text.

Thank you. I promise I'll think about it.

I bite down on my lip, my desire to get this woman to

say yes stronger than I can make sense of. Yet I have no choice but to sit back and hope she comes around.

How about we meet up at the wedding? You can tell me your answer then.

This time the silence lasts too long, so I start to panic.

I assume you'll be there since you're Becca's friend and all, I add.

When she still doesn't respond right away, I head to the kitchen to grab a beer then head back to my couch and pick up my phone to see that she'd sent another text.

I guess I'll see you there.

With a big smile, I take a swig of my beer then type back.

Looking forward to it.

CHAPTER FOUR

MEADOW

"We home tomowo!"

Tate's little voice squeals with excitement over the phone line. Tears well in my eyes as I realize my three-year-old is trying to convince me that it's okay, that a week apart isn't too much to handle. As much as I appreciated the time to get us settled, it feels like part of me is missing.

"Did you have a good day?"

"Mm-hmm. I wuv vacation."

A laugh bursts straight from my chest at the sound of him repeating something he surely heard my mom say. "I just miss you so much, my Tater Tot."

"I miss you, Mommy."

I hear my mom shuffling to get close to the phone. "Tell Mommy what you saw this morning."

Tate gasps like she just triggered his memory. "We see'd dofins!"

A tear leaks from my eye, and I swipe it away with a laugh at his excitement. "Oh, that's so cool. Bring one home for Mommy, okay? I want to see a dolphin too."

I hear my mom in the background feeding him more answers.

Tate lets out a high-pitched giggle. "No, Mommy. Dofin in da ocean."

I can imagine the serious scrunched-up look on his face as he lectures me. "Okay, then take some pictures for me instead."

"Otay, Mommy." He gets quiet for a second. "I wuv you."

My heart aches. "I love you too. I'll be waiting for you as soon as you get off the ship tomorrow, okay?"

He gasps as if he remembers something. "Gwamma and me on a boat."

"I know, buddy. That sounds like so much fun. And I hear you're going to a party tonight."

Tate starts to make zoom noises like he's playing with one of his Transformers, so my mom takes over the call. "He's already dressed up in his little suit. We're going to dinner, and then I'll let him hang out in the daycare room for an hour while they party it up, toddler style."

I laugh. "I bet that's a sight. He sounds so happy, Mom. Thank you for taking him with you this week."

"He's been the best little buddy. He definitely misses you, though. What about you? You getting all settled in?"

I don't want to worry my mom by telling her about all the difficulties I've had with my clients courtesy of the fender bender from last week. "I am. Work is already keeping me busy, and I think Tate will love what I did with his room. Oh, and I met up with Becca the other night. It was so nice to see her before her big day."

"Oh gosh," my mom exclaims. "That's today. You must be getting ready to go."

I walk in front of the full-length mirror in my bedroom and pat down my rose-red satin dress. It's an off-the-shoulder number with a cinched top and one full sleeve that puffs out around my wrist. The skirt portion is a floor-length dress in the back that slants into a miniskirt in the front, exposing one full leg up to my thigh. I chose tan heels with an ankle strap and left my almost-black hair parted down the middle to frame my face in long, thick layers.

"All dressed. I wanted to call early since I won't be able to talk tonight."

"Give Becca a hug for me. And Meadow..." I can hear the warning in my mom's voice before the familiar lecture comes. "Don't sit in the corner all night. Smile. Enjoy yourself. You deserve to have fun. Who knows, maybe you'll meet someone there."

I'm internally cringing as I do every time my mom says the exact words to me before I step out of the house. There's nothing like being thirty-three, single, and having your mom eagerly awaiting your next engagement.

"I promise to smile and have fun."

"Good," she says before telling Tate to take something out of his mouth. "Can't wait to hear about it tomorrow."

I say goodbye to Tate one more time before I hang up, grab my purse, and head to the venue. It's an elegant outdoor wedding set in front of a rustic, open-door barn. Pops of fall colors are everywhere, from the flower arrangements to ribbons strung through the trees and cloth wrapped around the tables and chairs.

I'm seated near the back on the aisle, so I have a clear view of everything. When Becca learned that I was moving home, even though we hadn't seen each other in years, she still wanted to make me a part of her wedding. I knew letting her bring me on as a bridesmaid would be too much, considering my move and her plans that were already in motion, so I assured her I was fine with being a guest. Still, I would have loved to be part of this setup. I look around in awe. Clearly, not a single thing was overlooked.

An orchestra plays from the side of the gazebo, and

when the music switches to start the ceremony, my heart is in my throat. I can't wait to see Becca walk down the aisle. Back in grade school, when we would have sleepovers at each other's homes, we would throw fake weddings. She was always the bride while I threw petals in her wake. Today, her vision will finally come to life when she marries the man of her dreams.

When the final groomsman walks through the thin fabric opening of the tent, I have to blink twice to make sure my eyes are working correctly. *It's him.* The jerk EMT guy who turned out to not be a jerk at all. In fact, he was actually kind of sweet.

My pulse quickens, and my palms feel all sweaty. It takes me a minute to realize my reaction has to do with how exceptional this man looks in a suit. All men look great dressed up like that, but *him?* He's simply mouthwatering. The way his black pants wrap his muscular legs like they could be glued to him, revealing every small movement. The way his thin seafoam green tie lies flat against what I imagine are washboard abs beneath a crisp, white button-down. And that's just his attire.

His chiseled jaw wears the same scruff I saw him with last, only it looks like the edges have been cleaned up a bit. His big steel-gray eyes hold the same wide-eyed innocence he carried when he was joking with me in the bar. And when he links arms with a bridesmaid at the start of the aisle, my eyes stay glued to him. I swear, after he offers her a polite smile, her cheeks redden with obvious lust. Then again, who wouldn't blush when they looked at him?

I remember the air that left my body when our eyes first collided and the way his fresh scent enveloped me when we were near. His friendly demeanor was almost irresistible. Almost. The man is charming, and that makes him dangerous, but I'd be lying to myself if I didn't admit wanting to know more about him.

He makes his way past me, parts ways with the bridesmaid, and takes his spot at the end of the line of groomsmen. He looks back down the aisle, toward where Becca should be appearing at any moment, and that's when he spots me.

My heart catches in my throat as a smile blooms on his face.

It's just my luck that I would run into this man, yet again. The only difference is that this time there's no escaping him.

I'm still swiping tears from my eyes when the wedding party escapes inside its tent. The ceremony was gorgeous, and Becca looked stunning in her long-train princess dress. I can't wait to give her a giant hug when she finally arrives at the reception.

We're all ushered away from the ceremony seating and toward the reception area, which is complete with a long buffet, round tables, a stage with a DJ, and an empty dance floor that will surely be full as soon as the drinks start flowing. By the hooting and hollering that went on during the bride and groom's kiss, the reception is sure to be a lively one.

The bar is packed already, so when a man in a tux walks by holding a tray of champagne, I take a flute with a thankful smile. A little liquid courage will go a long way right about now.

I may have grown up in the area, but Becca was the one who stayed close with most of our friends from grade school and college. So while there are several familiar faces, I definitely feel the anxiety of attending a wedding alone.

"I'm trying to figure something out, and I'm hoping you can help."

The moment I hear his voice, goose bumps shoot up all over my skin. I take a moment to breathe then turn around to look up at the devilishly handsome groomsman.

I tilt my head, amused. "Figure out what exactly?"

"What the universe is trying to tell us by putting us in the same place three times now."

I do my best to ignore the flipping in my chest. "Maybe the universe wants us to know that we have mutual friends who just got married? I must admit, though, it is quite the coincidence."

The man crinkles his nose, and he shakes his head. "I don't believe in coincidences." He narrows his eyes like he's thinking hard. "How do you know Aaron and Becca?"

"Becca and I went to grade school together, and she was my roommate in college. You?"

"Aaron and I work together."

Something clicks in my brain like I've already made the connection, but I can't seem to put my finger on it. "I don't know. It just sounds to me like we share mutual friends."

"You're such a skeptic."

I laugh. "What else could it be?"

"Fate."

A heat wave slams my body while he shrugs like the word isn't at all too magical to believe in.

"Think about it," he says, his eyes narrowing with playful excitement. "Out of all the bars in Tampa, you just so happened to be at Shipwrecked the other night."

"And how do you know I'm not already a regular?"

He flashes me a grin. "Because *I'm* a regular, and *you* just moved back to Tampa from California."

I bite down on my lip to stifle my smile. "Ah, you remember."

He nods, his metal-gray eyes peering deeply back into mine. "I do."

I suck in a breath from the electricity sizzling between

us. The air feels thick and humid. To make it worse, there isn't a cloud in sight, so the only breeze comes from the surrounding fans.

"Dane was giving me shit for not asking you for your number."

I practically choke on my next sip of champagne. "That guy you were with?"

"That would be the one."

I give him a small smile. "Well, I wouldn't have given you my number, anyway. I don't give my number to men I meet in bars. It's just a rule I have."

He frowns, the lines in his forehead scrunching together. "What about weddings?"

I laugh. "The chances are better, but there aren't any guarantees you'll be the lucky recipient tonight."

He's wearing a full-blown smile now. "Oh, so you only give your number out to one person per wedding? Is that it?"

"Something like that."

He narrows his eyes, his gaze back on me. "Then I guess we're even because I only ask for one woman's number per wedding."

I should not be entertaining this man, but there's something about him that I simply can't resist. I place my hands on my hips and tilt my head. "That sounds like a challenge." I regard him with raised brows and pursed lips. "You don't even know my name."

He grins. "That was going to be my next question."

I hold out my hand, offering to shake his, and he takes it firmly in his grip. "My name is Meadow. Meadow Matthews. And you are?"

His eyes widen slightly, and I swear it's as if he thinks he knows me. "Ah, now it's starting to make sense."

"Huh?" I shake my head and try to pull my hand away, but he only grips me tighter.

"I'm Asher Moore. I believe we've already met."

When he flashes me a gorgeous smile, my belly flutters, and my knees go so weak I have no choice but to latch on to his arm to steady myself. And when our eyes meet again as he steers me to the bar, I know in that instant that I'm in a whole lot of trouble.

CHAPTER FIVE

ASHER

When we get to the bar, Meadow sets her empty champagne flute on the counter and asks for a whiskey sour. I do the same, minus the sour, barely taking my eyes off her. The moment I spotted her at the wedding, I knew I couldn't let her get away again. It's been a long time since I've felt a pull to a woman in this way. I'm not about to ignore the blaring siren that wakes up some deep part of me I feared might have been lost along the way.

Maybe it's the fact that, other than the three times we've bumped into each other, we don't know each other at all that gives me a false sense of ease. She doesn't know my past, and I don't know hers, and there's a beauty in that.

"Are we really going to do this?"

I bend my brows, confused. "Do what?"

She gestures between us with one hand. "This—drink, talk—avoid the fact that you're going to spend all night trying to recruit me to be your photographer?"

One corner of my mouth tugs up into a smirk. "I won't spend *all* night trying to recruit you. Hopefully, it won't take that long."

Meadow blushes in response. "You're very optimistic."

She takes a quick sweeping gaze around the room, so I steal the opportunity to appreciate the way her dress dips and curves. It's only fair, since she already gave me the once-over. Her dress is a fascinating blend of classy and sexy, revealing just enough skin to make me want to see more. I'm especially enamored by the hint of silky-smooth skin at the top of one thigh.

"And persistent," I murmur, only half expecting her to hear me.

Her eyes snap back to mine, and I bite down on my bottom lip, debating how to phrase my next comment. "If it helps, I would have wanted to spend all night with you even if you weren't a fantastic photographer who I hope to recruit."

She narrows her eyes playfully. "You don't even know me."

I lean in slightly, my eyes never wavering from hers, fully aware of how thick I'm about to lay it on. "But I *want* to know you."

Her eyes grow wide. "Wow. You did not just say that."

I'm enjoying this way too much. My intense attraction to this woman surprises me. I can vaguely remember a time before Sheena when I acted in this same flirtatious way. Maybe I've still got it after all.

"It's true," I insist.

She rolls her eyes. "How am I supposed to believe that? You're way too smooth for me, Asher Moore."

The sound of my name slipping off her tongue draws my eyes to her pouty lips. "Trust me," I tell her, dropping the humor for a second. "I'm only as smooth as you are mysterious."

"Is that what you think I am—mysterious?" She laughs.

"Don't worry. I kind of like it."

Her blush deepens. "What about me makes me mysterious?"

"For starters, you're friends with Becca, yet I've never met you."

"Ah," she says with a nod. "Like I told you the other day, I grew up here, but I haven't been back in the area since college. Becca and I kept in touch but not as much over the last few years. I wouldn't have expected her to mention me. What about you? What brought you to Tampa?"

"My ex-wife, actually." I shift, almost expecting Meadow to run away at the mention of my failed marriage, but she doesn't even flinch. "She moved here while I was stationed in Afghanistan, so when I got out, this is where I wound up." The way her gaze lingers on me makes me eager to turn the conversation back to her. "You never did tell me where you were rushing off to before you got caught in that pileup."

She lets out a breathy laugh. "I had just come from one photo shoot and was heading to another. Unfortunately, the woman didn't handle the cancelation very well. She demanded I refund her for the missed appointment and reshoot."

"Tell me you didn't."

"I did." Meadow shrugs. "But she loved the photos and gave me a five-star review, so I guess I'll consider it a win."

Listening to her try to spin her shitty situation into something positive, I remember what Becca told me about how Meadow had been through a lot recently. While I want to know all the reasons, I decide now is not the time to grill the beautiful woman. Instead, I decide to take another approach to hopefully convince her that working with me will surely be the next best thing in her life.

"Things have a funny way of working themselves out, don't they?" I ask, smiling at her.

She regards me with wary eyes. "You're about to segue into how I should take you up on your firefighter calendar offer, aren't you?"

I laugh. "Maybe."

She frowns. "There must be dozens of photographers who would jump at the opportunity you're offering me. Why are you dead set on it being me?"

As soon as she asks the question, I instinctively want to jump to my own defense. I want to tell her how brilliant her website is and how no one is better suited for the job. That may be true, but I choose to tell her the real reason. "I kind of dropped the ball on finding a photographer." My insides are cringing as the admission falls from my lips. "Our first event is next month. We're holding a stair climb at Raymond James Stadium. That's when we'll scout out potential firefighters for the calendar, and we need a photographer there documenting the event."

Her brow furrowed. "So you bring these guys there then handpick the ones you want to be on this calendar?"

I chuckle. "Not exactly. Women are firefighters too." I wink. "And we only gather interest. From there, we'll interview each one, narrow them down to the top fifty, and then we'll have an auction event where the audience will vote for who makes it through to the calendar. If anything, it will be pure entertainment—and fun for you."

She looks to be considering my words. "Like I said, what you're doing is wonderful. I just—"

"Wait." Panic shoots through me, and I immediately aim for another tactic. "Don't make any decisions tonight."

Her eyebrows pinch together. "Why?"

I shrug and lean my elbow on the bar while my gaze traces the almond shapes of her eyes with mine. "We're at a wedding. There are rules."

She regards me suspiciously. "Rules like don't get so drunk that you make a fool of yourself on the dance floor?"

"Nope. That's a must. I mean the rule about not mixing business with pleasure. Tonight is all about celebrating. I won't mention the calendar again."

Her eyes widen, and she looks amused. "You won't?"

"Nope. Tonight, you're free from all business talk."

"Why do I feel like there's a catch?"

I grin. "If you call hanging out with me for the rest of the night *a catch*, then I guess you're on to something."

Her sweeping gaze takes me in from head to toe, and I'm desperate to know if she's even remotely as attracted to me as I am to her. But when our eyes catch again, I notice something else behind her stare. Something that was maybe hidden before but is plain as day now. Fear.

"Someone should have told you that you shouldn't put all your eggs in one basket," she says.

"But what if I'm only interested in this one particular basket?"

She shifts from one heel to the other as if considering her next words carefully. "Then I'd say you're a glutton for punishment. It's been a long time since I've been to a wedding. I forgot how intimidating they could be."

Electricity buzzes through the air during the next beat of silence. "Well, then," I say, unable to help my next smile. "It's a good thing you're sticking with me tonight."

In the flash of a second, something changes in her eyes. She goes from happy-go-lucky to somewhat serious. Then her mouth opens and closes before she finally speaks. "Okay, but I should warn you..." Her eyes search mine as if she's choosing her words carefully. "I'm not looking for anything serious."

Something tugs in my chest, but I push it away without another thought. Instead, I shrug and give her my best flashy smile. "You're in luck because neither am I."

Her entire demeanor visibly relaxes, and the smile that lights up her face is one I won't soon forget. "Well, good."

She lifts her drink. "Then you have yourself a deal. No business talk, and I'm all yours."

I lift my drink to hers, my smile widening. "I like the sound of that."

We clink glasses, and while I should be just as relieved as she is about our little deal, I'm not. Not in the least.

CHAPTER SIX

MEADOW

On my way to the buffet line, I spot Becca standing with a few other guests who are in mid-conversation. I catch her for the first time since the reception started. She smiles and waves, but then she looks at who's beside me. I can almost hear her thoughts as her eyes grow wide.

"*What the—?*" she mouths.

"We've been spotted," I say, gently nudging Asher.

Asher looks up, finds Becca, and chuckles. "Oh man, she's eating this up right now, isn't she?"

And then it dawns on me that Asher is Aaron's single firefighter friend who she wanted to set me up with. The one I venomously denied wanting to ever get to know, thanks to the fact that he, like my ex, has a dangerous career. That thought still lingers in the back of my mind, but I push it away because tonight isn't about meeting my next husband. Tonight is about having fun and letting loose a little bit. I deserve to have a night filled with no-strings-attached fun, and it sounds like that is exactly what Asher wants too. We couldn't be a more perfect fit—for tonight only.

Asher lifts a hand and waves tauntingly at Becca. Laughing, I pull his hand back down and shake my head. "Stop. Don't get her hopes up."

Asher chuckles and starts to say something when Aaron approaches, flanked by his other best man. "There you are. It's time for a shot. You're coming with." Aaron looks over at me with a smile. "Hi. I don't think we've met."

I stick out my hand, and he takes it. "I'm Meadow, Becca's friend. You and I met years ago at a quick dinner. I don't expect you to remember me."

His entire face lights up, and his palm moves to his head. "Of course. I do remember. You're the one who just moved back to town—from Cali. She was just talking about you the other day. In fact—" He gestures between Asher and me. "Did Ash talk to you about the calendar gig?"

I laugh. "Yes, he did."

"So you'll do it?" Aaron's entire face lights up, shooting guilt straight through me.

In my peripheral, I can see Asher cringe. "I made Meadow a deal that we wouldn't talk about business tonight. Don't get me in trouble."

Aaron raises an eyebrow at his friend, as though sending an unspoken message. "I see."

Asher slips an arm around me, causing a fluttering sensation in my belly. It's been a long time since I've felt this type of nervous excitement. I'd almost forgotten what it's like to feel that intense attraction to someone of the opposite sex. I'd even wondered at moments over the last three years if I'd ever feel anything like this again. It feels good—like there's hope for me yet.

So much had happened from the moment I left college until now that it almost feels like a blur. Like I was outside my skin watching my life unfold. To put it succinctly, I was the woman who had a quick engagement after finding out she was pregnant by her summer fling while at a monumental crossroads in her life.

It had taken three years after Milton's death for me to make that hard decision to leave California and move back home, but I finally felt like I was making a decision for me. Even with the crazy first week I've had in Tampa, I'm confident it was the right decision.

"Well, well, well." I turn to find a grinning Becca approaching with her bridesmaids close behind. "Looks like you found yourself a hot date."

I shake my head, quick to correct her. "*This* is not a date." I freeze when I catch Asher's raised brows. It's like he's challenging me to speak carefully. Between the heat in his stare and the burn in my cheeks, I could very possibly be melting right here on the spot. I turn back to Becca. "He's trying to seduce me so that I'll say yes to that calendar project."

Asher pulls me tighter against his side. "In all fairness, I would have tried to seduce you either way."

I roll my eyes and point at him while pinning Becca with a look. "Don't mind him," I tell her. "That's the alcohol talking."

Aaron claps a hand on Asher's back and winks. "Atta boy. Take advantage of that open bar."

Becca glares at me suspiciously before she wraps an arm around Aaron and bats her lashes at him. "Where are you off to, husband?"

Aaron leans down, placing a gentle kiss on her nose. "The bar, of course. I'm taking my boys to get a shot. Bring your girls, and we'll make it a party."

"Sounds perfect." She reaches out and grabs my hand, tugging me away from Asher. "I'll give her back to you in a minute."

Asher grins and takes off to the bar with the rest of the

wedding party, while Becca hooks her arm into mine and leans in closer. "Tell me everything," she hisses.

I give her the quick rundown about how I met Asher, and she regards me with wide eyes. "It's like the start of one of those romantic comedies we watched in college."

I let out a laugh. "Except neither of us is looking for anything serious."

She frowns. "You two say that now. But once you get to know each other, you'll both change your tune. I know I joked about hooking you two up, but seeing you interact only makes me realize how perfect a couple you could be. And Meadow, when I say Asher is a really good guy, I mean it."

He also spends his days jumping into fires, a voice in my mind argues. "I'm sure he's wonderful, but it's just not a great time for me to be focusing on a relationship." That's all I'm going to say. Tonight is Becca's big night. I don't want to spend our time arguing about why I won't date a man with the same dangerous profession as the one she just married.

"Fine. I'll drop it," Becca says. "I'm not fighting you on my wedding day." She winks and wraps an arm around me. "Come. Let's get a shot."

I smile and finally take in the close-up view of Becca. She's still wearing her white wedding dress, her gorgeous updo is still perfect, and her smile is the biggest I've ever seen. "You look beautiful, Bec. I'm so happy for you."

She squeals, tightening her hold on my arm. "I can't even believe it's official. You know, after graduation when you left for California with Milton, I was so jealous you had found your person. And I was crazy angry at you for not inviting me to your wedding."

I cringe and give her a pleadingly apologetic stare. "You didn't miss anything special. I wish I could say it was as magical as your big day, but it just wasn't like that. I didn't get the fancy venue or high-strung wedding planner, or photographer following me around everywhere I went, or a five-star buffet. I got a small business suite, a plastic pedestal filled with fake flowers, a cheap dress, and a quickly drawn-up contract."

She pouts. "You'll have a fancy wedding one day, Meadow. You deserve it all. So does Tate."

I know she wants nothing but the best for me, but the truth is, my perspective changed drastically after having Tate. While I used to dwell on the fact that I'd never gotten the fancy wedding, the venue and fanfare mean nothing in the grand scheme of things. If I ever get married again, it will be for all the right reasons. For now, all I truly care about is being a great mother to Tate.

Becca and I approach the bar, and we're immediately sucked into the swarm of a wedding party. Becca stands between Aaron and me, and Asher is on my right. Shots are being passed out, and Asher takes two, setting one in front of me. He leans in low enough that I can hear him. "Say anything nice about me?"

I narrow my eyes playfully. "Wouldn't you like to know?"

"I would, actually."

Chuckling, I shake my head. "Too bad. That's for me to know and for you to never find out."

He twists his lips and holds up his shot. "We'll see about that."

I recognize his challenge. Aaron yells out, "Cheers, bitches," and I toss back my shot and savor the burn that runs down the back of my throat.

In the next second, Asher's eyes connect with mine, and a small smile tilts his lips. "Another?"

I open my mouth to refuse out of fear that I'll get too tipsy tonight, but then I wonder why I care so much. I take in Asher's sexy stubble and the playful look in his eyes as he stares me down, and I say to myself, "Fuck it." It's not like I plan on driving myself home tonight, anyway. So I nod at him and decide to stop trying to play my cards so cautiously. "Let's do it."

After Aaron and Becca's first dance, the real party begins. The DJ plays Sam Hunt's "Body Like a Back Road" after a flood of faster dance tunes. Asher refuses to let me out of his arms on the dance floor. I haven't resisted too much, considering the man can actually dance. He doesn't miss a single beat as he twirls me and leads me around the dance floor like a pro. At the end of the song, he wraps a strong arm around my waist and dips me so low I can feel my hair sweep the floor.

He's grinning down at me, and I have the strongest desire to lift my head a few inches and plant my lips on his. It would be so easy, especially considering my stomach is swimming in a pool of alcohol and butterflies. I can't remember the last time I had this much fun.

Asher lifts me back to standing as the music transitions into the slow Chase Rice song "Eyes on You," and without a second of hesitation, he tugs me into his arms and locks me in his hold. It feels good—natural—and I'm just tipsy enough to imagine I've known the guy longer than I actually have.

"You look beautiful tonight."

My heart leaps at the surprise compliment, and my skin bristles with excitement. His mouth is near my ear, with his scruff tickling my cheek. Instinctively, I tighten my hold on him. Suddenly, I'm afraid to let go. Tonight feels like a dream—a dream I'll have to wake up from eventually. But I don't want to think about tomorrow, not when I'm in Asher's arms tonight.

"Thank you," I say, turning my cheek slightly. He leans back some so his eyes are locked on mine. Our mouths are close enough to kiss. All it would take is one slight move forward, and our lips would crash together. The way his eyes dip to my lips and then back up to my eyes tells me he realizes all the possibilities of our proximity too.

"Aren't you going to tell me how handsome I look tonight?" he teases.

Heat creeps up into my cheeks for the hundredth time since we've been together, and I laugh. "I'm a little afraid of what that kind of compliment will do to your already inflated ego."

He bites down on his bottom lip, and he has to know just how sexy he looks doing it. "See, that just proves you need to get to know me better. I think you'd be surprised at the size of my *inflated ego*."

The way his lips pop with his words has my chest and cheeks burning.

"I'm sure it's quite impressive when stroked." My eyes go wide. I can't believe I just said that. While I don't make a habit of drinking as much as I have tonight, I'm well aware of the liquid courage it's been giving me. I clear my throat. "What I meant was—"

"Don't," he says with a laugh and a shake of his head. "Don't ruin it. I'll have something to talk about at the station next week."

I roll my eyes as far back as they'll go, completely mortified. "I'm going to be the laughingstock of the fire station. Great. That's one way to ensure I don't work on this calendar with you."

He gasps dramatically. "No business talk, remember? If you're going to reject my offer, it's going to be over dinner next week, not here at my best friend's wedding."

I can't stop the grin that pushes up my cheeks. "Dinner? Really? Asher—"

He places a finger to my lips and shakes his head, shushing me with a playful look in his eyes. "No arguing at a wedding. It's bad luck." He pulls his finger away.

"You are impossible."

He grins. "Impossible to resist, you mean." He bites down on his lip and then releases it quickly. "Look, you agreed, no business talk tonight. But that means we still have things to discuss outside of the wedding. So... one dinner this week. I think that needs to be added to our deal."

I study him. "How many amendments to the deal are we going to make tonight?"

He chuckles. "As many as it takes. What do you say? Let me take you to dinner to give me one chance to persuade you. After that, you can make your decision, and we'll go from there."

"That's it? Just dinner."

Asher nods, but his eyes hold a teasing glimmer, like he knows something I don't.

I narrow my eyes into slits for a few seconds, but I'd made up my mind the moment he suggested dinner. "I'd like to add an amendment."

He chuckles. "That's only fair."

"I will agree to go to dinner with you but only if you keep that whole *stroking your ego* comment to yourself."

"Deal." His answer comes without a hint of hesitation.

He holds out his hand to shake mine, and I stare at it for a second before lifting my hand to fit into his. We're in mid-shake when the wedding planner spots Asher and waves him over to the front of the room.

"Ah, groomsman duties await." He releases my hand. "We can pick up where we left off when I get back." He points at me. "Don't you dare find yourself another date. You're mine tonight, Meadow Matthews." He winks and then jogs off to join the wedding party, leaving me with a whole new mix of emotions.

You're mine tonight, Meadow Matthews.

I shouldn't love the sound of that, but I can't deny the way my heart beat when I heard it. After I spent the past few years dedicating myself to being the best mom and learning how to make a career out of my biggest passion, meeting a man wasn't even on my radar. I always make the excuse that my responsibilities don't leave me any time to date, but thinking about it now, the real truth is I just don't *make* the time.

Sighing, I start to make the rounds to greet the few people I know, acquaintances from high school and college who remained better friends with Becca than with me, for obvious reasons. But it's nice to see them again, and we share in old memories together over drinks—too many drinks.

By the time I see Asher again, the cake-cutting ceremony and the bouquet toss are already over, and everyone is back out on the dance floor. He takes my hand and pulls me away from the group of girls I'm dancing with. I stumble to catch up with him, giggle, and toss a quick apology over my shoulder to the girls before focusing on Asher.

"Having fun?" he asks, a glimmer in his eyes.

I pinch my lips together and bat my lashes at him. "Without you? How could I?"

He narrows his eyes and leans close to my ear. "Good answer."

He pulls away again, and I catch the scent of whiskey on his breath, reminding me of my own state of drunkenness. I need to slow down or my decisions tonight will no longer be my own but that of my alter ego. But just as the thought crosses my mind, Becca and Aaron come up to us offering us shots.

Becca is all giggles and smiles, and I'm thrilled to see her this happy. "Someone gave us these, but we aren't drinking anymore tonight. Take 'em?"

Asher shrugs, leaving the decision in my hands. I'm ready to turn them down when I see the hopeful smile on Becca's face. "Thank you."

Becca gives me her shot, Aaron hands Asher his, and then they take off through the dance floor crowd.

"No more shots after this," I tell Asher. "At this rate, I need to order a ride home tonight." Almost as soon as the words come out, I regret giving him that information.

"I'm in charge of the limo tonight," he says. "I can give you a ride home."

The way he says it—so cool and confident, like he has no intention other than to do exactly what he's offering—should make me cautious, but for some ridiculous reason, I trust him.

"Okay," I say easily.

"Okay?" He's clearly shocked.

I laugh and nod. "I'm not going to turn down a free sober ride tonight." Before he can say anything else about it, I change the subject. "So, what did your groomsman activities call you to do?"

A wicked glimmer appears in his eyes. "Wouldn't you like to know?"

I drop my jaw in mock horror. "Are you keeping secrets from me already, Asher Moore? And here I thought our impromptu date was going so well. For all I know, you were out back necking with some woman on the dumpster."

He tosses back his head and gives a hearty laugh. "First of all, the only woman I'm necking with tonight is you." He winks. "And the last place I would do it is on a dumpster. You deserve much better than that."

I hold a hand to my chest and feign flattery. "I do?"

He nods slowly. "Yup."

"You need to give me more than that. What's better than a dumpster?"

He tilts his head and regards me with a playful smile. "I'll never reveal my secrets."

Maybe it's the alcohol talking, but I suddenly feel extremely courageous while staring back at this deliciously gorgeous man. "I can get it out of you."

One corner of his lips turn up in a heart-stopping smile. "I'd love to see you try."

Asher is frustratingly sexy in a way that revs up my core like we're at the start of a race. It's like I'm a completely different person around him. Or maybe I'm closer to myself than I've been in years. Either way, I'm not ready to let this night end as innocently as it began.

I take his hand and start to steer him from the dance floor toward the back of the room.

"Where are we going?" he asks, laughing.

"Away from here, so I can steal all your secrets," I say.

I head straight for a set of double doors where staff members walk in and out, but just as I'm about to push through the doors, the loudspeaker crackles, and the DJ's voice booms around the room. "All right, boys and girls. It's time for our newlyweds to make their grand exit. Please line up, and let's wish these lovebirds farewell. It's the end of the party for them, but their forever is only beginning."

Loud cheers and applause burst through the crowd as we freeze and turn around to find Becca and Aaron making their way back through the thick crowd of guests.

My mission will have to wait. "I don't want to miss this."

Asher nods. "Let's watch from here." He tugs me to one of the high round tables, grabs two glasses of champagne off an abandoned tray, and hands one to me. I probably shouldn't accept it, but at this point, what's one more? He moves to stand behind me and holds his champagne glass inches from mine. "To our matchmakers, Aaron and Becca."

I stifle a laugh and bite down on my lower lip, refusing to listen to the voice of warning in the back of my mind. *We're just having fun. Casual fun. Enjoy yourself, Meadow.* With that final thought, I clink my glass to his. "To Aaron and Becca."

We drink from our glasses, and I try to ignore the goose bumps that pop up all over my skin at our proximity. My eyes are focused forward where they should be, on the bride and groom. But all I can think about is the man scooping my hair over my shoulder and leaning down to place his champagne-flavored lips on my neck. His scent, his touch—it's all just as irresistible as I remember from the first day we'd met.

I lean back against Asher, dizzy from a mixture of drink and excitement. Something about the subtle move provokes a reaction in him. His palm splays on my stomach and presses me to his front while he runs another set of fingers down my arm, barely grazing my skin. "I really want to kiss you right now," he whispers.

A shiver goes through my entire body. Clearly, he feels it, too, because the next thing I know, his fingers cup my chin and turn me to face him, then he leans in and tickles my lips with his.

Asher is such a flirtatious tease, but he's also charming and funny. If my situation were any different, my subconscious mind would not reject all romantic possibilities with this man. He's simply too good to be true, which is precisely why anything more than casual fun would be too dangerous to explore.

A sigh slips past my throat as his firm lips press against mine. Something about the start of our kiss is innocent and tender, like neither of us wants to rush something so perfect, so new. I take the time to memorize the terrain of his full mouth and the way it moves against mine, giving and taking in a way that's commanding yet appreciative. Given the fact that it's been years since I've kissed anyone, I'm surprised that what's happening between us feels so natural.

My mouth parts against his, then his tongue sweeps my mouth. A moan slips past my throat, like I'm a woman possessed. It's just a kiss, but then why does it feel like a fireworks show is being set off in my chest? My head fogs, and my heartbeat strengthens. My pulse races, and my knees weaken. This feels better than something new, better than a fling or a night of casual fun. This feels like a first.

CHAPTER SEVEN

ASHER

An unfamiliar blaring wakes me from a deep slumber, followed by a loud groan not made by me. I turn toward the sound, my eyes adjusting to the morning light. A slender arm peeks out from my bedsheets, and a pile of dark brown hair is strewn on my other pillow.

My heart thuds in my chest as I pull together memories from last night. All I see is her. Meadow Matthews. The goddess of a woman I couldn't get enough of last night, especially after that kiss. Unfortunately, my memories after the kiss taper off rather quickly. Too quickly.

I scan the woman's body for any evidence that will help jog my memory. She's still wearing that sexy pink dress with the slit that reaches her upper thigh. Her leg is currently bent at the slit, exposing smooth and fair skin. I'm not exactly sure how, but I know how that skin feels.

I look down at my own attire to find that I'm fully dressed too. We probably stumbled inside from the limo and passed out.

She moans again, seemingly annoyed that the alarm is

still going off. I'm pretty sure I hadn't set it. I don't have any plans today other than to sleep and to work on some projects around my house. Meadow shifts and rolls onto her back. Hair falls around her face, and just like that, more memories from after our epic kiss come tumbling through my mind.

A series of cheering, hooting, and hollering had come from the front of the room. The sound of it had shaken us apart, and I'd looked down into Meadow's glossy, wide eyes and could tell she was just as surprised by our kiss as I'd been.

"Damn," I remember telling her, because what the fuck was I supposed to do after that kiss?

Meadow and I had come to a mutual agreement to have casual fun last night, whatever that loose description meant. To me, it had meant whatever happened between us would be up in the air, no strings attached, fun. But knowing that Becca and Aaron were gone, and the reception was about to wind down, scared the shit out of me. I didn't want the night to end. Not then, not ever. And when the music slowed, it felt like a subtle hint to the guests to start clearing out. I knew that after a few slow songs, the night would be over completely.

A panicky feeling lit in my chest, and adrenaline began to pulse heavily through my veins. "Dance with me," I asked—or, more like, begged—but she told me she had a better idea.

In one swift move, Meadow grabbed my hand and tugged me toward the double doors she had been leading me toward before we stopped to watch Aaron and Becca leave. I had no idea what was behind them or where we were going, but as soon as we entered the dimly lit room, she'd stopped, flipped around to face me, and our bodies—hands, mouths, chests—had come crashing together.

I sit up, letting my head drop back against the headboard in frustration. The last thing I'd wanted to do last night was sabotage my chances of getting to know her better. What if she woke up and wanted nothing more to do with me? Clearly, we hadn't had sex. But then...

Another memory flickers through my mind, of me lifting Meadow onto a stainless-steel counter and hiking her skirt up. Or maybe she hiked her skirt up. God, I wish I remembered. One thing I know for sure—it was her hand that grabbed mine and placed it between her parting thighs. It was her breathy whisper that begged me to touch her.

I'm getting hard just thinking about the wetness that coated my fingers as I slipped inside her soft folds, the way she clenched around me before she was about to come, like she was trying to hang on for dear life, and the way she tossed her head back before she came so hard her entire body shook with her orgasm. It was then that her foot banged into what we quickly figured out was a trash can. But that hadn't stopped our lips from crashing together again.

My memories are just fragments, but each one makes me dig harder into my subconscious for more. How had we ended up here? What had we *done?*

Meadow stirs again, and this time her lids begin to peel open as her hand searches the air in a hunt for the annoying alarm, which I finally realize is coming from her phone. At least, I think it's coming from her phone. I don't remember setting an alarm.

"I'll find it," I tell her. But just as I start to search, her eyes widen, and she gasps at the sound of my voice.

"Oh my God. We didn't."

I've had a few minutes to wake up enough to laugh at her shock. "That depends on what you're referring to, exactly."

She looks down at her body and pats her hands over her clothes. I give her time to analyze our situation and get up to walk around the bed to grab her phone and shut off the alarm.

"We didn't," she says again, this time sounding relieved. "We just... made out."

With a snort, I look down at her still sprawled out on my bed. "We did a little more than make out."

She shakes her head, refusing to look at me while appearing thoroughly confused. "I don't remember." Her head falls into her hands like she's ashamed. "I shouldn't have drunk so much last night."

I sit on the edge of the bed and cup her chin so she has to look up at me. Her sleep-filled eyes are the gorgeous light-green shade I remember. "No one here is judging you, Meadow. We both drank too much. C'mon, I'll make you breakfast and then take you home so you can sleep it off."

I place the phone in her lap, but she looks down at it, and her entire face lights up with horror. "Oh no no no." Her head snaps up to look at the bedside clock, as if confirming whatever she feared. She shoves me to the side and leaps to her feet. "I need to go. I can't be late." She looks around frantically then runs toward her purse, which is near the door.

I jump up and follow her, unsure of what's wrong but desperately wanting to help. "I'll take you to your car now."

"How far away are we from the venue?"

"Twenty minutes, give or take traffic."

She groans. "And then I need to go home, change... I'll be late."

I still have no idea why she's in such a hurry, but it doesn't matter. I hate to see her this way. "Let me help. Where are you trying to go?"

"The cruise port. Their cruise gets in in thirty minutes.

I have to be there when they get off the ship." She looks like she's about to cry.

"The port is only five minutes from here," I say and smile. I place a hand on her arm, hoping I can help calm her down. Whoever "they" are must be important. "C'mon, I'll take you straight there so you don't have to make two other stops. You have plenty of time."

She seems to be considering my suggestion and is probably thinking about what she's wearing, but I can read in her expression that she knows she doesn't have any other choice if she wants to make it on time.

"Fine. Okay." She gives in, her eyes settling back on mine. "Please tell me you have a spare toothbrush or something."

My chest swells at the sight of her relaxing some. I smile and start walking toward my bathroom. "Follow me. But please," I say, sneaking a peek at her over my shoulder. "Don't judge the mess. This house was built in the twenties, and it's going under renovations as we speak. I promise it won't look like this when I'm done."

I take a new toothbrush out of the bathroom drawer and start to hand it to her when I notice she's looking around the room. "You're going to do all the renovations yourself?"

I shrug. "Yeah, why not? I'm saving a ton of money, and I have a lot of days off. Projects make me happy." I grin and offer her the toothbrush. "I'll step out so you can have your alone time." I wink, knowing how completely awkward she probably feels in my home, without her car and wearing her same dress from last night.

"Thank you," she says, sending a bashful look my way. "I'll be right out."

After I use the hallway bathroom to freshen up a bit, I head into the kitchen to blend a quick smoothie. Meadow walks into the kitchen, and I hand her a plastic container of my special concoction and wink. "Thank me and call me in the morning."

"Ha," she says, accepting the drink. "What is it?"

"It's my hangover cure. Kale, spinach, celery, apples, avocado, flax seeds, fresh ginger, lemon, and water. Trust me, you'll feel amazing after you guzzle that down." I nod toward the door. "Ready to go?"

She nods, her face flushing as her gaze lingers on me. "Thank you for doing this. It was really sweet of you to offer. And for this." She holds up the drink. "And the toothbrush. If only you had a change of clothes that fit me."

"You wouldn't be here if I did." Our eyes connect for a second longer than I anticipate, and I swear there's an uptick in the energy between us. "Anyway, you don't have to thank me for any of it. I had fun last night. And not that I can remember much near the tail end, but I feel mostly to blame for you being late this morning. I think I encouraged you to have that last glass of champagne."

Her face lifts with a small smile. "Yeah, well, I didn't exactly fight you about it. I definitely got carried away with..."

"Me?"

She blushes. "Everything."

Her eyes slip down to my outfit. "You didn't change."

"I figured it was only fair, since you couldn't change."

Her expression softens. "That was incredibly thoughtful."

Something about the compliment hits me deep in the chest. So deep that I make myself push all thoughts about it to the side. "Let's get you to this cruise port."

She follows me to my truck. I open the door for her and walk around to hop into the driver's side. She's taking a long sip of the smoothie, so I wait and watch for her reaction. I swear her entire body shakes as the smoothie hits her throat. And all I can think about is her intense orgasm last night.

"This is heaven." She sighs and leans back in her seat.

Chuckling, I start the truck, back up into the road, and head toward the port. "Who are you in a hurry to pick up, anyway?"

She gives me a look I don't quite understand. "My mom and my son."

She's a single mom. A beautiful single mom. A beautiful single mom running a photography business.

The fact that she has a son just adds to the character profile I'm building for this woman in my head. I'm not just impressed. I'm turned on.

Meadow faces forward, and I wonder if it's because she's nervous about my reaction.

"They've been on a cruise for the past week to give me time to get settled in. We're staying with my mom for the short term. You know, until we get on our feet. I just want the transition to be effortless for Tate."

I nod, completely understanding. "Tate is your son?"

She nods. "He's only three, so I think he'll adjust well, but I thought it would be fun to have his room all set up with his toys so he didn't show up to a pile of boxes."

I steal a look at Meadow's profile, the gorgeous woman who in no time flat I've accidentally found myself wrapped up in. The visor mirror is open, and she's checking her appearance. She pauses and looks at me. "I'm sorry I didn't mention Tate earlier. I didn't expect to see you yesterday, and then we said things would be casual and fun. I just—I didn't think I needed to warn you or anything, but I feel like I should have told you."

I'm baffled that Meadow thinks she needs to apologize to me for anything. "Meadow, we've known each other for two seconds. You don't owe me anything. But I'm glad I know now." I smile, hoping to ease her guilt. "And you're right. Last night was casual and fun. It was just what we agreed for it to be."

She nods, closes the mirror, and brings the smoothie straw to her lips. She takes a sip and then looks at me again. "This is going to be awkward for you, isn't it? Picking up my mom and son when we don't even know each other."

"Well, we know enough." I tease gently. "I think it's safe for you to refer to me as your friend for now."

Her cheeks darken a shade. "For now?"

I shrug. "We'll see what happens."

She laughs, a light but true laugh that I remember hearing so many times last night. It had gotten to the point that I craved hearing it as much as I craved watching the way her lips curved up in that gorgeous smile.

"You are impossible. So, I take it you still want to take me to dinner this week."

I nod. "That was part of our arrangement. A deal's a deal, Meadow."

"I know, I know." She smiles. "You're true to your word or whatever. I get it." She raises her hands in surrender. "Don't worry. I'm not going to bail on you. I really do want to hear more about your organization."

"You do?"

She shrugs. "Well, yeah. Why wouldn't I?"

"I don't know. I was kind of worried that you waking up in my bed this morning might have changed your mind."

She cringes. "Yeah, well, it's not like I woke up naked or anything. Now, that would have been awkward."

I twist my lips, a fantasy version of two naked bodies tangled together rushing through my mind. "I don't know if I would use the word 'awkward'."

She slaps my arm with a playful swat, but I can't help but feel like it means more. Like she's into me, and maybe, just maybe, my fantasy won't be one for long.

"But," I add, "I'm glad we didn't go any further."

"You are?" I swear I hear a hint of disappointment in her question.

"Well, yeah. Because I wouldn't have remembered any of it." I sneak a look at her, our eyes catching for just a second. "And that's something I would definitely want to permanently tattoo into my mind."

CHAPTER EIGHT

MEADOW

Asher pulls into the parking lot at Port Tampa Bay, and the first thing I see is a giant vessel anchored near the dock. At first, I'm terrified I might have missed my mom and Tate coming off the ship, but then I look at the latest message on my phone.

They have us scheduled to depart in ten minutes. You here? Tate is so excited to see you.

Emotion clogs my throat as I type back. *I can't wait to hold him. And yes, I'm here in the parking lot. A friend drove me, so don't freak out. I'll explain later.*

I look over at Asher, who's already parked and looking at me as if waiting for some sort of signal. "They'll be coming off the ship in ten minutes." I smile. "We made it on time, thanks to you."

His gaze locks with mine, and the intensity in his eyes has an instant effect on my heart.

"It's no problem, Meadow. I'm happy to help." Almost as soon as the words are out of his mouth, his expression morphs into one of disappointment. "Shit. I don't have a car seat." He shakes his head, as if reasoning with himself.

"That's okay, I'll take you to the port then run to the store and pick one up then—"

"Asher," I say with a laugh while leaning over to pat his arm. He looks at me, eyebrows bent together. "My mom took a car seat with her on the ship for land excursions and stuff. We've got one. You're fine."

His face lights up at the good news. "Oh, good. Crisis averted."

I can't stop smiling. Everything about Asher has knocked me completely off balance since the moment I met him, literally. I'm not even sure what to think about it all. This morning, when I woke up and realized where I was, I nearly had a heart attack. I couldn't remember how I'd gotten there, or what we'd done, or what I'd said, or how everything would play out from then on. But he'd made me feel like nothing about it was weird.

"I'm going to walk up to greet them. You can stay here if you—" Asher is already opening his door and getting out of the truck. I'm so shocked that by the time I place my hand on the handle of the passenger door, he's already opening it from the outside.

"Such a gentleman." I let him help me out of the truck, and we cross the street to the sidewalk that leads to the port exit.

Many people stream out from the exit. Most of them head straight for the parking lot. Others appear to be waiting for rides. I crane my neck and search for my mom and Tate, gasping when I finally spot them. Tate's giant blue eyes search the crowd for me just like I did for him. My mom has a tight grip on his hand and is searching for me too.

I squeal, kick off my heels, and run forward as fast as my bare feet will carry me. Tate spots me before I reach him, and I'll never forget the moment he does.

"Mommy," he yells in his high-pitched voice.

He yanks his hand from my mom's and darts straight for me. I lean down just in time to catch him as he jumps into my arms. I pick him up, holding him tighter than I've ever held him before as my chest bursts with happiness. My throat clogs, tears prick the backs of my eyes, and we cling to each other as if our lives depend on it.

"I missed you so much, Tater Tot." I kiss his squishy cheek, and he squeezes my neck harder.

"I missed you, Mommy," he whispers.

I pull back slightly. Tears are pooling in his eyes, and I finally break, letting my own tears fall. Seven days is far too long to be away from my little guy. "I can't wait to hear all about your trip," I tell him with a big smile. "And I can't wait to show you your new bedroom."

"Bedwoom?" He gasps. "Toys?"

The smile that lights up his face is so contagious, my own cheeks start to hurt from beaming back at him.

I laugh. "Yes, baby. All your toys are there. New ones too."

I tickle his side, and he throws his head back and giggles. Then I set him down to greet my mom, who's finally catching up. I wrap an arm around her while still holding on to Tate, not missing the strange look she gives me before our embrace.

"I see you had a good time last night." Her knowing tone brings me right back to high school, when I would come home past curfew. But I can understand why seeing me in evening wear would bring out her suspicions.

"I told you I'd explain later," I whisper. "Don't make this any weirder than it already is."

I pull back to catch her raised brows and the way her gaze slides past me, locking on something above my shoulder. "My oh my. Well, that explains it."

After releasing my mom, I turn around to find Asher approaching, a sweet smile on his face. I step back toward him. "Tate, Mom, meet my friend Asher Moore. He was nice enough to help me out with my... um... car trouble this morning."

My mom laughs, not at all convinced, and reaches out her hand to Asher. "Nice to meet you. That was very nice of you to help my daughter out in her time of *need*."

"Oh my God," I mutter, so embarrassed I turn my head away. She did not just say that. Luckily, I can't stay mortified for long.

"Mommy, you a pwincess."

I look down to find Tate's big eyes all over my dress. "Do I look like a princess?"

He nods.

"Well," I say. "I did go to a fancy ball last night."

"Did you meet a pwince?"

Stifling a laugh, I sneak a look at Asher. "A prince? Well, I don't know if I'd call him a prince, but this is my friend Asher. He went to the ball too."

"Ashew," Tate attempts, but we're still working on his *R* sounds.

Asher crouches. "Nice to meet you, Tate. Can I tell you a secret?"

Tate nods, and by the look on his face, I can tell he's taking this secret very seriously.

"I think your mom might be a real princess," Asher says.

Tate gasps and looks up at me before taking a step closer to Asher. "She weal pwincess." He points at me. "And you a pwince."

I laugh and scoop Tate up in my arms before Asher can fill his head with any more fairy tales. Asher straightens, the glimmer in his eyes hard to look away from. "You're a troublemaker."

He winks at me and then turns to my mom, sticking his hand out to shake. "It's nice to meet you..."

"Farrah." My mom takes his hand and doesn't let go as she gives him her long, drawn-out once-over. "It's nice to meet you, Asher. I take it you two met last night at the wedding?"

"Not exactly," I say, internally cringing at the fact that in order for me to explain the story entirely, I'll need to tell her about the calendar project too. She'll undoubtedly want me to take the gig. "Asher is Becca's husband's friend. They work together."

My mom's eyes widen, and I can see the worry forming in them—not for her sake but for mine. She knows my fears too well. "So, you're a firefighter?"

Asher nods. "Yes. Well, I primarily work with our EMT units. I've been trying to convince your daughter to join my fundraising campaign as our photographer. She's very talented."

My mom looks between us as though the picture is quickly becoming clear. "Yes, that she is." Her gaze settles on me, and by the twinkle in her eyes, I know I'll be getting interrogated later.

I smile at everyone and plant another kiss on Tate's cheek. "You ready to get home?"

Tate rests his cheek against my chest and nods. I have a feeling my day will primarily be reserved for cuddling sessions, naps, and Legos.

"Let me get this." Asher steps toward my mom, taking the car seat first and then her suitcase. Then he leads us toward his truck.

I stand outside the back-seat door while he installs the car seat, half expecting him to turn around flustered and ask me to help him, but he's got everything locked in and tested in record time. When he turns around to me, I let out a surprised laugh. "You did that like a pro."

He winks. "Most firefighters are certified at car seat installation. I've taught a class or two."

He backs away, giving me room to put Tate in his seat. All the while, I'm the one who's completely flustered. Who is this man, and why do I feel like he's someone who will never escape me?

Once Tate is buckled up, I shut the door and face Asher. "Thank you for this. I'm sure you didn't expect to spend your day chauffeuring my family around."

He hooks my chin with two fingers, a smile lifting his cheeks. "I'm more than happy to do it, Meadow. Stop acting like I'm doing you a favor. If anything, you're doing me a favor by giving me a good excuse to make you hang out with me."

I laugh, trying to think clearly despite my knotting stomach and fluttering heart. "You're way too good at this charming act."

He makes an expression like he's been wounded, his hand falling from my chin. "Act? You don't think an extremely attractive firefighter can be sincere when he's flirting with an equally extremely attractive photographer?"

"You really know how to lay it on thick."

He waggles his eyebrows. "Now *that* I can't argue with. Between that and my oversized ego, I'd say my charm is the last thing you need to worry about."

Heat blasts me like a blowtorch at his innuendo. I should be mortified. I should be totally turned off by the man making subtle dick jokes while my mom and son wait for us inside the truck—not that they can hear our conversation. But I'm not turned off. In fact, I find his sense of humor insanely attractive.

Still, I need to be careful. My mom will take one look at me and know I have a crush on the guy. And then I'll have to explain all the reasons I can't date him. Not that he's asking to date me. He's not asking for anything more than for me to help out with an organization that has a great cause. The more I think about it, the more I question my reasons for being so resistant. It's like I'm looking for a reason to turn him down, but I've yet to find one. All I know is that these nonstop butterflies in my chest need to take a nap or something. I can't even think straight anymore.

Backing away from him to head around his truck to the other side, I shake my head. "You're something else, Asher Moore."

He grins. "Thank you."

CHAPTER NINE

ASHER

After I drop Meadow, Farrah, and Tate off at their car, I spend the next few hours in the hardware store buying all the material I need to finish the updates on my bathroom. When I bought my fixer-upper in Ybor City, I didn't have anyone to impress. It was just one big project to help me keep my mind off my failed marriage. I wanted to feel accomplished in some way. Besides, a man can only work out and go to the bar so much.

Up until my divorce with Sheena, I'd dedicated my life to loving one woman, in good times and in bad. And there was plenty of bad. For the longest time, I'd blamed myself for the toxicity that entered our marriage. After all, I was the one who had my heart and mind set on enlisting in the military straight out of high school.

Coming from a military family and having a passion to help others, I just knew I was born to serve my country in some capacity. If I hadn't fallen in love with Sheena senior year, I never would have questioned my decision. Unfortunately, I spent the next six years with the weight of guilt on my shoulders. And when I came home, it all only got worse.

Saying Sheena had been unfaithful would be giving her a lot more grace than she deserves. She basically lived her life like I didn't even exist when I was overseas, and according to her during one of our blow-up fights, she felt entitled to that lifestyle. She dated like she was in an open marriage and slept around like she was single. And when I came home, she spent all her energy showing me how much she resented me for being away.

Resentment turned into bickering and more of Sheena's infidelity, until I accepted an honorable discharge from the army and flew home to try to save our marriage. I was certain that if we were together again, we would find our way back to those two crazy kids we'd been in high school. Unfortunately, I'd been very wrong.

My cart is finally stacked with enough tile, fixtures, and paint to occupy me over the next two days. I walk down the horizontal aisle in search of a less-trafficked checkout stand when a cart nearly collides with mine.

"Sorry, dude," the guy says. He waves me on. "Go ahead."

As soon as I take a step forward, the woman to his right catches my eye. I have to do a double take to make sure my eyes are working properly. A familiar blonde with deep chocolate-brown eyes and a permanent pout regards me with as much surprise as I feel.

"Hey, Sheena."

It's not like I thought we would never see each other again. We live in the same city. We still have mutual friends. I just didn't expect to see her with one of the guys she was fucking when we were still married.

She looks absolutely mortified, which is unlike her. The Sheena I remember from the final months of our divorce had been cold, cutthroat, and vindictive. With the exception of the night of our divorce hearing, that is. We went across the street for farewell drinks—a terrible idea, in retrospect. Then she brought me to her place, and we had drunk sex. The kind that felt so wrong, I sometimes question if it even happened. But somehow, that meaningless night was exactly what I needed to confirm in my heart and mind that it was definitely over between us. I walked out of her house with no regrets, and that had been the moment I felt ready to start living again.

Seeing her with this dude doesn't aggravate me the way I would have expected. If anything, I feel sorry for them both. I can't imagine a healthy relationship coming from something that started in secret.

"Hi, Asher. H-how are you?" Sheena asks.

I pat the handle of my cart, not in the mood to stick around and chitchat. "Tackling some projects on my day off."

Her eyes dart to the cart and then back to me. "You always did love your projects." Her smile is faint but unmistakable. "What are you making today? A table? Some chairs?"

I stand there stunned, finding it completely ridiculous that she would even care. "Nothing like that." I pinch my lips together and do us all a favor by taking the first step to get the hell out of there. "Better get to it while the day's still young. Take care." I give them both a wave and push my cart toward a checkout line.

Take care. My own words have me stifling a laugh. If someone had told me when I was eighteen years old that I would be running fast and far away from Sheena, I would have had them confined to a mental institution. My, how things have changed.

I'm nearing the checkout lane when a message comes through from my buddy Greg.

Sorry I had to run off the other day. Had to see a friend. You get along okay with Owens?

It takes me a second to remember Dane's last name. *Yeah, man, he's cool,* I type back. *We might take the boat out some time and go fishing.*

Nice, nice. Figured you two would hit it off. Hey, how was the wedding?

An image of Meadow immediately infiltrates my thoughts, and my cheeks lift in a smile. *Better than anticipated.*

Ha ha. I hope that means a hot bridesmaid popped your cherry.

I bite down on my lip, thanks to the vague image of Meadow clenching around my fingers as she came. *I'll keep the sordid details secret for now.*

Atta boy. I'll get the juicy gossip from you later.

How about today? Want to help me renovate my master bathroom? I'm half joking. Greg is an anesthesiologist at Bayside Regional and has little time for side projects.

Wish I could. I've got to work on digging my way out of an impressive hole I found myself in over the weekend. Will explain later. Rain check?

I'll take you up on that.

I tuck my phone back into my pocket just in time to start checking out. When I'm done, I head for the exit, load up my truck, and return the cart to the nearest turnstile. And that's when I see it… the epic screaming fight between Sheena and her boyfriend. There are tears and then a glance in my direction that might haunt me for days to come. I can't hear what they're saying, but I don't have to. I know all of Sheena's moods—every expression, every gesture. And I know what the look she just gave me means.

Regret.

Steam from the shower seeps into my pores and caresses my achy bones after a grueling day of labor. I needed that. The release I get from hours of intense project-focused work is as satisfying as working out at the gym, even though I'll pay for it the next day. I'll sleep like a baby, that's for sure.

I notice an unread message on my phone when I climb into bed, so I tap on the notification to find the message is from Meadow. For the first time since I dropped her off, I smile.

Thanks again for today. I hope you were able to get some projects done.

I tap to respond and send her before and after photos of the bathroom, a feeling of pride at my accomplishment swelling my chest. *Master bathroom done. I'm going to start on my porch next week.*

Wow. That looks incredible. It doesn't even look like the same bathroom.

I'm not usually the type of man who needs my ego fluffed, but damn, it sure feels nice. *You'll have to come back and see it in person.* I add a winking face emoji.

That's very presumptuous of you—and highly unethical, if I do agree to work for you.

I grin. *You wouldn't work FOR me. You would work WITH me. Big difference.*

Semantics.

I chuckle. *Regardless, I sense you're coming around.*

Perhaps, but I'd still appreciate the sales pitch.

Ahh, you just want the free dinner.

I'll never tell.

I can get it out of you, I tease, in reference to her comment last night that ultimately resulted in us mauling each other in a dark room of the barn.

Good night, Asher.

Wait. My heart jolts to attention, and I sit up to quickly tap out a message. *I'm on call tomorrow, and I work Wednesday. Does Thursday night work for you?*

Yup. Can we do a late dinner, though? I'd like to put Tate to bed before I leave. Say seven thirty?

Perfect.

Good night, Asher, she types again.

Good night, Meadow.

CHAPTER TEN

ASHER

"Run through the pain, Becky!" I yell out to Beck, who's running the stairs at Raymond James Stadium. I try to keep my sassy grin from spreading. "You're almost there."

He grunts, probably at the sound of my favorite nickname for him, but he keeps going. Dane had been able to use his security guard connections to get Beck and me access to the stadium, and we made plans to meet up to prepare for the upcoming charity climb. That was before Beck told me he couldn't make it to the actual event. So now, I get to torture him just for fun.

I already finished my run, so I'm cheering him on while I think about all the stops I'm willing to pull out during my dinner tonight with Meadow.

She doesn't want it to be a date, but I'm finally going to get her alone to charm the shit out of her until she gives me the "yes" I want. Because at this point, I don't envision anyone else being right for the photography job. It has to be Meadow.

I smile at the sound of her name in my head, almost forgetting where I am. I snap out of it, just in time to see sweat dripping down Beck's face as he takes it one step at a time. He has three more to go before I'll let him call it quits.

"You got this!" I yell, this time with genuine encouragement. The dude is busting his balls with focus I've only seen him adopt while prepping for surgery.

I wait for him at the bottom of the ramp with a bottle of Gatorade. "You did it, man. Way to dig."

Beck takes the bottle and wobbles over to the rail, bending forward to catch his breath. "Sorry I'll miss the stair climb this year. You know I'd be there if I could."

I shrug, lifting one corner of my mouth in a sideways smile. "You made up for it today. Hell, I should've taken bets."

"At least I know you can revive me if I have a heart attack."

I chuckle, tossing him a towel. "You're good."

"Funny how fast it heats up in there," he says in reference to the stadium.

"Imagine that times a thousand when you're running into a burning building," I tell him as we walk toward the exit.

He shakes his head. "I don't know if you're a hero or just plain crazy. Or both." He laughs and then launches into a ridiculous knock-knock joke about a broken pencil being pointless.

Afterward, I squint up at him, the Florida sun already baking us. "Good to see you joking around again. I've been worried about you."

"How so?"

"You've been out of town the last two weekends, and I don't know. You just seem... broodier than normal."

Leaning against his Rover, he crosses his arms like he's considering his words carefully. "Let me ask you something."

I lean into a quad stretch while I listen. "Shoot."

"Say you have this thing in your past you've never told your girl. Nothing sinister like cheating—"

My chest clenches at the mention of cheating. "Oh, great. Well, if it's not cheating..."

"Don't be an asshole. I'm serious." Straightening from the car, he pulls one foot up in a stretch. "It won't change the past, and it would only cause her pain. Should I even bring it up?"

I narrow my eyes. "We're talking about a girl you like?"

"Yeah."

"A girl you want to have a long-term adult relationship with?"

He shrugs. "If she'll have me."

"And you're asking me if you should keep important information from her?"

"It's not important. It's more... coincidental."

"Would it matter to her if she found out what it was?"

"I don't know."

I straighten and clap his shoulder. "I think you do know, bro. I also think you know the answer without my input."

Beck is well aware of all the reasons my relationship with Sheena ended. Not revealing important information is as bad as lying, in my opinion. At the same time, Beck is one of my best friends for a reason. He's a great guy with a huge heart, and the fact that he's tormented like this makes me feel for him.

"She's finally opening the door to me again," he says. "Granted, it's only a crack, but it is a crack. Digging up the past will only hurt her. It doesn't matter to me. Maybe it won't matter to her."

I frown. "If it's causing you this much stress, it matters. The shit's in your head, so it's in your relationship. Whatever it is, you have to tell her, or she'll feel like you're holding something back."

He exhales deeply, and his eyes meet mine. "When did you get so fucking wise?"

I chuckle. "I'm not so wise. I just know you can't have secrets in a healthy relationship. "Why aren't you talking to Lars about it? This is her territory."

"Already did," he claps back as he pulls the door of his truck open. "She said the same thing."

I shake my head. "It all sounds heavy. Let me know what happens, okay? We'll miss you at the climb this weekend. The Halloween party at Shipwrecked too. Won't be the same without you this year."

"Let me guess," he quips with a tilt of his lips. "You're going as Mr. January."

I burst out laughing. "You know? I hadn't even thought about my costume." I punch him lightly in the chest. "Thanks for the suggestion, Becky. Maybe I'll even ask a little vixen to go with me."

Beck widens his eyes. "A little vixen, eh? And who are we talking about now?"

I grin. "Too bad you won't be at the climb. If all goes well, she'll be there. Her name is Meadow, and she's fucking gorgeous. She was at Shipwrecked the night we all met up last too. Turns out, she's good friends with Becca. Anyway, I'm trying to convince her to join the calendar crew as photographer." My grin widens. "She'll be stuck with me for months."

Beck chuckles. "I'm sure you'll convince her. Poor girl doesn't know what she's getting herself into." He winks. "Well, I hope it works out for you two. It will be hard to do worse than Sheena the she-devil, that's for sure."

I snort at the nickname and shrug. "We'll see. I have a good feeling about this one, though. She's funny, maybe even funnier than me." I waggle my brows. "And man, she knows how to keep me on my toes. She's sexy as fuck too." I dart a look at him, almost nervous to bring up the next fun fact about Meadow. "And she has a kid. The most adorable little boy."

Beck raises his brows. "No shit. She sounds like your dream girl, man."

I bite down on my bottom lip and take a step backward. "I think she just might be."

With a wink, I leave him at his Rover and jog over to my truck. I have a dinner date with Meadow to prepare for.

CHAPTER ELEVEN

MEADOW

It's early in the evening on Thursday when I decide to cancel on Asher. My stomach is in knots, and I can't quite make sense of the weight of disappointment in my chest, but I pick up my phone and call him instead of texting the way we've been doing the past few days.

"If you're calling to cancel on me, I'm going to hang up and pretend you never called." Asher's teasing voice lifts my spirits, despite the circumstances.

"I'm so sorry, but Tate's asthma is kicking in. It usually does this time of year. He gets super congested and can barely breathe. He'll be okay, but we've got these breathing treatments I need to give him every couple of hours until it clears." I know I'm overexplaining, but I need Asher to know I'm not making up an excuse to bail.

"Poor guy. Do you need any help? You know you are speaking with a trained medical professional."

I smile, my heart all aflutter the way it gets when he becomes flirtatious. "Thank you, but I think I've got it. We go through this every year. But..." I bite down, an idea coming to mind. "If you stop by, we can still have that talk about the calendar. I understand if you want to stay away, though." I laugh, immediately regretting my offer. Why would Asher want to hang out with a sick kid and a single mom?

I've barely finished my last thought when Asher says, "I'll head over."

I nearly choke on my spit in surprise. "You will? You don't have to—"

He chuckles. "Text me your address."

Stunned, I panic when we get off the phone and run around the house, straightening cushions and tossing Tate's toys into bins. While I'm rushing from the living room toward Tate's room to check on him, I spot my mom watching me with a narrowed slant of her eyes.

"Mind if I ask why you got the bug to start cleaning?"

I stop and take a breath. "Asher is coming over here, since I don't want to leave Tate to go to dinner. We're just going to discuss this whole calendar thing." I stop myself from saying too much. My mom can always see straight through me. "Anyway, he's on his way now, so I'm just straightening up."

She nods, and we both peek into the open door of Tate's room to find him sound asleep in his bed. I sigh, relief filling me. I was wound up at the thought of canceling on Asher, but I couldn't leave Tate's breathing treatments up to my mom. Not after she'd had Tate alone for an entire week.

"I see," Mom says, and the corners of her mouth turn up slightly. "You still want to convince me that this is all about charity and nothing to do with the fact that Asher is a gorgeous firefighter model?"

I laugh. Sometimes my mom can be so ridiculous. "He's not one of the models, Mom. He's *organizing* the calendar. Big difference."

She tilts her head. "You sure about that?" She struts a few steps to her room across the hall from Tate's, pops inside for a few seconds, and then comes back out with a twelve-by-twelve-inch calendar. "Take a gander at that, and then let me know what you think."

I pull the calendar from her and flip it around to the front, and there it is. The cover guy is staring straight back at me—shirtless and deliciously oiled up, with Herculean abs on the same strong arms that swept me into his web the moment he stopped me from falling at the accident scene.

"Oh my God."

My mom laughs. It's a full-on belly laugh, with her head tossed back. She's enjoying this way too much.

"Where did you find this?"

"In my closet." She's all giggly now, and I swear I'm staring at a completely different woman. "The girls and I went to this charity event last year at the mall, and these firefighters were there signing calendars. I thought Asher looked familiar the other day."

I flip to the first month of the calendar to find Asher again, only it's a different pose. He's leaning against a ladder and looking between the rungs to the camera. "Mr. January," I read out loud. My face and neck feel so hot, I know I'm completely exposed.

"He's a gorgeous man. Look," she says, pointing at a spot on his photo. "He even signed it for me."

Turns out my mom had met Asher before me. "Unreal," I say with a laugh. "So, this is what they want me to shoot." I continue flipping through the calendar. "This looks easy enough. I can't imagine needing more than a day or two to shoot."

"So you're going to do it?"

I shrug, closing the calendar and handing it back to my mom. "Maybe. That's why Asher is coming over. When I have all the details, I'll decide."

She pushes the calendar back to me and winks. "Keep it. You'll need it for research."

"I'm sure there's a lot to be learned here. Thank you." I laugh and shake my head, then I retreat to my bedroom to find something to wear other than sweats. I had a pretty dress picked out for dinner, but it would be ridiculous to wear that now.

"You think he likes you?"

I swivel around, surprised to find her sitting on my bed. I didn't realize my mom had followed me. "No, it's not like that." Even as I say the words, they don't feel right. I sigh. "He's not looking for anything serious."

"How do you know?"

"Because he told me the night of the wedding."

She narrows her eyes. "And why would he tell you that? Let me guess. You told him you weren't looking for anything serious, and then he echoed what you wanted."

I avoid her eyes, knowing my mom well enough to predict exactly how the rest of this conversation will play out. "Yes, but—"

"Oh, dear." She sighs. "How are you ever going to find a man if you tell all of them you aren't looking?"

"I'm not trying to find a man right now. I have enough going on as it is."

"Like what?"

My mouth hangs open as I stare back at her. I knew living with my mom would be difficult with her watching and judging my every move, but to have her question yet again why I'm not ready for a relationship triggers me in a way I don't quite understand.

"Like... getting my business up and running and getting Tate settled in a new place. Geez, Mom, we just got here. Give me a little time, okay?"

Her jaw clenches, and I know she's trying to bite her tongue. "You keep saying that. But it's been over three years since Milton died. And even then—"

"Please don't say it." I shake my head, feeling on the

verge of tears. "Look, just because I told Asher I didn't want anything serious didn't mean he had to say it back."

"Of course he said it back. He probably wants to make you feel comfortable."

"Or maybe he just doesn't want anything serious. I still don't know anything about him besides his profession and that we have mutual friends."

My mom raises her brow. "And he's funny and great with kids."

"Maybe so, but he's a firefighter. I always swore the next guy I ended up with would be a corporate type or a teacher. Something much less dangerous."

Her forehead creases as if she finally understands deep down what's holding me back. "Oh, honey. What happened to Milton was an absolute tragedy, but you can't base your entire future on fear. Besides,"—her face relaxes —"Asher primarily works with the ambulances, so there's already less risk."

I groan at her point and back away from her to turn toward my closet. "I can't do this right now. You're putting me in a funk, and it's not helping. I don't even know if I'm going to say yes to this charity thing. I don't know what the hours will be or how flexible they'll be if something comes up. He seems to think I'm the right fit, but I don't know."

My mom uncrosses her legs and leans forward slightly. "Okay, Meadow. I'm only going to say this once, because I know you don't need or want reasoning with, but please remember the reason you moved here. It's okay for you to lean on me and to ask me for things. It doesn't mean you're anything less than an amazing mother. I want to help. I want to spend time with Tate. So if you need to take this opportunity to help better your career while also doing incredible things for the Burn Foundation, then stop hesitating and just do it."

My throat tightens. "I just feel like I've failed Tate in so many ways already. And he's already lost one parent. What if I'm working so much that he starts to worry? And if I start dating..." I shake my head, unable to even comprehend the thought.

"You know what the key to Tate's happiness is?"

I look at her, waiting for her magical words to float through the air and make everything better. "What?"

My mom nods toward me. "You need to be happy first. Tate will feel that. Give yourself a break, Meadow. We all grow up with different circumstances. That's just life. And one way isn't better than the other. It just means we all have to find a way to make our own circumstances. You're not going to find your way if you're avoiding all the opportunities that come to you. And," she adds with a coy smile, "by avoiding all the handsome men who come your way."

I smile at her while a weight feels like it's lifting off my chest. After all these years, all it takes is my mom's words of reason as a reminder that I am being too hard on myself. "Thanks, Mom."

She stands, walks over to me, and hugs me firmly. "All right, well, I'll go check on Tate while you get ready." She starts to walk out. "And put on some lipstick. The matte. What's the name of that reddish-pink shade I like again?"

I laugh at how predictable my mom is and step into my walk-in closet. "Addiction."

"Yes, that one."

I change into a pair of white cutoff shorts and a lightweight blue denim button-down. I roll the sleeves up and tuck the front of my shirt into my shorts then detangle my dark-brown wavy hair with a comb. There. It's better than sweats. After giving myself another once-over in the mirror, I decide to add some mascara and a faint layer of lipstick to my otherwise plain appearance.

It's not like this is a date, I remind myself. *It's a business meeting. At my home. And my son is in bed, sick.*

I frown and push away from the counter to go see how Tate's doing with his nap. He's been sleeping on and off today. Most of the time, I have to wake him up for his breathing treatments, and then he has a hard time falling back asleep. Poor thing.

Tate is just waking up when I walk into his room, his deep cough having roused him. "Mommy," he croaks while reaching his arms out. His eyes are still half-closed, and hair the same color as mine is tossed in thick waves around his head.

I sit at the edge of his bed and pull him onto my lap. "How you feeling, babe? You hungry?"

He shakes his head.

"You thirsty?"

He looks blankly ahead for a second and then nods.

"How about we get you dressed then go into the kitchen, and I'll get you a big glass of water. And if you get hungry, I can make you your favorite meal."

His glossy eyes go as wide as he can manage. "Pasghetti?"

I smile and run my fingers through his hair. "That's right."

He presses his cheek into my chest and closes his eyes. I pick him up and grab a change of clothes for him then change him quickly before carrying him into the living room.

"You want to watch some TV while I get your water?"

He nods into my chest, eyes still closed. I prop him up in the corner of the couch, run to grab his water, and return to find his attention on his favorite dinosaur show. As soon as I hand him the water, a knock sounds at the door.

I head to the door, my chest doing that floppy thing it did when I was with Asher the other night, all the while convincing myself that I'm only into the guy for two reasons. He's safe—considering he doesn't want to get into anything serious. And he's obnoxiously gorgeous. Both reasons are superficial enough that no way could there ever be anything more with him.

But when I open the door, I'm blindsided—yet again. Asher stands on the doorstep with two large reusable grocery bags in his hands and a wide grin on his face. "Figured you'd still need to eat."

CHAPTER TWELVE

ASHER

The moment Meadow opens the door, I'm blasted with the memory of seeing her for the first time. Sure, my head wasn't in the right space at that time, but I knew the woman I had just caught in my arms was gorgeous. *Beyond* gorgeous. She was a breath of fresh air amid a chaotic storm of wind, smoke, and screams from the accident.

If not for Meadow, memories of that day would probably still haunt me the way they do my buddy Beck. After our workout earlier today, I finally pieced together that something happened on the day of the accident that triggered memories from his past. Since I've spent time in the military, I understand all too well how PTSD works, especially from my time overseas witnessing horrific trauma no one should ever have to live through. Memories of some tragic events have the ability to eat us alive if we don't learn how to gain control of them.

I lift the shopping bags I'm holding and peer over her shoulder to see if Tate or her mom are nearby. "This is okay, right?" I don't usually second-guess myself, but I'm still learning about Meadow, and the last thing I want to do is corner her in any way. "I just figured, since you had to stay and we couldn't go out to dinner, that maybe you didn't plan to make anything, so..."

The smile that lights up her face is like a jump-start to my chest.

"No. It's fine." She bites down on her lower lip. "It's more than fine. I'm just shocked, that's all. You didn't have to bring anything."

"I couldn't come over empty-handed. This way, you can look after Tate, I'll cook dinner, and then we can talk when there's time."

Meadow narrows her eyes, the playful spark from the wedding coming back. "You're pretty slick at this whole recruitment thing. If I didn't know better, I'd think you wanted more than a few photographs."

I grin. "Well, I'm going to need more than a few if you agree to this. How about I put the food down, and we start the negotiations?"

Meadow laughs and gestures for me to follow her into the other room, where Tate is nestled into the corner of the couch, his eyes drooping but locked on the television screen.

"Tate, remember my friend Asher from the other day? He's here to make us dinner."

Tate blinks up at her then at me. A wide grin spreads across his face. "Ashew the fiafida," he says.

"That's me," I confirm with a grin. I don't need to examine Tate in order to hear how congested the little man is. Then he coughs, and instinct kicks in. "Time for another treatment?" I ask Meadow.

She nods, her frown revealing how helpless she must feel when her young son is sick. "It's about that time again." She points toward the next room. "The kitchen is there if you want to put everything down. I'm going to go grab his nebulizer."

I walk to the kitchen and set the bags on the counter before coming back out to the living room to sit with Tate. "Whatcha watching, buddy?"

He sits up straighter, tucks his knees under him, then points at the television. The next thing he says takes a few extra seconds to decipher.

"*Dinosaur Train*?" I ask.

He nods so hard I think his head might fall off. He goes on to tell me in a very excited tone that the Pteranodon family adopted a *T. rex* named Buddy, and now Buddy is earning his conductor hat.

"You sure know a lot about dinosaurs and trains, huh?"

He reaches over and tugs my cap off my head, grins, and places it on his own. "I a conducto when I gwo'd up."

Laughing, I run my fingers through my hair. "You want to be a conductor? I can see why. Trains are pretty cool."

"Twains go fast," he says before using his hands to show me while following it up with zoom-zoom and toot-toot noises.

"Someone's feeling better, huh?" Meadow asks while walking back into the room, nebulizer in hand.

She plugs in the machine and sets it on the coffee table then drips the liquid medicine into the chamber before securing it to the mouthpiece. I watch her, impressed. "You're a pro," I tell her.

She smiles and picks Tate up to position him on her lap. She stretches the headpiece around Tate's head to get the nose and mouthpiece suctioned to his face before starting the machine. Tate looks like a pro too. He doesn't even put up a fight. When she verifies the vapor is filling the mask, she looks up at me. "We've been at this since he was eight months old. It's less frequent now, but necessary when his breathing gets like this."

I nod. "Bronchospasms are no joke. Albuterol is a miracle worker, in most cases. The hardest part is getting patients to relax when treating them, but your patient seems to be doing just fine."

Meadow reaches up and fixes my cap on Tate's head. "Looks like he found a new conductor hat."

I chuckle. "That he did. Looks better on him, anyway."

She smiles. "How long have you been an EMT?"

"I was a combat medic in the army. Earned my EMT cert there when I was only twenty. So, ten years now."

"Wow, really?" Meadow blinks at me in surprise. "So then when did you start working at the fire station?"

"Five years ago. I was lucky enough to find a job at the station quickly after graduating from the fire academy and getting my firefighting certification."

"Lucky? Wouldn't you be a shoo-in after your experience?"

I shake my head. "You'd be surprised. I've heard so many horror stories about the difficulties of finding a job after leaving the military. Especially if you're moving to a new town."

"That's right. I forgot your ex-wife moved you to Tampa. Where are you from?"

"Seattle."

"Really? Forgive my curiosity, but... why did your ex choose Tampa?"

I hate the way my insides clam up at her question, but it's something instinctual that happens whenever anyone mentions my ex-wife. As ready as I am to move on from that situation, I feel like I'm going to be answering for that time in my past for a long time to come.

"Her parents moved to Tampa to retire, and with me gone a lot, she said she felt lonely." I give Meadow an easy smile, hoping to show her that I'm over my ex. "By the time I was discharged, the decision was already made for me, and I made the best of it. I wanted her to be happy, you know?"

Meadow nods, her stare lingering long enough to make my chest feel jumpy. Afraid I'd said something that might have put her off, I stand up. "I'll start dinner. Is your mom around? There's enough for everyone."

Meadow starts to speak, but another voice beats her to it. "Oh, whatcha making?"

I look up to find Farrah walking into the room, carrying a book.

"Spaghetti sound okay?"

Tate gasps. "Pasghetti?"

We all laugh at the robotic tone of his voice, thanks to the mask strapped to his face. "Do you like spaghetti, buddy?"

"It's his favorite," Meadow says with a smile.

"Mine too," Farrah adds.

Meadow rolls her eyes. "Thank you again, Asher. That was really sweet of you to bring dinner."

I wink at her. "Just remember how appreciative you are when I pitch the calendar to you."

After returning to the kitchen, I find my way around, grabbing pots and pans and emptying the grocery bags. But not even cooking can distract me from the questions swirling through my mind regarding Meadow's silence after we discussed Sheena. I don't know what Meadow is thinking, and I hate that.

I also don't know what's going on between Meadow and me. I know I find her insanely attractive. I know she's an incredible mom and a true talent in her profession. She seems to have the drive and a desire to stand on her own two feet. I admire her as much as I want to strip her naked and finish what we started the other night. I also know I'm terrified to lose whatever connection we've started to build —a connection that goes deeper than anything a casual encounter could satisfy.

I'm stirring the sauce when Meadow walks into the kitchen thirty minutes later.

"It smells like heaven in here," Meadow says. She comes closer to the sauce, her eyes sparkling back at me. "Want to know the secret to Tate's heart?"

I raise my brow. "You mean my favorite hat wasn't enough?"

She laughs. "Not even close." She points at the sauce. "Add a little bit of sugar to that, and he'll be your best friend for life."

I clutch my chest in mock horror. "Sugar in spaghetti sauce? Are you trying to hurt me with your words?"

She reaches into the cupboard and pulls out a plastic container of sugar. "Trust me. Just a quarter cup should do the trick. It's not like you eat spaghetti for the nutrients, anyway."

Okay, she has a point. I sigh and grab the sugar from her with a playful glare. "Fine. But only because I really need a new best friend now that mine got hitched."

Meadow lifts herself onto the counter beside me, and my eyes immediately fall to her exposed legs. Her white shorts expose her sexy thighs—thighs I thoroughly enjoyed running my fingers between the last time she was on a counter in front of me.

I tear my eyes away from her legs and meet her gaze. "Can I ask you something?"

She tilts her head. "Sure."

"Why in the hell are you single?"

Her cheeks darken a shade, and while my question is very direct, she seems to be flattered. "Um, well... my husband died, actually—just before Tate was born."

Something twists in my gut as more pieces of Meadow's puzzle click together. "Shit. I'm sorry to hear that. So,

Tate never got to meet his dad." God, I hope that didn't come out too harsh. I'm just—shocked. I wasn't expecting that at all.

She bites down on her lip as if deciding how to word what she's about to tell me. "Tate knows his dad died a hero, and he's very proud of that." Her eyes mist a little. "Milton was a cop. He... um... got shot while intervening with a robbery."

"That's awful."

Meadow nods. "Yeah, well, now you know my deep, dark secret." She gives me a soft smile. "I lived in Cali for three years, just Tate and me, and while we made it work, I just didn't feel like it was the right place for us anymore. So here we are." She shrugs. "Back in my hometown, trying to make it my home again."

"You will." I don't know where the assertiveness in my tone comes from... "I think we all gravitate toward where we're meant to be."

"You think so?"

I nod. "I know so."

It now makes sense why Meadow has no interest in getting into anything serious. Her marriage hadn't ended the way mine had. She wasn't given a choice. Her husband was ripped from her clutches, and she'd become a single mom because of it.

A timer goes off, alerting me to the bread baking in the oven. I grab some mitts to slide them out and then take them off, turn to Meadow, and clap my hands. "Dinner is ready. I'll start dishing it out if everyone is ready."

Meadow hops off the counter. "I'll round up the troops."

She starts to walk away, but something squeezes in my chest. I reach out for her and grab the tips of her fingers before she can get too far. "Hey, Meadow."

She swivels around, her eyes wide with surprise. "Yes?"

"I want you to know that I'm totally capable of being a friend, if that's what you need right now."

Her smile is faint, and her eyes dart to mine before she takes a step back. "Thanks, Asher. That means a lot."

She opens her mouth to say something else then snaps it shut again. When she walks away, I get a gripping feeling in my chest, and my eyes squeeze shut for a second. Sure, I initially contacted Meadow with a completely innocent job offer. But after spending time with her, it isn't just Meadow's photography services that I want. Still, I know beyond a shadow of a doubt that I'd rather be her friend than lose her completely.

CHAPTER THIRTEEN

MEADOW

"Mommy," Tate says before a big yawn brings tears to his eyes.

"What is it, Tater Tot?"

"Ashew make good pasghetti."

A tug in my heart accompanies my smile. I run my fingers through his thick hair and nod. "I think so too, babe."

"Not betta dan Mommy's doh. Mommy make da bess pasghetti eva."

"Aww, you are the sweetest."

I kiss his little cheek until he giggles, then he curls closer into my chest like he wants to burrow himself there and closes his eyes. "Night, Mommy."

"Night, my love. Have sweet dreams, okay?"

"Otay, Mommy," he whispers.

A few seconds later, I hear Tate's deep breathing and look over to find his mouth partially hung open. I give him a kiss on the forehead, grab the baby monitor, and walk out of the room.

Asher is in the kitchen with my mom. They're cleaning up and chatting away like old friends.

"I can get all that tomorrow," I insist.

My mom waves me away then gives Asher a little shove away from the sink. "You two go. I've got this."

Asher grins and walks toward me. "Where to? Dining room? Living room?"

"How about out back? It's nice tonight."

He shrugs. "Lead the way."

I start to walk to the back door when I have a thought. "We're going to need these." I stop, grab a bottle of whiskey from the counter along with two old-fashioned glasses, and then lead Asher to the back patio table. The pool is brightly lit, and the screened-in porch provides much-needed protection from the mosquitos.

"All right." I pour us each a shot to sip. "Let the pitch begin."

"Just like that, huh?" Asher leans back in his chair and brings his whiskey to his lips, eyeing me over the rim. "You'd think I'd have this all planned out by now."

I gasp. "You don't? I expected flip charts, reenactments, and PowerPoint presentations."

Asher grins. "Maybe I should have thought about the flip charts and PowerPoint, but reenactments? C'mon. How exactly would I reenact the making of a firefighter calendar I've never organized before?"

I narrow my eyes. "Then who organized last year's calendar?"

I swear he almost chokes on his drink. "How did you know about that?"

My lip hurts from biting down on it to contain my smile. "Did you think I wouldn't find out?" I release my lip and laugh. "*Mr. January.*"

His eyes practically bulge from his head.

"Nice ladder work, by the way. And that water coming down around you... Was that actual rain, or did someone run a shower for you in front of the station?"

Asher sets his whiskey glass down, nearly choking on his laughter. "Look, I can explain."

A laugh bubbles from deep in my belly. This is far too much fun. "Please. Explain how you got your abs to look all shiny like that. I need to know. For research purposes."

He tosses his head back in a full belly laugh. When he catches his breath, he shakes his head. "Okay, tell me how you found out about the calendar."

I give a cocky shrug of my shoulders. "My mom might have a signed copy lying around."

His mouth drops open. "You have got to be kidding me." He holds up a finger. "In my defense, we put that together almost as a joke, and when we realized we could profit off it, it became a bigger deal, and we donated all the money to charity. And that inspired what Aaron and I are organizing this year. I'm not going to be in the calendar this year, though. I'm just organizing it."

My heart swells in my chest at the mention of their charity donations. I love that they're volunteering their time and efforts for a good cause. For those reasons alone, I want to help.

"Tell me what you have planned for this year."

Asher launches into detail after detail about the events leading up to the actual calendar shoots, the release of the calendar, and then the signings that will take place well into January. It's obvious he and Aaron have thought of everything—thanks to their experience last year, no stone has been left unturned. They've even got a local Top 40 radio station working with them to spread the word.

"I only have one question left," I tell him, once I feel like I've heard enough.

"Let's hear it." He takes a quick sip of his whiskey and leans back in his seat.

"Why on earth did you wait until now to find a photographer? It seems like that's the first thing you should have done."

Asher cringes. "That one's all on me. I searched for months, interviewed a few people who would have probably been great, but at the end of the day, I just didn't pull the trigger for whatever reason. Then I got busy finalizing my divorce, and then I got hurt, and my head just wasn't in it. So I dropped the ball, but I'm glad I did because you came along."

I want to ignore the part about him finalizing a divorce and then getting injured at work, but I can't. "I'm sorry to hear about your divorce."

He shakes his head. "Don't be sorry. It was a long time coming. We'd already been separated for a couple of years, but everything kept getting delayed."

My stomach twists, but the knowledge that he's been separated for two years brings some relief. "And what about your injury?"

He chuckles. "I fell out of a two-story building. House fire. Twisted my ankle and landed on my back. It could have been worse, but it was enough to take me out of work for two weeks. Anyway, none of that is important. I slacked on finding a photographer, but now you're here. You're the perfect fit, Meadow. Please say yes. You can even bring Tate to the station if you need to. He can be our assistant, and just think about how much fun he'd have around all those engines."

I smile, picturing Tate's face lighting up at the sight of all the trucks and lights and uniforms. I groan because Asher has punched holes in every single ounce of defense I had. "Okay," I finally say. "I'll do it. I'll be your photographer."

The shock on his face is epic, like he wasn't expecting that answer from me at all. He jumps up, pumps his fists in the air, swoops me up out of my chair, and spins me around. "You said yes." He pulls back and searches my eyes like he's waiting for me to tell him I'm lying. "Say it again."

Laughing, I roll my eyes. "Yes, Asher. I will be your photographer."

He folds me into his arms again. "You're not going to regret this. And I promise to help you find more business than you'll know what to do with."

I'm still laughing when we break apart. Asher refills our glasses and holds his up to mine. "To new partners."

"Partners? You mean you won't be bossing me around?"

He grins. "Not if I can help it."

"Hmm," I say teasingly, giving him a playful glare.

"Just take the damn shot, Meadow."

I smile and raise the glass to my lips. "To new partners."

We take our drinks and walk to the pool. I sit down at the edge first and slip my feet into the water. He follows my lead, then our eyes turn up toward the full moon.

"I hope I haven't crossed any lines with you." His tone contains a mixture of hope and worry that squeezes my chest.

I turn to look at him. "What do you mean?"

He meets my stare. "I just mean that I'm attracted to you. Very attracted to you." He smiles, and I swear, even in the darkness, I can see him blushing. "And I haven't done a great job with hiding that. But I respect what you said about not wanting anything serious. After hearing your story tonight, I can completely understand why."

"You haven't crossed any lines. At least..." Now it's me who's blushing. I can feel the heat spread up my neck and into my cheeks. "At least none that I haven't wanted crossed. Besides," I say, nudging his shoulder with mine, "you also said you weren't looking for anything serious."

He smiles. "I did say that, didn't I?"

My eyes widen. "You didn't mean it?"

He laughs a little and returns to face forward. "I'm not sure. I mean, I married my ex straight out of high school, so dating is kind of a foreign concept to me to begin with. But it's also been two years since I separated from her, so it's not like it's too soon to move on or anything. I guess I'm figuring things out as I go."

I sit up straight. "As you should. I think that's what I'm doing too." My heart is beating fast when I look back at Asher. I want him to know I'm not set on what I said the other night either. At least, not anymore.

His eyebrows bend together as he searches my eyes, like he's still trying to figure out something about me. "So you're open to dating? I mean, if you found someone who sparked your interest."

I nod. "Yeah, I think so." I laugh. "Good luck to whoever is finding time to date me with my busy schedule between Tate, work, and this new charity project I'm taking on."

Asher leans toward me, pressing his shoulder to mine. "You never know, Meadow. You might just meet a guy at this charity project thing."

"You think?" I tease.

"I pretty much guarantee it." He leans in closer with just his head this time, his eyes dipping to my lips. "And what a lucky bastard he'll be."

His mouth is only an inch from mine. My eyelids flutter closed. "You're starting to sound like the jealous type."

His lips brush mine. "If that lucky bastard is anyone other than me, jealousy wouldn't even begin to cover it."

My heartbeat triples with his husky tone, the heat of his words enveloping me in a rush of desire that reaches deep down into my chest. This man is as dangerous as he is charming, and while those are reasons to stay far away, staying away is the last thing I want to do.

He presses his lips firmly to mine, and a groan erupts from my chest. It's like I'm experiencing his kiss for the first time all over again because in a way, it means something more now. Something that goes beyond a night of no-strings-attached fun.

Something that absolutely terrifies me.

CHAPTER FOURTEEN

ASHER

The crowd at Raymond James Stadium for this year's Burn Foundation stair climb is far more than triple the size it was last year. Every year, it grows, but I'm absolutely stunned by what our fire station has been able to accomplish with the help of the surrounding Tampa fire stations. Thousands of people have pledged money online for the event, and we're about to celebrate that by running the stadium steps.

The squad I pulled together consists of some of my closest friends from Bayside Regional and from my station. Aaron is part of my squad, too, but both of us will be more focused on our calendar project than anything else.

"Where is she, dude? Don't tell me she bailed." Aaron struts up to me, a wicked grin on his face.

When I told him I'd secured Meadow as the photographer, he was impressed and amused all at once.

"She'll be here any minute, you ass. How's the sign-up crew doing?"

Aaron pats the back of his clipboard and winks. "Great. They know what to do. They'll look for all the guys wearing fire crew shirts and pitch the calendar to them. If they're interested, we'll get them to fill out a contact form, and I'll invite them to the selection dinner on Monday." He flexes his bicep and pretends to kiss it. "All in a day's work."

I pinch my fingers around his arm, deflating his muscles and chuckling. "Too bad this wasn't the ladder climb. Those arms could use the extra workout."

I take off sprinting from Aaron before he can tackle me to the ground because I know that's exactly what he wants to do.

"You better watch your back, Moore!" he yells after me.

A few moments later, I catch up to the members of my squad who have already arrived and clap Dane on the shoulder. "Thanks again for coming, man."

He smiles, showing his appreciation. "No problem. I'm looking forward to the climb. Greg said he was coming by. You seen him yet?"

I shake my head. "Not yet. I'll keep my eye out."

We chat it up for a few minutes until I spot another friend in the distance. It's none other than Lars, who I haven't seen since our last group happy hour. I'd done a little begging to get her to join my squad today, not that I should have had to. We've been friends since she started her residency in the area years ago, but now that she's a full-time psychiatrist at Bayside Regional, our run-ins are as frequent as our meetups at Shipwrecked. After a recent fishing trip with my new buddy, Dane, I found out he's into her, so I decided to do a little matchmaking. I would love to see Lars loosen up a little, and if anyone can help her do that, it will be Dane.

Judging by the lustful look on Dane's face, he's already spotted Lars, so I leave him and head off in the opposite direction. As soon as I start walking, a vision in yellow enters my sight. Applause booms from the spectators sitting in a section of the stadium roped off for observing, and if I didn't know better, I would say they were clapping for her. Meadow fucking Matthews. *God, she's gorgeous.*

She's wearing a long shirt with rolled-up sleeves and dark jeans that cling to gorgeous curves. She carries the same professional camera I remember seeing at the scene of the accident. I think Meadow's choice of outfits is one of the things about her that attracts me the most. She has a classy yet sexy vibe that feels as effortless as it is to spend time with her.

I haven't seen Meadow in ten days, which made me think I was going to go crazy. Between her work schedule and mine, we hadn't found a time to get together. We'd texted each other here and there, but I was afraid to be pushy after finally getting her to agree to this whole calendar thing. I wasn't willing to risk messing it up, even after that firework of a kiss we'd shared.

"Is that a big camera in your hand, or are you just happy to see me?" As soon as the terrible joke spills from my lips, I cringe internally.

Meadow cocks a brow, not even pretending to be amused. "Really? Ten days, and that's how you're going to greet me?"

"You've been counting down the days too?"

She smiles. "I guess I have. So," she says with a slap of her hands on her hips, "where do you want me?"

Her question triggers an automatic response in me that's far too crude to repeat aloud. So, instead of telling her that I'd just envisioned her stripped down naked at the fifty-yard line, writhing, with my face between her thighs, I give her the next best answer. "With me. I'll give you the lay of the land, and then I'll let you do your thing."

I take her around the section of the stadium sectioned off for the stair climb and show her where the members of the different squads sit while they wait for their turns. I point at a woman holding a clipboard. "She's one of a dozen volunteers working with us to recruit firefighters. The more the merrier."

Meadow nods. "Right, because then everyone interested will show up at the selection dinner next week to be voted in or out."

I grin. "That's right. Think Miss America, calendar-boy style. The dinner is a huge fundraising opportunity for us. The entry fee alone brings in a ton of money, but donations will continue to pour in all night."

"Sounds great." She looks around. "So, how do I know who the firefighters are versus everyone else in attendance?"

"Easy." I walk forward to a guy who's filling out a contact form. "See his shirt?" I point at the firefighter logo on the back. "All the different organizations show their field of service. Just look for the firefighter logos and snap away. We'll use all the photos in slideshows at the upcoming events, and we'll auction off the photos later to raise additional funds."

I show her around the concession area and then down to the sidelines of the field, where a squad of firefighters does synchronized push-ups. "Right there." I point at them. "That's the kind of shot we want."

She's quick to the draw, pulling her camera to her eye and stepping forward to capture different angles. At one point, I look up to find my buddy Greg standing a good distance away with a curvy brunette I don't recognize. He gives me a nod, and I can't help the slight squint that I give him, signaling that we definitely need to catch up soon so he can fill me in.

When Meadow's done, she walks back over to me and lifts the viewfinder up to start scrolling through the photos. "Like this?"

I peer over her shoulder, her addictive peach scent drawing me close so that my front is just barely touching her back. It takes everything in my power to keep my hand from finding the small of her waist to lock her in closer to me.

I'm so entranced that I almost forget why I'm standing here to begin with, until she tosses me a look over her shoulder, and I have to glance up from her neck.

"Well, what do you think?"

"Come to a Halloween party with me tonight," I blurt out.

The pink in her cheeks darkens. "W-What?"

"There's this party at Shipwrecked. They always have one on the Saturday before Halloween. They have a DJ, and they clear out all the tables, so it's just one big dance floor. You should come. You don't even need to dress up if you don't want to."

She appears to be thinking about it. "I have to see if my mom's okay with watching Tate tonight, but it sounds like fun." She smiles. "I'll try."

She starts to drop her camera, but I reach for it and look into the viewfinder while it's still in her hands. The shot is simple enough, but something about the way Meadow captures the absolute best angle where the lighting hits her subjects just right makes a simple photo come to life.

"I think I hired the right woman for the job."

She laughs and lowers her camera again. "*Hired* implies that you're paying me."

I wince. "Ouch. True. I suppose you don't accept sexual favors."

As expected, her blush deepens. "Well, if I did, I would probably need to get to work, wouldn't I?"

I grin and take a step back, gesturing for her to snap away. "By all means. Don't let me stop you from earning your keep. I'll be with that squad over there if you need me." I wink and take off in a jog to reach my squad, more than ready for the festivities tonight.

CHAPTER FIFTEEN

MEADOW

Tate is already asleep by the time Asher gets to my house. My mom passed out not long after Tate did, taking the baby monitor with her so that she can hear if he wakes up. Tate has been sleeping so well lately, though, that I have a feeling he won't wake up until late tomorrow morning.

When I swing open the door, my jaw drops so far, I swear it might hit the floor. I knew Asher was taking me to a Halloween party. He told me he was going to dress up as a firefighter. I guess his buddy Beck planted the idea in his mind as a joke. But I didn't expect him to show up wearing nothing but a baggy pair of bunker pants and oil that covers his amazing upper body. Seriously, the man is as gorgeous as he looked in that calendar, and that's when it hits me.

"You're Mr. January, aren't you?"

He holds up a large piece of cardboard I hadn't even seen him carrying. January is written at the top, above where a hole is cut out for his head to go. Below it is a grid of dates, mimicking a real calendar.

"Wow. You really outdid yourself."

He grins, lowers the fake calendar, and gestures to me. "Your turn."

I grab the belt of my trench coat to ensure it's secure, clutch the plastic bag holding accessories for my costume, and shake my head. "Not until we get there. If I show you now, I'll chicken out."

He lifts his brows. "Damn. That good, huh?"

I laugh and take a step forward to lock up behind me. "I was able to pull something together last minute. I'm pretty proud of it, actually."

"Can't wait to see it."

He walks me to his truck, helps me inside, and then walks around to his side. The entire time, I can't take my eyes off his amazing body. Asher is already drop-dead gorgeous, tall, smart, and funny—it's unfair he has to look like that without a shirt on too.

"So, how did today go? I didn't see you much after you got going with taking pics."

"It went well." I perk up, excited to tell him about some of the candids I was able to get. "I got some shots of the crowd and stadium, too, in case you need to use those for anything, but I think you'll be happy. I uploaded all the raw photos to my server. I just need your email address so I can send you the link. And if you need me to edit anything, then I'm more than happy to."

He sneaks a glance at me when he reaches a stop sign. "Thanks, Meadow. Already going above and beyond."

I sink back into my seat and face forward. "Just doing my job."

"*Job* would suggest that I pay you," he teases, using my joke from earlier today.

I bat my eyelashes at him, feelings of bold flirtation taking hold. "I thought we worked out a payment plan."

He narrows his gaze at me before facing front again.

"All that teasing is going to get you in a whole lot of trouble, I hope you know."

"I'll take my chances."

What started out as a joke earlier today suddenly doesn't feel like one anymore. While I'm not afraid of a little flirtatious banter, I certainly don't engage in this kind of talk with just anyone. I can't even wrap my head around how Asher makes me feel. All I know is that I want more of him.

Shipwrecked looks packed by the time we arrive. The parking lot is full, but we get lucky finding a spot when someone pulls out. I hop out of the truck and strip my trench coat off then toss it inside before closing the door behind me. Asher rounds the corner and stops in his tracks. I think his eyeballs might pop out of his head.

"Holy fuck." His jaw drops, and his greedy eyes peruse my body from head to foot, drinking in every last inch of me—short black skirt, white cutoff tank stretched over my chest, red suspenders, and a red firefighter hat I borrowed from Tate's toy collection. His eyes settle on my breasts, and I watch as he silently reads the words Miss January, which I'd written in permanent black marker. He smiles. "You just threw that together, huh?"

I shrug. "Thought it was pretty clever. You said you were going as a firefighter, so I thought I'd match." I give him a little twirl. "With a twist, of course."

"Well, damn. Now I don't know if I want to rescue you or let you rescue me."

I grin and strut by him, throwing him a playful look over my shoulder. "I think you're going to need all the help you can get tonight."

He catches up to me and threads his fingers through mine. "I think you might be right, Miss January. You better stay close."

My chest is like a container for wild butterflies at this

point. I don't remember ever feeling so giddy over a man before—or so wanted. It feels good.

Asher knows everyone who works at Shipwrecked, so he's able to steer us straight through the entrance, skipping the long line of characters still waiting to get in. Once we're inside, I take a sweeping gaze around the thoroughly decorated room. Spiderwebs cling to every light fixture, laser images dance on the walls, fog blows steadily across the dance floor, and haunting music beats through the surrounding speakers.

Asher squeezes my hand and nods toward the bar. "I'm not going to drink tonight, since I have to work tomorrow, but I'll get you whatever you want."

I shake my head. "I'm good. Tate and I have a big day tomorrow."

"What are you going to do?"

"Oh, you know, the usual. Carve pumpkins, visit a haunted house, go trick or treating. He wore his Elmo costume all day today. He can't wait to wake up and put it on again."

Asher laughs. "I need to see that." He squeezes my hand. "In fact, I'm working a haunted house tomorrow. It's a scary one, but they have a kid zone with a spooky house that's just for fun and laughs. If you come, I can get you in for free." He wiggles his brow.

I smile, once again amazed by Asher and his many surprises. "Firefighters work at haunted houses?"

"EMTs do."

"I thought you work for the station."

"I do, but I volunteer my time for an ambulance service on the side, too, since I can use the hours toward becoming a paramedic. Anyway, we're just at the haunted house on standby in case anything goes wrong. You'd be surprised by the amount of heart attacks and injuries I see at this time of year."

"That's terrible."

He nods. "Yeah, unfortunately, it happens. It's a law now that if you have a haunted house, trained medical professionals need to be present."

"On that note..." I laugh through my discomfort. "Sounds terrible, but I'm sure Tate and my mom will love it. Count us in."

His smile widens, unleashing more flutters in my chest. "Now that that's settled, let's dance." He tugs me to the dance floor and wraps me in his arms as a sexy Camila Cabello song starts to play. Even without alcohol running through my blood, I'm drunk at the firmness of his hold, the flirtatious glimmer in his eyes, and the way our bodies fit together like they were made for that purpose.

I love when he walks me around the room a few songs later to introduce me to some of his friends. Since Shipwrecked is located on Davis Islands, right next to the hospital, it makes sense that Asher would have a small group of tight-knit friends who work in one of the wealthiest areas of Tampa.

"Nah, Beck couldn't make the climb today, so I don't expect him to be here," Asher tells his security guard friend, Dane.

I look to Dane's right and notice a stunning blond woman with light-brown eyes and an awkward smile. She sticks her hand out. "Larsen Belle."

I accept her hand, giving her an easy smile. "Meadow Matthews. Nice to meet you."

My focus moves to her shirt, which is a plain white number. I wouldn't have thought anything of it, but the chalky black handwriting catches my eye. *Pickled Pecker Picker*. I burst out laughing.

"Yeah," she says with a laugh. "I find myself doing ridiculous things lately."

With a quick look over at Dane, I see that he's wearing

a matching shirt that just says *Pecker*. Now it all makes sense.

I smile at her. "Well, you have my vote in the costume contest."

Asher says he sees someone he knows and guides me back through the crowd. Someone squeals out my name, and I turn just in time to catch a drunk Becca in my arms. Aaron is right behind her, greeting Asher with a fist bump.

"Becca, where have you been? I haven't seen you since the wedding."

She gives me a dramatic pout and nods. "I know. I've been meaning to call. After the honeymoon, we moved into the new house, and it's just been nuts. Aaron dragged me here to let loose a little. Surprised to see you," she says before her eyes drift over to Asher then snap back to me. "Oh."

I laugh, hoping she doesn't make too big of a deal out of the whole thing. "I love your costume," I tell her, trying to divert the conversation before it even begins.

She does a little twirl for me in her sexy Maleficent costume. It appears that Aaron is her dragon, although he's shirtless and only wearing a tail and dragon wings, so that's only an assumption. My attempt at a diversion is short-lived. She plucks at my red suspenders and drops her jaw at the writing on my top.

"*Miss* January? Holy shit, Meadow. Are you and Asher, like, an official couple?"

I cover my face with my hands, embarrassed. "It's not like that, it's..." I'm about to say, *"It's nothing,"* when I catch Asher and Aaron watching me, waiting for me to answer. "My mom found last year's calendar, and I had to tease him. I didn't know he was going to go as Mr. January."

There, I turned the tables and avoided a terribly awkward situation. Although when Asher narrows his eyes playfully at me, I'm not totally in the clear.

"What can I say? I lack creativity, unlike this one." He winks at me, then he nods at Aaron. "What the hell are you supposed to be?"

Becca runs her hands over her husband's abs. "He's my sexy dragon man, that's who," she slurs.

Asher and I laugh before he pulls me back onto the dance floor, this time moving even closer than before. He doesn't even bother to move his hips much. He stays close, not breaking eye contact until he's got me backed against a wall. His fingers dance on the bare skin of my stomach while his other hand grips my waist.

"Have I told you how sexy you look tonight?"

I shrug. "No, but I could have guessed by that drool running down your mouth."

He leans in, our lips inches apart. "Get it for me?"

With a smile, I close the distance, connecting us with yet another heart-stopping kiss. All the sound in the room muffles as the scene blurs to nothing but bright lights and a sea of faceless bodies, dancing all around us. But all I feel is Asher. My hands land on his chest, and I boldly run them up the terrain of his cut body, appreciating every dip, valley, and peak, like a new explorer on her first real adventure.

He groans as he pulls away from my mouth and buries his face in my neck. "This outfit is making me want to do all kinds of dirty things to you, and I'm not even sorry for it." He leans back slightly and lets his fingers drift up my skin until he's grazing the lower part of my bra. "You know what's unfair?"

My heart is beating so fast that I can barely breathe, let alone speak. "What's that?"

"It's unfair that I've already touched you, but I was too drunk to remember every single detail."

I swallow. At this point, I'm convinced Asher and I are

completely on the same wavelength because I've been bothered by the exact thing. "What *do* you remember?"

He blows out a breath, his other hand slipping to the bottom of my skirt. "I remember your pretty pink dress with the high slit on this leg." He draws a line with his finger over the cloth of my skirt. "I remember fitting between your legs on that counter and badly wanting to fuck you on it, but I was a good boy."

I bite down on the inside of my lip, desperately trying to keep it together. "You were very good."

He nods. "I remember how wet you were, how fast you soaked my fingers, and I remember how you strangled the shit out of my fingers when you came."

God, it's hot in here. "Sounds like you remember quite a bit."

His eyes narrow. "Not enough. I can't remember what my fingers looked like when they pumped you, or if you made any noises when you came. And it's been killing me, Meadow." He lowers his minty breath to my ear. "I need you to help me remember."

"And how can I help you with that?"

My tease is throaty and breathless, and it's all the answer he needs to pull me away from the wall, to the staff door, and down a narrow hallway. He pushes open the door to a dimly lit room filled with furniture that normally fills the restaurant. His mouth is on mine again, hungrier this time as he backs me up against a table and slips his hand beneath my shirt. He cups my breast and groans as he squeezes. I swear I can feel the length of his cock growing hard between my legs, and I'm just intoxicated enough by his kiss to reach inside his pants and stroke him.

Before I can think to make any sort of move, he pushes my suspenders off my shoulders, reaches beneath my shirt at my back, and snaps off my strapless bra so that it falls to the floor.

"Goddamn, you're sexy." His fingers brush my erect nipples, softly at first, but just like his kiss, his fingers grow hungry too. He shoves my shirt above my breasts, gazes down at them like the view is agonizing at best, and then takes a swipe at one while gazing back at me.

It's like he's trying to torture me with slow, deliberate licks while gauging my reaction. I'm so focused on his eyes and the feel of his mouth wrapped around my breast that I almost miss the fingers crawling up beneath my skirt and between my thighs until they're running circle patterns on the cloth above my clit.

Greedy for more, I climb backward onto the table and spread my knees wider. I want his mouth on me as much as I want to feel him deep inside me. I grab his hand to reposition it over my opening then push his two fingers inside me until I shudder.

"Holy fuck." He sighs. "Meadow, you're so wet. Are you always like this or is it just for me?"

I bite down gently on his bottom lip. "This is all for you, Asher."

My words are a torch to his already blazing inferno of desire. "Good. Because I know just how to take care of you."

He presses me down so my back is lying on the cold table while he pushes my skirt up to my waist and buries his mouth between my legs. He doesn't even try to be gentle as he tastes me where I ache for him most then suctions his lips to my clit and flicks his tongue like he's punishing me.

A guttural moan flies from deep in my chest, only making him greedier as he grips my thighs and sucks me until I explode.

"Fuck." His breathless curse is the only thing I make out in my post-coital fog. "I think I remember now."

"Me too," I pant out, recalling the memories of our

escapade in the staff room at the wedding reception. "You and your big ego," I tease.

He chuckles. "Yeah, except you never did stroke it."

I frown. My memories from late that night are a little less vague now, but I think he might be right about that. He made me come with his fingers that night, but I gave him nothing in return. I can't make that mistake again.

He yanks me back to a sitting position, his mouth catching mine. I can taste myself on his tongue as it glides into my mouth. Still coming down from my orgasmic high, I undo his pants, tug them down, and let them slide to the floor before I slip down Asher's body to join them.

He stands tall above me, his stomach muscles heaving, and he stares down into my eyes as I grip the elastic of his bright-red boxer briefs. I look down and swallow at the sight. His dick is so hard that I can see skin through the flap in his underwear. It looks too snug, like it's suffocating, and I'm the only one who can rescue it. So that's exactly what I do. I peel the fabric away, coming face-to-face with an exceptionally endowed Asher Moore.

"Shit, Meadow. I don't know if I can—"

I don't know what he was about to say, but he gives up on the sentence when my mouth wraps his tip. I don't fully anticipate his size until my mouth stretches around his girth. Geez, he's big. I guess I should have assumed that much, given his build, but how could I have ever anticipated *this*?

My core aches at the thought of trying to fit him and his many inches inside me. Fitting him into my mouth is hard enough. He hits the back of my throat, and I nearly gag at the sensation.

"You have a very talented mouth, Meadow Matthews."

I twist my wrist at his base and slurp him at his tip, earning a guttural groan that slips past his throat. I sink back around him, teeth sheathed and jaw stretching, and his fingers slide through my hair.

I can't remember ever feeling so powerful. Here I am, on my knees for a gorgeous specimen of a man, yet it's me who has complete control over his pleasure. There's no greater high than knowing that.

"Fuck yes. Oh my God, I'm going to come," he growls

.I'm sure he expects me to move away, but I'm too invested in my mission out to leave now. I take him deeper, swallowing at the same moment he pushes against the back of my throat. I stay there and move only in tiny pulses before a stream of hot, sticky fluid glides down the back of my throat.

I sit back on my heels and swipe at my mouth while looking up into his glossy, sex-filled eyes. "You weren't kidding about that ego of yours."

He lifts me to my feet and slides his mouth to my ear. "Don't worry, Meadow. When the time's right, I'll fuck you nice and slow until you've gotten used to me."

I suck in a breath and swallow against my nerves. "And then...?"

I can feel the curl of his lips turn up against my cheek. "And then I'll show no mercy."

CHAPTER SIXTEEN

ASHER

"Since when did you become a little fuck boy?"

I stop walking and glare at Aaron, who's in front of the stove stirring his ramen meal. I just stopped by the station to meet up with Pete before we head out to the haunted house gig. He's the one who told me about how to pick up extra hours with AMR, the private ambulance company he works for on the side.

"What the hell, dude? Where did that come from?"

Aaron chuckles. "I'm just kidding, dude. Becca and I saw you and Meadow with your dirty paws all over each other last night. How'd that staff room work out for you?"

The grin that automatically brightens my expression might be a dead giveaway, but I don't care. Last night was well worth any flack I'll get at the station today. "Worked out well, thanks for asking." I wink and start to walk off.

"Wait up one sec." Aaron turns off the stove and turns to face me. At his serious expression, a weight drops in my stomach. "Maybe we should talk about this Meadow thing."

I hold up a hand to try to get him to stop. "Dude, no.

Please. If you're about to give me a lecture about messing around with Becca's friend, then just stop now."

He sighs. "It's not just that, Ash. She's our photographer now."

I let out a laugh. "Yeah, I know. Thanks for the lead. Look, I didn't expect for any of this to happen, but I'm glad it did. I like her."

Aaron nods. "What's not to like? She's beautiful, talented, and she's a great mom."

The way he enunciates the last part of that sentence stirs something in my chest. "What do you mean by that?"

He drops his head and shakes it a little. "I just hope you know what you're getting yourself into, is all. I know you, Ash. You're a loyal motherfucker. You stayed with She-Devil even after all the shit she put you through, and you still put your everything into it. I just don't want you to get swept up with someone else so soon and get hurt if it doesn't work out."

"So what do you suggest? I play the field instead?"

Aaron lifts his hands in surrender. "I'm not suggesting anything. You're a big boy. I just don't understand why you couldn't test the waters a bit. There's something to be said about not putting all your eggs in one basket. It's not like it's hard for you to find a date."

I roll my eyes. "You sound like my buddy Dane."

"Dane from our stair-climb squad?"

"That would be the one. Dude is hopeless. Can't even keep it in his pants for a second, I swear."

Aaron looks to be fighting a laugh. "You sure? He seemed into Lars last night."

I chuckle. "He did, didn't he? I can't wait to see how that one plays out. They're an oddly perfect match."

He shrugs. "I guess when it's right, it's right. Take me for example. I never thought I'd settle down until I met Becca."

I take another step toward the main bay. "Look. I'm happy, okay? And right now, Meadow is all I see."

He nods. "Right on, man. I hope it works out. I really do."

I walk out into the main bay with Aaron's concern lingering on my mind. Beneath his playfully competitive nature, Aaron has always been a protective friend. He even went as far as unfriending Sheena on social media when I gave him the highlights of what led to our divorce. I get why he wants me to be cautious, but he's forgetting about the last two years. Sheena and I may not have had legal documentation solidifying our divorce, but that wasn't what stopped me from dating. I just hadn't met anyone who intrigued me... until Meadow.

When I finally meet up with Pete, it's time to take off for AMR. We hop in his car and head the twenty minutes to the facility. Then we check in, change, find our assigned ambulance, and begin our pre-trip inspection of the vehicle.

He pats the driver's door when we're done. "All set."

I clap him on the back as I pass him, round the front of the ambulance, and hop in. The ride to the Fisher Avenue warehouse is short. Every October, the owners convert it into a haunted house, topping themselves each year with crazy effects, realistic makeup, and custom costumes.

Pete and I take turns making rounds through the haunted house and down the line of waiting customers. The line is already at least three hundred people long, and it's not even dark out. I make my way back to the front of the building and from a distance spot Farrah and Tate, in his Elmo costume, walking toward the kid side of the entrance.

Meadow is with them, and my heart catches at the sight of her dressed in a more-clothed version of her firefighter costume. A different white tank is tucked into a pair of baggy pants, and her lips are void of that scandalous red lipstick she had on last night. Lips that slipped up and down my cock like it was a fireman's pole. I must have jerked off three times before bed just replaying our escapades—from the first swipe of my tongue on her pussy until the sight of her taking my release like she was dying of thirst. I could have fucked her on that table. We were so hot and tangled up in the moment, I'm sure she wanted it too. But even in my post-orgasmic state, I wanted more for us. Meadow deserves more. So do I.

Looking at her now, with her hand wrapped around Tate's as they laugh at the pumpkin-carving competition going on right in front of them, I know exactly why my attraction for her goes beyond the physical. Being in my prior relationship for ten years had taught me the good, the bad, and the ugly when it came to relationships. I know what I want. I also know what I don't want. But if I had to pin my failed marriage on one thing, Sheena's cheating aside, it was that I wanted a family. Desperately. And Sheena didn't.

Tate sees me coming first and his eyes get so big, an instant smile tugs at my cheeks. He points and tugs on his mom's hand. "Ashew! Mommy, it Ashew."

Meadow looks toward me, the beginning of a smile lifting her cheeks. "Hey, Asher."

"You made it." I ruffle the top of Tate's Elmo costume and give him a thumbs-up. "And I see you brought Elmo with you. But where's Tate? I thought you were bringing him too."

Tate grabs my hand and flashes me a cheesy grin. "Me Tate." He giggles and pulls down his hood. "See! Me Emmo costume."

I kneel to get a better look at Tate's red, fluffy onesie. "It is you. Nice costume, buddy. You ready to go inside and check things out?"

Tate points at a nearby table filled with other kids who are carving pumpkins. "I wanna punkin."

Meadow laughs. "He spotted them before we even parked. What if we carve pumpkins first and then go through the spooky house?"

Tate squeals and takes off toward the table, tugging Meadow with him. I stand and pull out my wallet to pay for the pumpkin, but Meadow beats me to it, tossing me a playful glare. "Thank you, but I've got this."

I shrug. "Okay, but the spooky house is on me." She opens her mouth to argue, but I shake my head, not allowing her to win this one. "I invited you here. Besides," —I stick my tongue—"they let me in for free, remember?" I pluck at my collar and wink. "It's the uniform. It's practically a ticket all in itself."

She rolls her eyes. "Cocky much?"

"Nope." I shake my head and take a step closer to whisper in her ear. "Big ego, remember?"

Farrah must notice her daughter's flaming red cheeks when she looks over. "What are you two kids whispering about?"

"Nothing," Meadow and I both say. We look at each other and smile, then Meadow helps Tate climb onto the chair while the pumpkin she bought gets set down in front of him.

I join them, offering to carve out the lid so Meadow doesn't have to get her hands dirty. I pull off the top, and some of the stringy orange guts and seeds also get pulled out. Tate gasps. He's so dramatic about it, too, the way his eyes widen to the max and his two little hands cover his mouth like he can't believe what he's witnessing. Every time I've been around Tate, I swear I can't stop smiling and laughing just watching him.

"Ooh," Meadow says to Tate. "Now you get to dig out all that stuff inside like that." She points at another kid who's getting down and dirty, scooping out the guts and slamming them onto the table.

Tate jumps to his feet so he's standing on the chair and claps his hands while Meadow spots him from behind. "Guts, guts, guts!" he squeals.

"Tate is a hoot," Farrah says to me. "I'm so glad Meadow moved here with him. I'd be missing out on so much more than I already have."

I smile at Meadow's mom, loving the relationship the three of them have. "I'm glad they decided to move here too. You know," I say, realizing I haven't even told Meadow this, "my mom was a single mom."

Farrah looks surprised. "Really?"

"Yup. My parents got divorced when I was still a baby. My dad got remarried right away, but my mom stayed single until I was a teenager. We were always really close when I was growing up. Single child and all."

"And where's your mom now?"

"Seattle. She loves it there but visits me often. I actually have plans to extend the third bedroom in my house so she has a little suite of her own when she comes to stay."

"Well, aren't you a sweetheart? Sounds like she lucked out with you."

I shake my head, my heart swelling with emotion. "I'm the lucky one. She devoted her life to raising me. So much so that I worried she would never find someone, you know? But she did, he's great, and they've been happily married for fifteen years now."

"Your mom sounds like a wonderful woman," Farrah says, her gaze traveling to her daughter and grandson. "Maybe I'll get to meet her sometime."

The twinkle in her eyes tells me she's leaving something unspoken.

I look over at Meadow, who's digging around inside the pumpkin, showing Tate how it's done. "Maybe you will."

"Your turn now, Tate. Just stick your hand in there and get it," Meadow says.

Tate wrinkles his face and reaches his hand down into the pumpkin while turning his head away like he's afraid to look. When his hand comes up filled with guts, he looks down, and his face morphs into absolute horror. He claps a palm over his mouth as Meadow laughs behind him.

"What's the matter?"

Tate mumbles something I can't quite make out.

"You don't like the way pumpkins smell?" She's obviously trying to keep herself from laughing any harder. "What do they smell like?"

"They smell like poop!" He drops the guts back into the pumpkin and waves his wet, sticky hand in the air while his other hand stays over his mouth. "I done now."

"You're done? You didn't get all the guts out."

"I said I done," Tate sasses then turns around and smacks his dirty hand on Meadow's shirt, creating a faint handprint on one breast.

Beside me, Farrah is in a fit of infectious laughter. I have to stifle my own in an effort to be polite. Meadow looks up at us and shrugs. "Guess we aren't carving pumpkins after all."

Farrah steps forward and grabs some paint and brushes, saving the day. "How about we paint the pumpkins instead?" She helps Tate into his chair while Meadow walks up to me, looking amused but maybe a little defeated too.

I wrap my arm around Meadow's shoulders and kiss the top of her head. "In little dude's defense, pumpkins do smell like poop."

She shakes her head at me. "He's such a little diva—never wants to get his hands dirty. I thought boys were dirty and stinky."

"Just wait until he's a teenager."

"Great," she says with a laugh. "Thanks for inviting us, by the way. Are you busy tonight?"

"Earlier, yes, but nah, it's been pretty tame so far, but it's still daylight out. Want to check out the haunted house?"

Meadow looks over at the long, winding line then up at me. "Oh, I don't know. I get scared pretty easily."

I grin and hold her tighter against me. "Good thing I'll be with you the entire time."

She sighs but finally agrees then tells Farrah and Tate we'll be right back. I weave my fingers between hers and walk her to the front of the line, where a staff member lets us through. Meadow makes me walk in front, but the beginning of the haunted house is deceiving, with only mechanical objects on timers jumping out in an attempt to scare us.

"This isn't so bad," she says.

"Then you walk in front," I tell her, scooting her around me.

"Wait, no." She laughs. "I don't want to be up front."

"Too bad."

I wrap my arms around her from the back and make her lead. I have been through this maze a few dozen times today, so I know exactly when the first true scare will come. Fog billows around the next corner, and she walks through it, emerging on the other side as a man with a plastic chainsaw and realistic makeup comes charging toward us.

Meadow screams and flips around, burying her head in my chest while I tighten my hold around her. I help her past the chainsaw man but not before giving him a fist bump for the great scare.

We're almost to the exit when I get a panicked feeling in my chest. It's the same one I get every time we're about to part. I hate leaving Meadow. I hate being away from her. And even though all of this is new for us, I hate the fact that we haven't put a label on anything yet. But I also have respect for her wanting to take it slow.

Just before we enter the final room of the maze that spills out to the exit, I tug her through the opening of a black curtain marked Exit. The door leads to a small empty room with a kitchen, a few tables, and chairs.

"Another staff room? What is wrong with you?" She laughs.

I guess I do have a thing for dragging Meadow into staff rooms, now that she mentions it. "Sue me for wanting to be alone with you."

She slides her arms around my neck and laces her fingers together. "Alone time is hard to find when you have a three-year-old. You sure you want to get all wrapped up with me?"

I lean down, brushing my lips against hers. "I'm afraid it's too late for that."

Our lips find each other's, but unlike last night, this kiss isn't rushed or frantic with need. This one is more like a slow dance to a symphony filled with measured beats, synchronized instruments, and a metronome made of two hearts becoming one.

It's too soon to tell what happens from here, but I've never been more excited to find out.

CHAPTER SEVENTEEN

MEADOW

My heart hasn't stopped beating fast since Asher pulled me into the exit space at the end of the haunted house—even after he had to get back to work, and I rejoined my mom and Tate for pumpkin painting. After putting the pumpkin away in the car, we head back to try out some of the games situated around the perimeter of the warehouse. We eat hot dogs and dance to live music playing on a small side stage, and finally it's time to get Tate to go in the spooky house.

"Don't push him, Mom. If he doesn't want to go, then he doesn't have to."

My mom scoffs and waves Asher over. "Tell Tate the spooky house is for kids and not at all scary."

Asher looks down at Tate, whose eyes are filled with a mixture of curiosity and fear. "What's the matter, buddy? You afraid?"

Tate sighs and shrugs, not saying a word.

"He saw one of the mummies walk out of that haunted house." I point at the main entrance of the house that Asher and I visited earlier in the night. "But I told him there aren't any super scary monsters in the spooky house."

Asher bends down. "Your mom's right, you know? There's nothing scary about the spooky house. But there are really cool costumes, just like your Elmo one."

"Weally?" Tate asks.

Asher nods. "Yup. I wouldn't lie to you. See this uniform?" He points at the EMT logo on his chest. "Do you know how I got this badge?"

Tate tilts his head then shakes it.

"I earned it, like in Boy Scouts. To earn something like this, you have to save people and protect people from danger. I wouldn't lie to you, little dude. Do you believe me now?"

Tate nods. I cheer and pick Tate up, planting a kiss on his cheek. "You're so brave, Tate. Let's go now so we have time to get home for trick-or-treating." I look over at my mom, who's grinning from ear to ear. I don't even want to guess what fantasies about Asher and me are running wild through her mind. "You coming?"

My mom shakes her head and waves us on. "I'm going to sit this out. Asher can go with you two."

I do a double take between them. "You don't have to, Asher. I know you're working."

"Ashew come," Tate squeals.

Asher chuckles and gestures for us to walk ahead of him toward the entrance. "I have to make my rounds through there, anyway." He winks. "After you."

I believed Asher when he said the spooky house would be nothing but smiles and laughs for the kids, but I didn't expect Tate's nonstop giggles throughout. We're about halfway through when Tate does something completely unexpected. He leans toward Asher and raises his arms, inviting Asher to take him from me.

Asher smiles, and, like it's the most natural thing in the world, takes him from me and balances him on his hip before pointing out the long, funny mirror that makes them look four times their size.

My throat tightens, and my chest squeezes. Bringing Asher into Tate's life has seemed natural so far. I haven't even stopped to think of the repercussions of what will happen if things don't continue the way they've been going. We've made no commitment. No reason for him to stick around. Asher could walk out of our lives and go on about his life as if we never existed.

My stomach knots, and I watch him hold Tate in front of the mirror, their laughter and smiles lighting up the whole room. I could get used to this. And for that reason alone, I know I should also be scared. Asher and I may not have slept together yet, but whatever is happening between us feels real. I didn't even see it sneaking up on me until it was too late. I'm quickly falling for Asher Moore.

"See, that wasn't so bad," Asher says to Tate when we're leaving the spooky house.

Tate is all hyped up like he just ate a pound of sugar. He raises his arms. "I did it!"

Asher looks at me, my eyes lock on his, and I swear, everything freezes. Right now, this moment, this is the start of my forever. I'm not sure how I know it, but it feels so right. My chest buzzes, my head spins, and every muscle in my body feels weak for a man who fits into my life in a way I never could have imagined. It almost feels too good to be true, but he's right here, taking my hand in his while Tate smooshes his face between his two palms. I laugh. Truly laugh. For the first time in a very long time, my heart feels free to soar.

Outside of the spooky house, we walk down the ramp that will deposit us in front of the building. Asher slows his gait. I look at him, curious, and notice that his eyes are pointed on something ahead of us. Tate is oblivious and still playing with Asher's face. But Asher's expression says it all. He's just spotted something that makes him uneasy.

I follow his stare and find a gorgeous blond woman looking back at him in the same way. They know each other. I get a sinking feeling in my gut. Her gaze flicks to me then back to Asher and Tate, and I swear she goes as pale as the ghost costume behind her.

"Asher," she says, her voice thick with emotion.

"Hey, Sheena," he says before releasing my hand.

Shit. It's his ex-wife. I can't remember if he mentioned her name before, but I know that's her.

Stung by the loss of his hold, I instinctively reach for Tate to take him from Asher. Whatever is going on here is no longer safe for my son. Asher's forehead creases like he doesn't understand why I'm taking Tate.

Sheena steps forward, with a pointed look toward me. "Well, isn't this a surprise?" She pinches out a smile and extends a hand to me. "I'm Sheena, Asher's..." She pauses while looking back at Asher.

"Ex-wife," Asher enunciates clearly.

Sheena laughs. "After twelve years, it feels so weird to hear that."

"More like ten, but who's counting, right?" Asher chuckles after his correction like he's trying to lighten the mood. Discomfort swirls through the air. "Sheena, this is my... friend Meadow and her son, Tate."

When he doesn't elaborate on who I am, I get a sinking feeling in my chest. We haven't talked about what we are to each other, so I can't fault him for that, but I certainly considered myself more than a friend. More than that, the animosity between them brings me the most pain. What does it mean? Do they still have feelings for each other? Questions and doubts begin swirling in a tornado of insecurity, and all I know is that I need to leave right now.

"Right," I say, giving them both the best smile I can

muster. "We should go before it gets too late. I need to get Tate home for trick-or-treating. It was really nice meeting you, Sheena." I take a step away from Asher, refusing to look him in the eyes.

"Wait," he says, coming after me. "I'll walk you to your car."

Not wanting to make a scene, I nod. I gesture to my mom, who's sitting on a bench near where the music is playing, that it's time to go. She's not stupid. I can see in her eyes that she senses something is wrong. She takes Tate from me and walks ahead, while Asher grabs my hand and squeezes.

"I'm sorry about that," he whispers. "I didn't expect to see her."

I shake my head. "It's fine. You don't have to apologize."

"Then why do you look so upset?"

I open my mouth then close it again, suddenly feeling ridiculously petty for my reaction. "I just—I wasn't expecting that either."

"Don't worry about Sheena, okay? She's my past."

A hint of jealousy creeps into me. "That's not what it felt like back there. It felt like she's not over you, and you're still mad at her. And Asher, I completely understand if there's lingering feelings there, but I don't think it's safe for me to get involved with you if that's what's going on."

He shakes his head, his eyes wide. "That is not what's going on. Not at all." He squeezes his eyes shut before opening them again. "I'm going to try to explain this without being disrespectful to Sheena, but you have to understand that we were separated for two years before our divorce was made final. In those two years, everything became clear. I was able to get my closure and move on. I knew long before appearing before that judge that Sheena and I were not meant to be in each other's lives any longer."

I swallow. "What about her? Did she get that same closure?"

Asher looks up to the sky before locking eyes with me again. "She didn't want the divorce."

That explains so much about their interaction, but there's still something I can't shake. "We're just friends, anyway. Right? It shouldn't even matter what your history with her is."

His expression falls like he's defeated. "You know we're more than friends, but we haven't talked about it."

"I know."

He squeezes my hand. "The only reason I haven't brought it up is because I didn't want my feelings for you to freak you out. But even then..." He stops walking and places his hands on my hips so we're facing each other. "The only reason I didn't call you my girlfriend back there was because of Tate. I'm not sure what you want, or what you want him to know, but *you* need to know that I am all in with you."

My throat tightens, emotion lashing through me to the point that I feel like I could cry. "You are?"

He lets out a breathy laugh. "Yes." He leans down so our foreheads touch. "Tell me you're all in with me too."

I close my eyes, my chest swelling, because even an admission of how much I truly like Asher feels big. My fears of him having a dangerous career feel so small in comparison to how important he's become to me. "I am all in with you."

He sighs heavily, and I swear I can hear the relief escape his chest. "Thank God," he says. Then he sweeps his lips over mine. "I'm off tomorrow. Spend the day with me. And the night."

I smile, wanting desperately to say yes. "I can't." I bite down on my lip. "I have back-to-back appointments all week, including calendar events, which means I need to be home with Tate when I can be."

He groans, his lips brushing mine again. "You torture me."

My smile grows so wide I can feel the sting in my cheeks. "Look, it's your fault, you know? If you didn't beg me to be part of this whole calendar thing, I'd have much more time on my hands."

He grins. "Are you trying to get fired?"

"Is it working?"

He shakes his head. "Not even a little." He swats my butt and presses his lips to mine. "I'll just have to make sure you get plenty of breaks. You know, to spend time with your needy boyfriend."

My entire body grows hot at the term *boyfriend*. I haven't called anyone my boyfriend since college. "I don't doubt you'll find a staff room or two when you're feeling extra needy."

He waggles his eyebrows then steps away from me and grins. "See, you already know me so well."

I know a ridiculous grin is on my face when he jogs over to my SUV to tell my mom and Tate goodnight, and it grows even bigger when he returns and kisses me hard on the mouth.

Laughing, I watch him turn around and jog back to work while I bask in the happiness that Asher has brought me in just a few weeks. I soak it in and look forward to whatever our future has in store when my gaze slips off into the distance to find Sheena still standing where we left her. She has a hard, cold look in her eyes... aimed directly at me.

CHAPTER EIGHTEEN

ASHER

Meadow is a fluid machine as she works to set up an impressive lighting display. She came fully equipped for our first day of photo shoots with gear I didn't even know she had—backdrops, green screen, tripods, and the laptop she uses for editing. She stretches her arms up to adjust one of the lights, giving me a glimpse of skin where her white blouse lifts away from her jean shorts.

She looks good. Better than good. In fact, every time I've seen her these last ten days, she's looked better than the day before. Today, she has her dark hair pulled up, and all I can think about is how great her high ponytail would look wrapped around my wrist while her painted pink lips slid up and down my cock the way they had at Shipwrecked. I would gladly return the favor after stripping her free of those shorts and spreading her out on one of the fire trucks.

Okay, so maybe fucking her with my tongue while she's laid out on a fire truck would be a no-no, but I'm sure I could find an equally scandalous location that won't get me fired. It's been agony keeping my hands off her in an effort to stay professional.

Three days after Halloween, we had the calendar selection event, where local celebrities came out to choose their top fire servicemen and servicewomen. They cast their votes like judges on *American Idol* as the contenders strutted their stuff and showed off their unique talents on stage.

Five days after that, we had an invitation-only auction with the final models, where Meadow snapped pics of all the fun. Not once had I found time to sneak her into the nearest staff room, and I'm incredibly disappointed in myself for that.

Someone grips my shoulder and jostles me out of my daydream. I turn to find Aaron grinning ear to ear. "I take it things are still going well with Miss January?"

I cock a brow. "You can say that."

I sense him wanting to ask something, but he looks around first, like he's trying to see if anyone is within earshot, and then leans closer to me. "Any more Sheena sightings?"

My body immediately tenses at the mention of my ex-wife. After Halloween, I told Aaron about our two random run-ins and how awkward the exchanges were. He said it wouldn't surprise him if Sheena had staged the last run-in, knowing I'd worked at that same haunted house for the four years prior to this one. "No more sightings, but I had to block her from calling and texting."

Aaron's eyes get big. "No shit. She's blowing you up?"

I shift uncomfortably, not liking that this is something Meadow doesn't know. But I feel like mentioning it to her will only add to the worry she expressed the night we ran into Sheena. "She was. Said she wants to get together for coffee. Said she has something she wants to talk about."

Aaron makes a face. "Since when does Sheena drink coffee? And what could she possibly want to talk about?"

I shake my head. "Who knows, man. And honestly, I

don't really care at this point. I gave that woman over a decade of my life. Why put in the effort now when it's over and done with?"

He claps me on the back. "One hundred percent. I think blocking her was the right thing to do. You don't owe her a single thing."

My jaw clenches, and I nod, completely agreeing with that sentiment. Aaron leaves me and focuses on the first guy up to be photographed, a firefighter from the Hyde Park station who got selected as Mr. February based on his love for his wife and twin baby girls. He got all the oohs and aahs from the crowd on that one.

"So," Meadow says to me once she's all set up, "I thought with this one, we could reshape the hose to make a heart and put him in the center. What do you think?"

Come to find out, Meadow isn't just an amazing photographer—she's a creative director. Every idea she's pitched so far has been something totally original.

I nod. "Let's do it."

I whistle to Chief Boone to help me round up some guys on duty to help move equipment around. Since we're working at the fire station, they could get called away at any second. I don't want to take or move anything that will sabotage a quick getaway.

Once everything is set up to Meadow's specifications, she begins shooting. No angle goes uncaptured, I swear. She calls a wrap on Mr. February and immediately scrolls through the images in her viewfinder.

I creep up behind her. "Can I see?"

She jumps and turns to look at me over her shoulder then presses the viewfinder into her chest. "Let me edit them first."

"What?" I ask, surprised. "I want to see them."

Her expression eases into a smile. "Just let me edit this

one so I can show you what I envision first. Then I'll let you see all the raws. Please?"

She's so cute when she begs, of course I can't deny her. "Okay fine, but after this I get to see all the raw pics."

"Deal."

She sticks out her hand, and I take it, refusing to let it go right away for the mere purpose of holding on to her a little longer. She tugs a little to take her hand back, but I give it a light squeeze.

"And you have to have lunch with me."

She narrows her eyes. "Fine."

"Fine."

Her glare disappears, and she smiles at me, and our good mood continues until the next guy struts in thirty minutes later. The new Mr. January, Samuel Waters. He was in last year's calendar, too, and earned quite the reputation for himself.

The guy is a walking, talking douche canoe, with a perma-smirk, the hair of a wannabe rock star, and a sex life that no man should be proud of. Not even Dane holds a candle to this guy.

The first thing Samuel does when he gets onto the set is yank his shirt over his head and flex for Meadow, who's taking candid shots of him walking in. To make things worse, she's laughing.

My blood is already boiling, and we haven't even gotten started with his official shoot.

"Geez, remind me how we let this guy slide through the screening process to auditions," Aaron whispers when he comes up beside me.

I snort quietly. "Beats me. We need guys who are role models, not class-A pricks."

Aaron nods. "He needs a woman to tame him. Maybe the calendar will change his ways."

I look at Aaron with doubt creasing my forehead. "Seriously? Between the club nights and all the signings we have lined up at sorority houses, Waters will be milking it all year long."

Aaron makes a disgusted noise in the back of his throat. "You know what that means, right?"

I tilt my head, unsure.

"We're going to have to babysit him. We can't let him ruin our reputation just because he doesn't care about his own."

Shit. He's right. "Well, that's just great."

"What are you two whispering about?"

Our heads snap toward an approaching Meadow.

"Just business," Aaron tells her and winks. "Need any help setting up your next shot?"

She seems to forget about her curiosity quickly because she starts to order Aaron around, asking him to pull out a ladder and bring it to the front of the station. I navigate the chaos, helping wherever I can, but I mostly study Meadow and try to figure out what she's got planned for the next scene.

Meadow hands me two empty buckets and smiles. "Can you fill these up with water for me, please?"

I look down at the buckets. "What for?"

She laughs and turns away. "Thank you."

Feeling dejected, I walk off to find the nearest hose and start filling up the buckets. When I return with them, the entire scene seems to be set up, and Meadow is standing in front of Samuel. Too close. A tube of oil is in her hands, and she's lathering up the turd so he's nice and slick for her camera. But that's not even what boils me to my core. He's looking at her with a lust-filled gaze while his tongue slides against his bottom lip.

"No fucking way," I mutter under my breath.

I start to walk forward to stop her from rubbing on him any further when Aaron hooks his arm around me, holding me back. "Don't you dare. He's no threat to you. But if you cause a scene on the first day of photography, you will regret it."

As much as I hate to admit it, Aaron is right. Plus, Meadow doesn't need the embarrassment of me swooping in like Tarzan to steal her away into my treehouse. As much as I want to do exactly that. I stand back and watch while Samuel poses with the ladder, and Meadow shoots him in various positions—through it, above it, under it, holding it. I think she's captured every angle that she can, but then she sends Aaron to the top of the ladder with the two buckets and asks him to release the water onto Samuel's head. And just like that, magic happens.

Water pours down on and around Samuel like a waterfall splashing over a tall rock. At first, he almost looks paralyzed by the sensation, but then he looks back at the camera with a fierce expression that even I can admit is gold. It's like a nod to last year's calendar but executed better. I can't wait to see the photos.

"Perfect," Meadow calls out, excitement lighting up her tone. "That's a wrap."

Everyone cheers. Even me.

I walk forward to stand beside Meadow. "You heard the woman. That's a wrap for Samuel. Let's take a lunch break. I want the crew back here in two hours." I look at Meadow and lean close to her ear. "You're coming with me."

"You said we were going to lunch."

I shut off my truck engine and nod to my house. "We are. We're making sandwiches."

Meadow laughs and narrows her eyes. "Why do I feel like you're just trying to get me alone?"

"Because you're smart." I wink and walk around my truck to let her out, then I take her hand in mine and lead her to my front door.

My insides are still boiling over seeing her lather up Samuel with baby oil, only because if there's anyone she should be rubbing her hands all over, it's me. I push open the door to my house and let her walk through first. As soon as we're inside, she turns around, leveling me with her gaze.

"Okay, tell me. What's up with you and Sammy?"

"Sammy?" I choke out. "You two are on nickname basis now?"

I can tell by the way she bites down on her bottom lip that she's holding back a laugh. "He told me all his friends call him Sammy. I take it you two aren't friends."

I shrug. "He's kind of a creep, so no, we aren't friends."

Her mouth falls open. "A creep? Really?"

I clench my jaw. "He was part of the calendar we put together last year. The guy was messy. He's in his mid-thirties, but he acts like he's still in college."

The corners of her mouth carve up into a small smile. "You sound jealous."

"Of Samuel Waters? No way. I'm not jealous of the guy. I just don't trust him."

Meadow steps forward and wraps her arms around my waist. "But you trust me, don't you?"

"Of course." There's no hesitation, because for some reason, I do trust Meadow. Even after everything I went through in my previous relationship.

"Well, you acted like you didn't trust me today." She points a finger at me. "Don't think I didn't see the way Aaron had to hold you back from flying at Sammy earlier."

"Yeah, because your hands were all over him. And stop calling him that."

She throws back her head and laughs. "No, they were not. I was just doing my job, Asher."

"Your job is to take the photos. Let one of the volunteers lube up the guys. Your hands belong on me and me only."

Her mouth shapes into an O, revealing her surprise. She slips a hand under my shirt and runs it up the front of my chest, taking her time while blinking up at me with her sexy eyes. "Is that so?"

My jaw clenches, and I nod, not giving a damn how demanding I sound. "Yes, but you're forgetting something."

Her eyes open wider. "I am?" She lifts my shirt over my head, presses her mouth between my pecs, and kisses me there softly. "Was it that?"

I shake my head. "Nope."

Her cute forehead wrinkles in confusion. "Then what did I forget?"

I lift her so that her legs straddle my waist, and I walk her toward my bedroom. "The lube."

CHAPTER NINETEEN

MEADOW

Asher's mouth slams into mine, his intentions clear as he carries me to his bedroom. He's so fired up. I can feel it in the tension that radiates from his body. I can taste it in his bruising kiss. I can hear it in the way his heart thuds furiously against his chest. He wants a release. He needs it. And he wants me to give it to him.

He sets me on his dresser and peels off my shirt before his mouth is back on mine. Then he undoes my shorts and pulls them off me, leaving me in nothing but my sheer pink bra and panties.

"Fuck, you're sexy," he mumbles after he gets an eyeful.

I bite the inside of my cheek. "And here I thought you were bringing me here to eat."

He shrugs, his eyes locked on the space between my thighs. "Isn't that what we're doing?"

I ignore my growling stomach, reach for the waistband of Asher's pants, and tug him to me until he's fitted nice and snug between my legs. "I don't know," I say, slipping my hand down his front until I grip his length. "I'm pretty hungry."

"Don't worry." He slides a finger against the fabric

covering my opening then hooks it and shoves it to the side. "We're going to work up an appetite first." His middle finger sinks into me, then his ring finger follows. It doesn't take long for me to reach a climax. Not when he's aiming all his focus on my pleasure while his erection fights its way through his jeans. I throw my head back with my release, absorbing his thick fingers as my orgasm squeezes around him.

"You're going to feel so good wrapped around my cock."

I gasp at his dirty words. Asher is a flirtatious guy and charming to a fault, but when he talks to me like this, I can't help but feel an ache between my thighs that only he can quell. "Then what are you waiting for?"

He smirks and slips his dripping wet hands from between my legs. "I finally have you alone in my bedroom. I'm not going to rush this."

He takes a step back and unbuttons his jeans. He slides them down, bringing his boxer briefs with them and revealing his monster of an erection.

"Jesus," I breathe, taking in his massive size with eyes I know have gone wide. I've seen him before. I've felt him, tasted him. But everything appears so much more *intimidating* in daylight.

I stand, push down my panties and undo the clasp of my bra so I'm standing naked before him too. It would be so easy to feel self-conscious with Asher, since this is the first time anyone has seen me naked since I was with Milton. But the way his gaze scrolls appreciatively over my body gives me more confidence than I've ever felt in my life.

He reaches for me and pulls me toward him as he backs up to the bed. He sits, bringing me down, too, and places my knees on either side of him. His mouth meets mine, a gentle sigh shuddering between his lips before we kiss slowly and deeply. Every time we've been together has felt so rushed. I want to take advantage of this moment to explore him like it's the very first time. So that's exactly what I do.

I run my fingers through his hair while my tongue finds the space between his lips. His arm wraps my waist, holding me tightly to him, rocking me against his length so that my slick opening is riding him. He feels so good against me, but I'm feeling greedy and want more.

I reach down and grab hold of him, lifting his shaft and pressing it to his stomach, then I lift my hips and lower them so I can feel him against my clit. I wrap my hand around his length while I move, stroking him while I stroke me too.

He tears his mouth from mine, his lips parted and his gaze turning down to where we meet. "Holy fuck," he gasps.

My eyes flutter closed as my second release builds. I can feel this one tensing through me slower than the first. It builds and builds, until the intensity gains strength between my thighs. But just when I feel like I'm about to explode, Asher adjusts me so that his tip buds up against my entrance.

"I need to be inside you."

I feel him shift again and look down, surprised to find a condom in his hand. He rolls it over his engorged length. "I'm on the pill," I say, desperate to feel him bare.

He lets out a breathy laugh. "Fuck, don't tempt me, Meadow. But I don't think I'll last long without this."

I nod, my pending release catching my breath. "Okay."

There's no question that I want this as badly as he does. I wanted it the night of the wedding when we barely even knew each other. After weeks of getting to know him and declaring that I'm "all in," I'm desperate to know Asher in every way possible. And to his credit, he's been extremely patient with my lifestyle, my schedule, and me. He's never made me feel bad about them in any way. That only makes me want him more.

He finishes rolling on the latex, grabs my hips, and holds me to him while he enters me slowly, stretching me, as we both watch every inch of him disappear. He groans, his hooded gaze meeting mine. We begin to rock together, finding our rhythm while our breaths sync as one.

His hands never leave my hips, his fingers gripping me tighter as our pacing quickens. His tongue swirls around my hardened nipples, one at a time, until he locks in on one and sucks it into his mouth.

I groan out a warning, and I swear he thickens inside me. He slides one hand around to my front, locating my clit, and rubs gentle circles over it, bringing on an intense release that hits me deeper than the first. This one radiates through me, exploding in a wave of heat and mini pulses that I hold on to for as long as possible.

When my orgasm subsides, my muscles weaken, and Asher takes over completely. He lifts me, spins me around, and moves me to the bed, never separating our bodies as I spread wide for him and take every delivered thrust.

"I knew it," he says in a breathy voice as he hammers into me again. "I knew you'd feel so fucking good, Meadow. You're a goddess, you know that? I was already addicted to you before, but now..." He beats into me again and again as sweat beads across his forehead and chest. "Now I'm ruined for anyone but you."

I slide my arms around him, bringing his mouth down to mine so I can taste his words as they linger in the air. No man has ever made me feel this way—so wanted, so desired. It's not just Asher who's addicted. I'm a complete goner for this man, but I'm too busy savoring the realization to think of all the reasons why I should be more careful.

"I feel the same way." My words float across his lips. "All in, remember?"

His thrusts grow more intense, filling me deeper than before. "All in," he repeats. With that, he lets go, spilling his warm release inside me.

When I think it's over—after he's trashed the condom and crawls back onto the bed—he kneels above me while my legs are still spread wide and lowers his mouth. "One more," he demands. Then his mouth moves between my thighs.

"That's so generous of you." My words are breathier than I intended, but how can I breathe when he's swiping the length of me with his tongue and licking my clit like I'm his last supper? I run my fingers through his hair and lock eyes with him as he laps and sucks me to yet another brink of madness.

I think I'm floating.

Asher and I are still in bed naked and wrapped up in each other. I never want to leave. I stopped counting orgasms after three. *Three.* My mind is blown, but it's the feel of his arms around me, the snug, safe hold that he always seems to wrap me in that I don't want to escape.

Groaning, I look over at him. "We should get dressed. I don't want to be late."

Asher looks back at me and nods. "I don't want you to be late either. Can we steal five more minutes? I just want to lie with you a little bit longer. We can grab snack bars on our way out, and I can make you dinner at your place tonight."

He looks so hopeful, it's adorable. "Okay. But I don't know how you're going to top spaghetti."

Asher grins. "Just wait until little dude tries my tacos." He runs a hand through my hair and starts twirling it on its end. "Was it weird for you?"

I raise my brows, confused. "Was what weird?"

His throat bobs like he's nervous.

"What we did. You said it's been a few years since... I hope I wasn't too aggressive."

I smile, my chest fluttering. "You were perfect. Better than perfect." I reach up and touch his face, gliding my palm against his stubble. "Sometimes it seems like you're too good to be true."

Asher's eyes flicker to mine. "That's how I feel about you." He opens his mouth and then closes it again, and I can tell something is on his mind.

"What is it?"

He shakes his head. "I was curious about something, but I don't want to be disrespectful."

I squeeze his arm. "Just ask."

He blows out a breath. "I just... sometimes wonder about your late husband. The things he missed out on. The things you probably miss. No one should have to face a tragedy like that, but then you had his child. I can't imagine how hard that must have been for you."

There's not really a question in there, but I think I know what Asher is getting at. "Yeah, I think about it a lot too." I suck in a breath and let it out in a slow release. "It's not easy to admit this, but Milton and I weren't getting along all that well before I got pregnant. To be honest, I'm not sure we would have gotten married otherwise." A tear slips from my eye, and I swipe it away. "It feels so terrible to say aloud. Because he's gone, and I promised myself I would do everything in my power to protect Milton's memory for Tate."

Fingers thread through mine. "And you are. You're doing a damn good job, Meadow. Tate is lucky to have a mom like you."

I swipe at another tear and smile. "That's sweet to say."

"I mean it." He turns onto his side to face me. "Let's just say I have a soft spot for single moms."

"Because you were raised by one?"

He smiles. "Your mom told you."

"She did. That and how I shouldn't get so crazy jealous over your ex-wife when it was you who ended things."

He chuckles. "Crazy jealous, huh?"

"Well," I tease, "not as jealous as you got today."

He leans down, touching his forehead to mine. "I guess that just means we care about each other."

"I guess so." I kiss him then pull away slowly, unable to shake a nagging question in the back of my mind. "Can I ask why things ended between you two?"

Asher nods. I sense that the subject is not an easy one for him to communicate, but I hope that he wants to discuss it with me. It takes him a few seconds to start talking.

"Like you and Milton, Sheena and I definitely rushed into things for the wrong reasons. We were young and in love, and I was set on joining the military. She was furious about that, and for some reason I got the dumb idea that I could make it up to her by proposing. Anyway, she hated it. She hated me being gone, she resented me when I was home, and then one day she just started living her life as if we weren't married at all."

His story is shocking, yet I know he hasn't even scraped the surface. "But you said she didn't want the divorce."

Asher shrugs. "She didn't. And for the longest time, I didn't either. Even when I knew she was cheating. Her infidelity was the whole reason I chose not to reenlist. I blamed myself for being gone so much. I thought that if I was home, we'd get back to where we started."

"And that didn't solve it?"

He shakes his head. "Nope. We'd both changed so much by then. I felt grounded and ready for a family, but suddenly she didn't want kids anymore. Maybe she never did. But it was like she was addicted to this new lifestyle she'd created when I was overseas, and she couldn't let it go."

"Even the cheating?"

He coughs out a laugh. "Especially the cheating. I thought serving her the divorce papers would be the wake-up call she needed to give our relationship one final shot. I was an idiot."

My heart feels like it's beating out of my chest. "You are not an idiot. You're a good man who wanted to make it work with your first love. There's nothing wrong with that, Asher. That's loyalty. That's commitment. You stayed true to your vows even when she couldn't stay true to hers." Silence lingers between us as he nods. "So, what happened next?"

He sighs. "She begged me to stay, said she changed her mind about having kids, but I—" His voice cracks with emotion. "I gave it six months and then realized the damage was already done. I didn't love her anymore, and I knew in my heart that I would never get there again. That's when I packed my bags and left for good."

My throat is so tight with emotion I could cry, but I don't because I want to be strong for Asher. "That explains why Sheena isn't over you. She was finally ready to give you what you wanted, and you walked away."

He shakes his head. "She only said those things because she didn't want me to leave, and that's no reason to have a child."

Our eyes connect as if he knows without me saying anything that I completely agree. "Is she going to be trouble for us, Asher?" The fear buried in the back of my mind slips past my lips before I can even stop it.

"No. I won't let that happen." He moves so he's hovering over me and using his elbows to keep his weight off of me. "I'm crazy about you, Meadow. If I haven't made that clear yet, then allow me to try again." He dips down and kisses me hard on the mouth. "And again," he whispers. He dips his mouth to my neck and places a sweet kiss there while opening my legs with his knees. "And again." This time, his words drift along my neck while he reaches for a condom, rolls it over his length, and fills me with his promise.

A promise I know deep down isn't up to him to keep.

CHAPTER TWENTY

ASHER

"Are you sure?" Meadow looks down at her camera then back up at me with worried eyes. "If I'm not taking photos tonight, should I even be there?"

I chuckle at her sweet, innocent reaction to me banning her camera from tonight's private dinner event. We're going to reveal the final edited calendar images to the firefighters and staff involved in the "making of," and I want Meadow to enjoy her night. After all the work she's put in, she deserves to celebrate along with the rest of us.

"I'm sure. And of course you should be there. We're showing off the photos *you* took, silly." I pluck the camera from her hand and set it on the end table by my couch. "No one is working tonight. Besides, everyone will be taking pics on their phone, so we can just ask the guys to submit photos if we need them."

Her eyes light up. "We can have a slideshow playing when everyone walks into the unveiling."

I cup her face with my palms, excitement pinging my chest. "You're brilliant."

She sighs. "You give me way too much credit, Asher."

I press my lips to hers. "You deserve all the credit, Meadow. Now, let's go before I change my mind and keep you here all night." My gaze takes an appreciative sweep of her strapless black dress. It's fitted to her body on the top, revealing her fucktastic body, and flows out from her hips down to the tops of her thighs.

She drove herself to my house tonight because she arranged to spend the night. As soon as I opened the door, I thought about tearing her clothes off right there. I've always had a healthy sex drive, but it's different with Meadow. For one, I don't see her nearly as often as I would like. Between her schedule and mine, I feel like I'm always looking forward to those few hours we can have together. With Tate too. Sometimes, I'll go to their house for dinner. Other times, I'll make a pit stop at Meadow's after a shift. But it seems the most time we get together is when we're working on things related to the firefighter calendar.

"Okay, let's go celebrate." She smiles. "I can't wait to see everyone's faces when the photos are revealed."

It's adorable how nervous Meadow is. I give her ass a little squeeze to lighten the mood. "Everybody's going to love them."

She makes a face. "You sure? Samuel seemed intent on wanting approval first before those photos get printed."

I roll my eyes, fire heating my chest at the reminder of how difficult Samuel has been to work with during the past week. The day after his shoot, I started hearing rumors circulate about Samuel and his risky behavior—binge drinking, picking fights with his station brothers. Clearly, he's going through something, but if he can't clean up his act, then we're going to have to replace him.

"Yeah, well, Samuel got the cover vote, so we're stuck with him."

Meadow frowns. "He does realize the point of all this is to raise money for charity, right?"

My jaw clenches, hating the distaste I have for the guy. My reaction to him is so unlike me, but then again, Samuel has done no favors for himself in the likability department. "If he doesn't want to play along, then he's going to get a rude awakening. Just like any fire station, this calendar crew is a team."

Meadow smiles, easing the fire in my chest. "You're sexy when you're all passionate like that."

I chuckle and bury my face in the crook of her neck, taking in her flowery scent. She smells as divine as she tastes. "I'll make sure to remember that when we get home."

It takes all my self-control to leave the house for the sake of getting to the restaurant on time, but I manage. We're even the first ones to arrive at the private room, with Aaron and Becca following suit. Tonight is for the organizers, the volunteers, and the firefighters along with their significant others. We'll have drinks and dinner and then unveil the selected images that Meadow doctored up.

One by one, the firefighters arrive dressed to impress. The drinks start flowing, and the chatter is cheery while the appetizers are served, even when several voices echo the fact that Samuel still hasn't shown up.

"He's what?" I ask Aaron in a booming voice when he pulls me outside the private room to tell me the news.

"He's not coming." Aaron looks just as ticked off as I feel.

"Why the hell not?"

He blows out a heated breath. "Fucker went on a bender and landed himself in jail last night. He got suspended and everything. Things aren't looking good for him right now."

My jaw drops. "What the hell? Is he okay?"

"Does it matter?" Aaron shakes his head. "Guy's a fuckup. We need to cut him."

"You want to cut Mr. January? What are we going to do for the cover?" I push off the wall and pace the hallway, so infuriated I can barely think straight.

"We can find someone else," Aaron says, taking on the role of the calm and collected one.

"We go to print in three days!"

Meadow chooses that moment to come out into the hall, and by the way she's darting looks between us, she knows something is going on. "What is it?"

"Samuel is out," I say, cutting straight to the point. I agree with Aaron on that much. If Samuel is going to cause this much drama before the calendar has even been printed, then he can't be trusted.

"Okay," Meadow says. "So, now what?"

Aaron folds his arms and looks at her. "So, we need to find a replacement, and we need to shoot him in the next two days."

I shake my head, already by Meadow's side. "No way. Meadow has already put in more hours than we can ever repay. Maybe we just use one of the guys twice. What about Rev?" I snap my fingers at the idea. "We took shots of him in his paramedic shirt and in his bunker gear."

Aaron cringes. "I don't know, man. Our audience isn't dumb. They'll recognize him."

I shrug. "So what? We need more representation outside of just the fire crew. We don't even have an EMT this year."

The air goes silent, and I feel like I might have said something wrong. When I look between Meadow and Aaron, and they're both staring right back at me, I get a sinking feeling in my chest. "Wait. Why are you both looking at me like that?"

Aaron chuckles. "C'mon, dude. You were in bunker gear last time. We'll reshoot you in your EMT getup. It's the perfect solution."

Meadow nods. "I'll shoot it. It won't take much time at all, and I don't mind."

I blow out a breath, staring at both of them like they're out of their minds. They must be. "I was January last year. I can't take the spot again."

"Why the hell not?" Aaron asks.

I point at him. "Why don't you take the spot? You're decent looking." Even in my heated state, I find the humor in all of this and smile.

Aaron flips me off and shakes his head. "You know Becca would freak. I can't do that to her, especially on short notice like this. Besides, she has all these vacations lined up for us next year. I'll miss all the events. You're the obvious choice."

I find myself stuck between a rock and a hard place, and I feel like no one is jumping to my defense. Then again, I'm starting to lose sight of what my defense is. "Fine, as long as everyone else is okay with it, I'll do it." I look at Meadow, pinning her with my stare. "You realize this will make me the most wanted man in all of Tampa, don't you?" I tease.

She pouts, though amusement is in her eyes. "You poor thing."

I tilt my head, with every intention of driving her as crazy as she makes me feel lately. "You sure you want this?"

She shrugs as if it's no big deal. "I guess it's a good thing you only have eyes for one woman." She slips her arms around my waist. "And she happens to be crazy about you."

Jesus. Just like that, she douses the flames with the sweetest sentiment that I plan on returning later.

I sigh and look at Aaron. "You heard the woman. I guess I'll be returning to my role as Mr. January."

The second Meadow and I get back inside my house, I close the door and push her against it, immediately finding her mouth with mine. I can taste a hint of whiskey from her one drink earlier in the night, and I deepen our kiss in an attempt to savor it. "I've been wanting to do that all night," I murmur against her lips.

"Is that right, *Mr. January*? Lucky me."

I chuckle and shake my head. "You're going to keep calling me that, aren't you?"

She nods while bringing her mouth to my neck. "Oh yes. Just wait until I get you in front of my lens."

My cock twitches, and I swear it's got a mind of its own when it comes to Meadow. "I can't wait."

"Just think. It'll be you I'm lathering up with oil this time."

I chuckle. "Maybe that's a bad idea."

She starts to unbutton my shirt, her innocent eyes flipping up to look at me. "I think it's a great idea. You'll just slip your shirt off like this." She slides the shirt off my arms. "And I'll cover you with lots of baby oil, just like this." She runs her palms up my stomach to my chest. "I won't miss a single inch of this body, I promise you that." She unfastens the button and zipper of my pants then slides it down. "I'll even give you my VIP service." Her eyes follow her palm as she drags it down my chest and into my boxer briefs.

"And what service is that?" I can barely breathe out my words.

"For starters, I'll make sure you're nice and relaxed."

I'm fully hard when she grips me then starts to move her hand with slow and steady strokes.

"You know, massage out all your kinks for as long as you need." She tightens her grip while quickening her rhythm just a little. I press my palm against the door and groan. "You really know how to treat your VIPs."

A small smile lifts her lips. "I'm glad you're pleased with my services, Mr. January."

Fuck if I don't harden even more when she says it like that. I reach for the front of her dress and pull down the top, revealing her sheer strapless bra. "You're full of surprises tonight, aren't you?"

She lengthens her strokes. If she keeps this up, I'll blow in seconds. "Wait, Meadow." I intend to ask her to slow down, but she's too focused and too determined on pleasuring me that I give up. "I wanted to take my time with you tonight."

"There's still time," she says before kneeling and shoving my underwear down my legs.

Before I can take another breath, she's got me so far down her throat I can barely see the base of my shaft. "Holy shit."

She flips her lids so she's looking directly into my eyes as she takes every inch, her perfect lips stretched and glistening around me. I come in seconds, giving her fair warning before I'm spilling down her throat.

"What did I do to deserve that?" I'm panting like I just ran ten miles.

Meadow swipes at her lips and rises to stand before me, a shy smile transforming her face. "I realized that I haven't thanked you."

I'm so confused. "If that's how you thank me, then feel free to do it as much as you want, but you're the one doing us all a favor here. You've already taken on so much more than I expected."

She tilts her head. "I was put off by the idea when Becca brought it up. I don't even know for sure why. I think I was just stressed with the move, and the idea of working with a bunch of firefighters terrified me to no end." She laughs lightly. "I'm so glad you were right there to convince me to take the gig. I've had so much fun, and I love that this is all going to a great cause."

I smirk a little, biting my tongue to keep from saying, *I told you so.* "You're forgetting to mention all the new clients you raked in, just like I promised."

She narrows her eyes. "See, I was trying to thank you, but now I'm afraid of that inflated ego of yours again."

I bring her in so we're flush together. "I think I've demonstrated there's nothing to be afraid of when it comes to my inflated ego. In fact, I'm up for another presentation if you are."

Her pretty pink lips part as a shallow breath escapes. "I'd be lying if I said I wasn't curious."

"Good, because I'm going to need a volunteer from the audience." I skim my mouth against hers while running a hand beneath her short dress. "What do you say? Care to be my test subject?"

Her breath hitches, and she nods.

I grin. "Right this way." I walk her backward toward the couch. My hands are still beneath her dress when I find a thin strip of fabric over her hips then follow the line down to her soaking wet pussy. I apply pressure with my thumb, rubbing circles over her clit, knowing Meadow and her reactions to my touch. At this rate, I'll be hard again in no time. "Turn around."

She does as I say, turning to face the armrest of the couch. I sweep her hair over her shoulder, exposing her neck. "You're delightful in every way, Meadow Matthews."

My nose finds the small of her neck, and I take in her floral scent and groan. Unable to control my hands, I ease her down so that she's folded over the armrest, her breasts hovering in the air. I bring the bottom of her skirt up, revealing her luscious ass. A small strip of black fabric runs between her ass cheeks. I hook my finger into the top of her thong and slip it from her body.

A shudder shakes through me at the sight of her, her center glistening before I've even entered her. I get on my knees, using my fingers to spread her wide before swiping her with my tongue. Her legs shake, causing her heels to wobble by my sides, so I hook her legs with my arms while continuing to devour her sweet juices with my tongue. I suck her hard into my mouth, pulsing there until her screams fall muffled into the couch cushion.

I rise slowly, my muscles tense, my adrenaline soaring, and it takes everything I have not to ease my bare cock into her from behind.

"Stay here," I warn while backing away from her.

She turns to look at me over her shoulder. "Where are you going?"

Without a word and without taking my eyes off her, I find my pants, slip out my wallet, and pluck out a condom. I tear the casing with my teeth and roll the latex over my eager and ready shaft.

Meadow doesn't move as requested, and when I begin to ease inside her, I know this won't be one of our normal slow fucks. Like Meadow said, there's still time.

I bury the rest of myself inside her in one quick thrust, and that sets the pace. It's dirty. It's rough. I'm relentless in my pursuit of making her come first, but by the time she does, I'm right there with her. Just the way it should be.

CHAPTER TWENTY-ONE

MEADOW

After assuring Asher that I could do a reshoot with him as Mr. January, it took a full day for the panic to set in. We go to print tomorrow. *Tomorrow.* And we haven't even started shooting yet.

My palms are sweaty, and my mind feels foggy as I try and fail to come up with another original idea to set Asher's photo apart from all the others. This all came to me so easily before, but after twelve unique photo shoots under raging pressure, I'm fresh out of ideas. To top it off, any chance of natural lighting is destroyed, thanks to the storm brewing from the east.

The sky rumbles, and a crack of lightning strikes like a tease to my senses. I'm running out of time.

My eyes narrow at the gloomy sky outside the square window in the room Asher set me up in. It's his sleeping quarters while on shift, complete with a single bed in the corner, a large cabinet that fills most of one wall, and the wood desk that I'm sitting behind.

He's been gone for the last two hours, responding to a fire, and I'm secretly grateful for the alone time to plan. I just thought I would have come up with something by now.

The click of the door makes me shift my gaze to Asher, who makes his way across the threshold. "Hey, you still in here?"

I sigh and set my pencil down on the blank sheet of paper and shrug. "Yes, and no closer to coming up with anything remotely mind-blowing."

He chuckles and sits on the top of the desk. "We're not asking for mind-blowing, Meadow."

I peer up at him without lifting my chin. "You're the cover, Asher. It has to be mind-blowing."

"Why don't you just redo the ladder shoot?"

I point at the gloomy view outside the window. "Because of the weather. There's no way we can do anything outdoors. We'll have to use my studio lights, but we've already used the ambulance in the paramedic shoots."

He shrugs. "What about other angles?"

Frustration shakes through me. It's like I'm having some sort of creative block. "This has never happened to me before." I put my forearms on the desk, fall forward, and moan.

Asher must stand up, because I can hear the footfalls of his boots as he positions himself behind my chair. What is he doing? Strong hands wrap the tops of my shoulders and squeeze at the tension rolling through them. Holy shit, that feels good. "Oh my God," I moan, more seductively than I planned. At this point, I don't care. "Yes, Asher. More, please."

He chuckles and keeps at it, working the tight muscles of my neck, shoulders, and back like a trained professional.

"Was massage therapy part of your training too?" I ask.

"No, but I do understand how the body works, and you, my little firecracker, are in dire need of a good stress reliever."

I bite down on my lip, a smile breaking out across my face anyway. "Isn't that what we did all last night?"

"Well, yeah, but I think that might have backfired. You're too tired to think straight."

"No shit." I sit up and look over my shoulder at him with puppy dog eyes. "Can you push the print date? We just need another day. I promise I'll get my head straight for tomorrow."

Asher smiles. "I'll see what I can do. Just relax tonight. Go home, take a hot bath, drink some wine." He waggles his brows. "Think of me while you finger that tight pussy."

The temperature of my entire body spikes. I stand, a smirk playing on my lips. "Thanks for the idea."

He slips his arms around my waist and pulls me close. "Does this mean you have to leave right now?" He brushes his lips against mine. "Maybe you can stay for lunch? Aaron's cooking something up. He's actually pretty decent, but don't tell him. He'll think he's better than me."

I smack his chest lightly. "You two are so ridiculous to each other. And yes, I'll stay for lunch. But then I need to go home and take my hot EMT boyfriend's advice."

He steers me out of the room, down the hall, and into the main bay, where it seems to be pretty quiet save for a couple of guys walking around the vehicles like they're inspecting them. My gaze catches on the ambulance, and an onslaught of images flood my mind of the first time I saw Asher.

He was laser focused on his mission. I could tell that by the way he jumped out of the passenger seat and immediately jogged to the back doors of the vehicle. It was as though he knew what his mission would be before he even headed toward the horrific accident. He was a fluid machine, yellow stretcher tucked under his arm, eyes set straight ahead. I couldn't stop staring and didn't notice the person stumbling to get out of their car until they pushed me forward and straight into Asher Moore's arms.

I thought I was dreaming when I blinked up at him, his steel-gray eyes hard and staring directly back into mine. For a flash of a second, a single heartbeat, I thought he might feel the same connection. But then he spotted my camera, and a different version of Asher came out. One I've yet to ever see again.

"Meadow, you coming?"

The images dissolve in my mind's eye, except for one. I blink, my heart beating fast, and it's like I've been knocked on my ass all over again. "No," I tell him, snapping my head around to look at him. "Let's do the shoot."

He lets out a bewildered laugh. "Seriously?"

I nod, the spike of adrenaline hitting me with an intensity I've never felt before. "Yes." I grab his hand and steer him toward his sleeping quarters. "Let's get you oiled up."

He doesn't argue as I close the door of his room behind us and begin unbuttoning his shirt. He seems stunned by my sudden change of mood, and I don't blame him. I also don't have time to stop and chat about it.

After grabbing the baby oil from the desk, I squirt a healthy amount in my palm and smear it all over his chest until he's a glossy canvas of the most beautiful mountain I've ever seen. For a split second, my mask of professionalism falls, and I look up at Asher, my heart stuttering.

"You ready?"

He looks down at his shirt that I'm buttoning back up. "That was really fucking hot, Meadow. You're going to need to give me a minute."

I step forward, my eyes dipping to the erection fisting its way through his trousers. "As much as I want to take care of that for you, I'm afraid we're losing precious time."

He adjusts a little and takes a deep breath. "Okay, I'm

good. Let's go." He claps his hands like we're breaking from a huddle. "So, what's this great idea of yours?"

I don't need my lighting gear, so I grab my camera off the desk and walk Asher back out to the bay, where I point at the ambulance. "Can you move that outside?"

Asher shrugs. "Sure. Let me grab Pete."

While Asher takes off to find someone to move the ambulance, I step out onto the drive and stare up at the grumbling sky. A raindrop falls on my nose, and I smile. "Perfect."

As soon as the ambulance is where I want it, Asher warns me that they could get a call any second.

"We'll make this quick. Promise."

Rain begins to fall harder, and he looks at me and squints. "Are you sure about this? Won't your camera get wet?"

"It's waterproof. Stop stalling."

Wind blows against his wavy, light-brown hair, and a chuckle vibrates through him. "All right, let's see what you got." He raises his arms. "I'm all yours."

My grin widens, and I move my gaze to the viewfinder. "Good. Now go grab that yellow stretcher thing. The one you were holding the day we met."

"The transport basket?" he questions, his smile amused.

I wave my hand in the air, dismissing him. "Yes, that."

He opens the back doors of the ambulance and pulls out the same yellow stretcher I remember him lugging around that first day we met. Blood pumps furiously through my veins.

"Now, jog along the ambulance like you're heading somewhere."

He starts to jog with that sexy, serious look on his face that stunned me on that first day.

"Perfect," I call out. "Now unbutton your shirt while you're jogging."

He doesn't even stop to question my ridiculous request. He does as I say as the rain falls harder from the sky. And in the next moment, at the perfect moment—as he whips his head to clear the hair from his face, and his fingers pull open his shirt—a flash of lightning lights the sky, so big I'm blinded long enough that I don't know if I got the shot.

My breathing is labored as I fumble with my camera to turn it around. I shakily adjust the screen to show the last series of images. I panic when the screen shows nothing but black.

And then *bam*. There it is. A shot that looks more like it's been photoshopped than captured at the perfect moment. I gasp and laugh, my hand clapping over my mouth. Excitement bubbles up in my chest. I'm so happy I think I could cry.

Asher jogs over to me, sans the stretcher, and stands behind me to see what all the fuss is about.

"Holy fucking shit, Meadow. How in the hell did you do that?"

I shake my head, my chest so full I can barely breathe, let alone speak. So I give myself a minute to catch my breath, then I look up at him. "I guess we have the new cover, Mr. January."

After showing off the photo to Aaron, who's as astonished by it as we were, we go back to Asher's sleeping quarters. It will be easy to edit the photo and get it off to the printer in plenty of time to meet Asher's deadline.

Tension releases from me in droves as I lean back

against his desk. "Guess I don't need that stress reliever after all."

He narrows his eyes and steps toward me, pinning me to the desk. "No, but we should certainly celebrate." His hands drift up my sides, lifting my dress some. I can feel his growing hard-on working its way between my legs. I'm so high on life right now, I don't even care that we're at Asher's work while he's on duty, or that he's still soaked from the rain that poured down on him. I'm desperate for this man in a way I've never felt before.

My fingers move to the edges of his open shirt, his slick chest illuminated in all the best ways. "I don't suppose they give you sex breaks here, do they?"

Asher's hooded gaze darkens. "Fucking you right now is the only thing I want to do, but you should know that comes with a risk."

"We could get caught." I nod, trying to talk myself down from palming Asher where he wants it most.

Asher shrugs. "Well, yeah, but that wasn't the risk I was talking about. Think of me being deep inside you and having you on the brink of madness when an alert comes through the speakers." He groans and presses against me. "I can't finish fucking you if that happens. I'd have to pull out so fast you'd mistake me for the Flash, and I can't think of a worse way to leave you."

The mental image of Asher buried between my thighs and rocking his sexy hips into me makes me dizzy with want. "I think I'm willing to risk it."

He blows out a breath, his fingers gripping the bottom of my dress and shoving it up to my hips. "Then we better make this quick."

His suggestion acts like an alarm bell of our own. I frantically undo his belt buckle, unsnap his pants, and unzip him. His finger slides against me, and he lets out a curse at my slickness.

"Thank fuck," he says. "We don't have time for foreplay. Looks like you're ready to go."

I groan and slip down his pants, along with his boxers. "Where's your condom?"

Another curse flies out of his mouth as he reaches down to grab his wallet. "Panties off," he growls.

I do as he says, slipping my panties down to the floor and stepping out of them just as he wraps the latex around his girth and rolls it up as far as it will go. His cock is already so swollen, it looks angry—I can feel my heated lips quivering in anticipation. Backing against the wall, I try to steady my breathing, but it's impossible.

He stalks toward me, palms the meat of my thighs, and hoists me up like I weigh nothing. I rush to rest my arms around his shoulders, hooking them behind his head. My back slides up the wall then back down before I meet the tip of his shaft right before it plunges into me, fast and hard.

I gasp, and Asher claps a hand over my mouth. "Quiet, or I'm going to have to stop," he warns.

Desperate for him to continue, I jerk my head up and down in a nod.

His other arm supports me while his hips rock up, and he lifts me up and down so I'm bobbing on him. My breasts bounce while he continues pounding into me without mercy.

Without warning, he releases his hand from my mouth and moves me away from the wall so only he supports me. He looks down at where he enters me, his mouth parting like he's found his own personal heaven. He's so outrageously gorgeous, so strong, so... unlike any man I've ever had the pleasure of knowing intimately. He makes me absolutely come undone in such an effortless way.

My muscles constrict around him, the first signs of my

orgasm building quickly, impatiently, and I know it's only a matter of seconds before I burst.

"Come with me." I'm not above begging.

He grits his teeth as he brings me down faster. "Are you ready?"

I gasp at the release taking hold of me. "Now," I half moan, half scream.

He doesn't try to quiet me this time. He's too focused on his own release emptying inside me to control my reckless sounds. So I clap a hand over my own mouth while one arm continues to be hooked around his neck. I ride out the rest of my orgasm while he spills every last drop into me.

The universe must be wholly on our side because an alert chimes over the loudspeaker. Asher rushes out of the room while I collapse, completely satisfied, onto his desk.

CHAPTER TWENTY-TWO

ASHER

I pull up to Meadow's house at six o'clock on the dot, in plenty of time to grab her, head to Raymond James, and have time to tailgate before we take our field seats to see the Bucs play the Giants in a *Monday Night Football* game. I might have paid a mint for the tickets, but Tampa Bay is Meadow's favorite team, yet she's never been to a live game. I couldn't resist giving her the experience of a lifetime.

The door swings open, and Meadow looks back at me, wearing an apologetic expression. She's not even wearing her jersey. My heart sinks. "Oh no. What's wrong?"

"I'm so sorry, Asher. I assumed my mom would be home tonight to watch Tate, but apparently, she left for a casino cruise hours ago. I had no idea she'd already made plans until I got home from work. She won't be back until well past midnight, and I have no one to watch Tate."

As disappointing as that is, I completely understand. "It's okay. We can go another time."

She gestures to me, sweeping her eyes over my Bucs jersey, cap, and jeans. "You should still go. Maybe Aaron will go. Make it a boys' night."

I roll my eyes. "Aaron's a Panthers fan, believe it or not."

Meadow bites her lower lip. "What about Dane?" Her eyes light up. "Or one of your Shipwrecked buddies. Greg, Beck, Larsen..."

I shrug. "I can ask one of them. Sure."

Just then, a shriek fills the air, Tate barrels toward me and jumps into my arms. "Ashew!"

I laugh, my heart nearly exploding out of my chest at little dude's excitement. I ruffle his thick mane of dark, curly hair. "Hiya, Tate. Nice to see you, buddy."

Meadow looks like she could cry. "I'm so sorry, Asher. I know you got fancy seats and everything."

I look over at Tate and tilt my head as a thought springs to mind. "Why don't I take Tate to the game, then?"

Surprise fills her eyes as she looks down at her son. "Really? I mean... it's late."

I pluck the arm of the Tampa Bay Buccaneers jersey Tate is wearing and grin. "Looks like this guy would have been up late watching the game anyway. Am I right?"

Tate nods, then, as if on cue, raises his arms and emits a loud cheer. "Goooooo Bucs!"

I laugh and look back at a smiling Meadow. "See, he'll be the loudest one in the whole stadium. We don't even have to stay the whole game if he doesn't want to."

Meadow twists her face, appearing amused. "I think you'll be surprised. I've never seen a kid so young so into football. He loves rewatching all the games, and he already knows every player's name, jersey number, and position. My mom is always quizzing him."

I scrunch up my face, ready to call her on her bullshit. "You're lying."

She shakes her head. "Not at all. Try him."

"Hey, Tate," I say, quickly thinking up my question. "What is Tom Brady's jersey number?"

"Tweff," he bursts out in no time at all.

"C'mon," Meadow teases. "Too easy."

I look at her, completely baffled. "Who wears number eighty-one?"

Tate giggles. "Antonio Bwown." *Antonio Brown.*

No way. "What position does he play?"

"Wide weceva." *Wide receiver.*

I look up at Meadow, amazed. "You weren't kidding."

She shakes her head. "Nope. He watches every live game and replays them all week long. Sometimes, he'll even call the plays before they happen."

My mouth falls open, then I set Tate down and crouch to meet him eye to eye. "Hey, Tate. How would you like to go to a Buccaneers game with me tonight?"

He tilts his head, seemingly confused, and points at the TV. "Game on tonight, Ashew."

I smile. "Yup, but how would you like to sit in the stadium and watch the game live, right in front of you?"

His gorgeous green eyes widen. "Weally?"

"Yes, buddy. Just you and me. Would you like that?"

Tate squeals again and wraps his arms around my neck. He clings to me so tightly my chest feels like it could burst. When I look up at Meadow, she's got her arms folded and a defeated smile on her face. "This is a lot to ask of you, Asher."

"Good thing you didn't ask." I wink and pick Tate up. I lean over and kiss Meadow. "He's in good hands."

She makes an annoyed expression. "I have no doubt about that."

"Is that a yes?"

Meadow takes Tate from me. "Okay, fine." She glares at me, her eyes sparking with amusement. "But you're moving the car seat over."

For the entire ride to the stadium, Tate sings nearly every song that plays on the Kidz Bop Radio I found on Spotify, and I can't stop smiling. I'm quickly realizing just how great a memory the kid has, and with every passing minute, he gets more animated and talkative. We park in a gravel lot facing the stadium, and I help Tate out of the truck. After taking pit stops at the bathroom and the concession stand, we make our way to our seats.

Clearly, Tate didn't totally realize exactly where we were headed because the look on his face when he stares out at the field is something I'll never forget. His eyes get huge, his mouth drops wide open, and for the first time since we left the house, he appears speechless.

I make sure to catch it all on video and send it to Meadow then continue snapping pics while Tate pans the field. "Dat Bwady!" he squeals.

I chuckle and pick him up. "Yup, and look over there," I say, pointing at another player. "Do you know who that is?"

"Yup," Tate says proudly. "Dat's Wyan Succop, da kicka." He wiggles a little in my arms, his excitement practically exploding out of him as he names every player he sees. He gasps, his hands covering his mouth like he can't believe his eyes. "Dat Mike Ebans, Ashew. See." He points frantically at one of the Bucs' wide receivers.

As much as I wanted to bring Meadow here today, I wouldn't change this experience for the world. Being with Tate reminds me of great times with my family, my dad especially. When he brought me to the games, I could barely contain my awe—not just over the players and their skills. Nothing beats the adrenaline rush you get at a live football game.

Tate's excitement doesn't quit, not even at halftime when we have down time to rush to the restroom and grab one last snack before the game starts again. He's still wide awake, and I don't think he missed a single play in the first half.

"Ashew," he says while shoving a handful of popcorn into his mouth, "aw you my mommy's boyfwend?"

I bite down on the inside of my mouth to keep from bursting into a smile. "I sure hope so, little dude. What does your mommy say?"

He nods. "She say you hew boyfwend, and I like dat."

My chest squeezes. "You do?"

He nods bigger this time. "You fiafida, so you save Mommy fwom fia."

This time I can't help but release the gentlest chuckle at the sincerity of his words. "Yes, buddy. But don't worry. Your mommy won't get caught in any fires." I wink.

A worried look flickers across his face, then he smiles wide like I eased some of his biggest fears. "My daddy was hewo like you."

I take a slow, deep breath, choosing my words wisely. "Oh yes. Your mommy told me all about him. Your daddy was a very brave hero. And I bet you'll grow up to be a hero one day too."

He looks out at the field and points at Tom Brady. "I wanna fwo footballs like Bwady."

I grin, ignoring the fact that he wanted to be a conductor not long ago. "Well, then, we better start practicing. How about I come over this weekend and throw some balls with you? Would you like that?"

He does one of his famous squeals and squeezes his fists tight. "Yes, yes, yes."

We make it through the rest of the game, and I'm almost surprised when Tate starts to yawn during the fourth quarter. I wait until what I think might be the last big play of the game and use the next timeout as an opportunity to leave so we can try to beat some of the traffic. Before we head to the parking lot, I stop at the merchandise booth and grab a few things for Meadow and Tate. When I set the Bucs cap on Tate's head, he smiles so big a faint dimple pops in his cheeks.

"Tank you, Ashew."

I rub his head. "You're welcome, buddy. Ready to head home?"

He nods as another huge yawn takes over his face.

I help Tate into the truck, he hops into his car seat, and I'm buckling him into the five-point harness when he stops and looks at me while tilting his head. "Ashew, what you intensens with my mommy?"

It takes me a second to figure out what he'd said. "Did you just ask me what my intentions are with your mommy?"

Tate nods, as if his question wasn't the least bit adorable. "Do you have howwible intensens?"

I almost choke on my next breath. "Do I have *horrible* intentions?"

"Honiwwible," he says more slowly, this time adding in another letter so I think I've cracked the case.

"Oh, honorable. Tate, did you just ask if I have honorable intentions with your mommy?" I try to keep a straight face but think I might die from laughter later with that one.

He nods, totally oblivious to why his question amused me. "My gwamma says she hope you have honiwwible intensens."

"My intentions are nothing but honorable, little dude. Make sure to pass that on to your grandma, okay?"

Tate nods, another yawn hitting him harder than the last. The kid will be passed out for sure by the time we get home.

I transfer Tate from his car seat into Meadow's arms. While she tucks Tate in, I run out to my truck to transfer the car seat to her car. When I'm done, she's waiting for me at the door, a sweet smile on her face. "Come in. I want to hear all about it." She leads me to her bedroom, shutting the door and locking it behind us.

I raise my brows while sweeping her over with one swift gaze. Her black tank top is stretched tightly over her chest, sans a bra, the bottom seam ending just above her adorable belly button. Her matching cotton shorts reveal a hint of her ass cheek, and I can't help but hope she chose this particular outfit just for me.

"You want to hear about the game or all the secrets Tate told me about you?"

Her cheeks lift, and she takes my hand, tugging me to her bed. The backs of her knees hit the edge of the mattress, and she stops. "I don't really want to hear about the game right now, Asher."

"Oh really?" I ask like it's a challenge. "So you don't want to hear about my horrible intentions?"

She laughs, appearing confused. "What?"

"Tate asked me if my intentions with you were honorable, and I thought he said horrible at first." I scan her body again. "I can't say my intentions are all that honorable right now. But I thought you said you wanted to hear about the game."

"That was just a ploy to get you into my bedroom."

My hands move to her hips. "You don't need a ploy for that." I slide my hands up her sides, taking her shirt with them. Her breasts are so supple and her dark brown nipples so hard, they look like they're aching for my touch. My thumb finds one nipple, rubbing it softly while I bring my mouth down to hers. God, she smells good. Like a cool winter's day at the strawberry fields. She feels so good too. I squeeze her breast in my palm.

"Does this mean you're inviting me to spend the night?"

She gazes back at me for a beat then nods. "As long as you promise to keep quiet."

I bring my mouth to her ear, knowing it drives her crazy. "I believe it's you who can't stop from screaming when I fuck you."

She shudders, her body weakening as she molds herself to me. "Is that a challenge?"

I lean back slightly so that I can peer deep into her eyes. "Absolutely."

CHAPTER TWENTY-THREE

MEADOW

I'm a ball of nerves walking into the Vault, an elegant venue in the heart of Tampa's downtown arts district, where we'll unveil the firefighters' calendar for the first time to the public. After weeks of work, shooting, and editing each of the twelve photos, I feel a level of pride in my work that I've never felt before. To think that I almost walked away from this opportunity is mind-blowing. I've gained so much since accepting—new clients, new friends... a boyfriend.

My heart beats harder at the term. *Boyfriend.* Such a silly word for what we've become in just a couple of months, yet it fills me with that same fluttery feeling I remember from my teen years. And my heart isn't the only thing Asher makes flutter.

"There she is."

Speak of the devil. Asher crosses the room, and I can't keep my eyes from drinking in every single inch of him. He's wearing a shiny gray suit, a white button-down shirt, and a heart-stopping smile.

"Wow." I reach for a lapel of his jacket and drag my eyes up to his. "I guess I know who the subject of my aim will be tonight." I gesture to the camera in my hand with a little shake. "Say cheese, Mr. January."

He narrows his eyes and grips my hips. "You know better than to call me that in public." He peers around me. "Although I spy a staff door at the back of the room. I think I can manage to steal you away later."

The twinkle in his eyes is fuel to my already-racing heart. "You just want something to talk about with your station buddies."

His mouth drops open in mock admonishment. "I would never."

It's my turn to glare. "How will I ever know?"

He chuckles. "Because they'll tell you the next time they see you. We may be a tight-knit group, but that only makes them bigger assholes. Nah," he says, tilting his head. "I think I'd rather keep you and our intimate details between us."

"Good. Considering half of them are my clients now, that's probably for the best." I take a step backward, intending to get to work, but Asher pulls me back in and plants a kiss square on my mouth.

"Sorry," he murmurs against my lips. "I couldn't resist."

I run my thumb against his stained pink lips. "You might want to wash that lipstick off before your fans see you."

He grins. "Better for them to know I'm very much taken, right?"

"Good point." I lift onto my toes and kiss him again, this time harder and longer. I drop back onto my heels and laugh. "Can't wait to see you strut your stuff down that runway."

Still laughing, I walk away before he can stop me again. I have photos to take. Asher couldn't stop me from bringing my camera this time. As a thank-you to everyone involved in the making of the calendar, I wanted to send them all some final photos as mementos of their special night.

I spot Becca soon after leaving Asher, and she tells me the line for tickets extends down the block—and that doesn't even include the presale passes. Tonight's event will be a big one for everyone involved. The event will start with the introduction of the calendar models and will lead into a fashion show of sorts, beginning with Mr. January. While the calendar models are strutting their stuff and dancing, their calendar photos will pop up on screens located all around the room. When the main event is over, guests will have an opportunity to buy calendars and have them signed by the guys. Then it will just be a party.

Becca mostly hangs out with me while I walk around snapping photos. Aaron is in the back with the guys, pumping them up before the start of the show. When I snuck back there with my camera, a half dozen firefighters with their shirts off were doing push-ups and sit-ups while the others were lifting weights or giving interviews.

At one point right before the show starts, Becca clutches my hand. "Don't look now, but the ex-wife is here."

My heart sinks, but I don't know why. Nothing about Sheena intimidates me... other than the fact that she had Asher's heart for over a decade. While I know that's just part of life, a tinge of jealousy is still buried deep down in my chest. It also doesn't help knowing that she never did get over him and quite possibly still wants him back.

I look up, spotting the gorgeous blonde quickly. She's in the back of the room, alone, and she's wearing a bright-yellow dress with an empire waist and ruffled sleeves. Geez, the woman reminds me of one of those *Desperate Housewives* characters with how manicured to perfection she is. Not a hair is out of place, and while she's clearly wearing makeup, it's subtle enough to look natural. Her lips glisten with a coat of gloss, and the smile she wears seems to come naturally, but there's an air of discomfort in her stare, as though she knows she shouldn't be here.

She shouldn't. While this is a public event where anyone can buy tickets, why show up on Asher's big night after an already uncomfortable run-in at the haunted house? And I'm convinced she'd gone to that haunted house knowing he would be there, seeking him out because she wanted to talk about their relationship. I'm baffled by it all and now furious that she's here at all.

"That woman has some nerve."

Becca steps in front of me. "Don't stare. She-Devil will see you. It's best that you just pretend you never spotted her at all."

I drop my jaw, letting out a noise in the back of my throat. "How can I? Becca, should I be worried?"

She shakes her head quickly and with obvious sincerity, filling me with some peace. "Definitely not. But this is for Asher to deal with, not you. Whatever she's up to, and I'm sure she's up to something, will be on Asher."

Becca makes sense, but an instinct inside of me kicks in that wants to protect Asher from any more pain than Sheena's already put him through. And that's when I realize that my tension over Sheena isn't even about jealousy and the time she'd spent with Asher—it's about Asher's heart.

I take Becca's advice to heart and focus on my job instead of on Sheena's looming presence. Out of my peripheral vision, I catch sight of her yellow dress from time to time, so I know she's tucked away in the back corner of the room.

After introductions, the emcee introduces Mr. January to the crowd, and my heart beats faster. I set up my camera on my tripod and wait impatiently for Asher to pop out from behind the red velvet curtain. Having missed the rehearsal earlier in the evening, I have no idea what to expect.

The moment the sound of sirens plays through the speakers, I know that what we're all about to witness will be entertaining, to say the least. But then an upbeat Fergie song begins to play, and that's when Asher jumps—yes, jumps—through the opening in the curtains.

"Oh my Lord."

I bury my head in my hands before peeking through my fingers at the wicked grin lighting up Asher's face. He's fully dressed in his EMT getup, his shirt buttoned to the very top, but the second he grabs the sides of his shirt, my entire body grows hot with embarrassment.

The crowd—mostly filled with women—is going insane in every way. Women are on their feet, throwing their arms around, and screaming like they're at a boy-band concert. It's all well-deserved attention, I must say.

Asher tears open his shirt, revealing his well ripped and oiled upper half. The man is a treasure chest of surprises that I can't wait to claim later tonight, after the couple hundred audience members ogle the hell out of him. I can't blame them.

Asher isn't just a gorgeous specimen of a man. He's got charm, wit, and great dance moves too. All of the above combined make for one swoon fest of a show. He uses every note of the song to parade around for the crowd as he slowly makes his way down to the end of the runway where I'm waiting for him, ready to capture shots of him up close and personal.

What I don't expect is for him to spot me at the end of the stage, point, and then jump onto the floor in front of me while wearing a devilish grin. I have no idea what he's up to until he picks me up and straddles my legs around his waist. He lays me back on the stage and thrusts the air in my direction, like I'm the lucky lady who got plucked from the crowd in a Magic Mike show.

I cover my face with my hands again, unable to contain the laughter bubbling up inside me. I'm so mortified and turned on at the same time, I don't know what to do with myself.

He sets me back on my feet and smacks my ass, and I realize I've got an ache between my thighs he's going to pay for later.

I'm almost relieved when he walks away but not as relieved as I am when I catch sight of a bright-yellow dress in the corner of my eye and turn to watch Sheena walking straight to the exit.

Too many glasses of wine and hundreds of autographs later, Asher and I drive back to his place. I park in the driveway behind him and walk toward his front door, giving him a warning glance when his eyes connect with mine. I haven't had a chance to scold him for the show he put on earlier tonight, but I don't plan on letting it go anytime soon.

"You have yet to feel my wrath, Mr. January."

He bites down on his bottom lip and wraps his arms around me, dropping his hands so his palms grip my ass. He squeezes me to him, and I can feel him getting hard already. "Oh yeah? Whatever did I do to deserve your wrath, Miss January?"

"Hmm." I pretend I'm thinking about it, twisting my lips while my eyes look up and away. "Let's see. Maybe it's the part of your catwalk where you bent me over the stage and dry humped me in front of hundreds of hungry women."

He throws his head back and laughs. "What? Do you

know how many one-dollar bills I could have gotten if I chose some random woman from the audience?"

I cock an eye, daring him. "Oh, I'm sorry. Maybe you should have warned me first so that I could have been prepared with some dollar bills."

"C'mon. You're not really mad at me, are you?" He looks genuinely concerned.

I bite down on my lip, letting him wonder for a few seconds longer before smiling. "Not at all, but I do think you owe me a private show." I cock a brow.

He pushes open the door and tugs me over the threshold. "Now, that sounds like a plan."

CHAPTER TWENTY-FOUR

ASHER

I wake before the alarm sounds, my hand finding the silky skin of Meadow's perfectly shaped ass. It's no secret to her that I have a fascination with her body. I love the way her natural curves and the small of her waist make her ass and tits look voluptuous, despite her petite size.

She stirs, causing the sheet to slip away from her nude form, revealing every inch of her. The way the early morning sun peeks through the blinds in streaks of gold against her skin is intoxicating, to say the least. I run gentle fingers along her skin, from her shoulder to her hip.

She stirs again, a moan slipping past her throat as she pushes her ass against me. "Asher." She sighs, like she's still in a deep sleep. Maybe she is. Maybe she's dreaming about me.

I lean down, kissing her shoulder then running my lips against her back. I had every intention of letting her sleep in, but my growing erection seems to have other plans. Still, I'm cautious as I take in her scent—the floral lotion she applied before bed rising from her skin and infiltrating my senses.

My fingers skip over her hip then slowly slide back up to her waist, earning another groan from her. She pushes against me again.

My breath shudders as she starts to move slowly, gliding her ass cheeks around my still-rising cock. Fuck this woman and what she does to me—to my heart, my mind. She's an addiction I never want to quit.

"Oh Asher, you feel so good." Her voice is drunk with sleep.

I slide my hand to her front, taking hold of one breast as though I need the leverage. "Good morning, beautiful." I kiss her shoulder again, but this time I can't resist adding a little bite.

She pushes against me harder. "I need you."

I smile, slipping one hand between her legs while the other snakes under her neck so she fits in the crook of my arm. "Just tell me what you need." I slip my finger between her folds, confirming her eagerness by her slickness, but I don't give her any more than that. This time, I'll wait for her request.

"Please."

"Please what?" I tease. "Just ask, and you shall receive."

She grabs my hand and pushes two of my fingers against her slick skin. "Touch me. Please, Asher."

The way she says my name, with desperation in her sleepy morning voice, has my heart beating fast. "As you wish."

Her clit is so slippery, I have to focus harder than normal to keep up my rhythm. Not that I need to focus for long. She gasps so loudly, I have to slam my mouth to hers to swallow her reactions to what I'm doing to her.

Her body quivers then stills completely, but I'm a determined man when it comes to Meadow Matthews, and one orgasm simply isn't enough. She must have the same idea, because she flips up to gaze at me, a wicked smile playing on her face. "Think you can do that again with your fingers inside me?"

A challenge I happily accept.

I waste no time lifting myself to gain deeper access and slipping two fingers deep inside her warmth, my cock jumping at the sensation. While it waits impatiently for entrance, I take my time bringing Meadow back to the brink, this time covering her mouth with one palm as she screams out her release.

Her body goes limp, and I uncover her mouth, watching her breasts heave with each breath. "Want me to do it again with my cock?"

She laughs and shakes her head. "Not yet."

My jaw drops, wondering how long Meadow is going to make me wait to get mine. I look down at the throbbing beast still propped between her ass cheeks and grit my teeth. "I might need to take care of this." I back up and grab my length, stroking it a few times, desperate for a release of my own.

She rolls to her side, climbs on top of me, and straddles me. Meadow has never been on top before. The realization makes me pause my strokes and grip her thighs to thoroughly take in the sight of her.

"Fuck me," I beg.

She's still smiling as she leans down, her ass hovering in the air while she grazes her lips against mine. "Okay, but I want you bare," she says.

I think I might choke on my next breath. "O-Okay."

We've teased the conversation before. Eliminating the condom so we can finally feel each other, skin to skin, but we never actually committed to the act. This time, she doesn't hesitate in lifting my unsheathed shaft, fitting it to her, and beginning to slide down around me. I gasp, the feel of her almost too much, so I tighten my hold on her thighs to slow her pace.

Her pussy swallows me, inch by inch, until she reaches my base and then begins to move. Her hips rock, her breasts thrust into the air, and her palms push deep into my chest. I can't stop watching her as she moves. At one point, her mouth parts, and her entire body shakes. I think she's about to let go, but then her pace quickens.

I lift my hips to meet her, deepening our connection as she moans at the new sensation. I'm not going to last long at this rate.

Sex is great, but sex with Meadow is something so much more. An intimacy between us exists because of the relationship we've built outside the bedroom, and it only gets stronger every second we're together.

"Come with me," she begs, her whispered words reaching straight to my heart.

I sit up and wrap my arms around her waist while she works us both to the edge of what feels like the tallest mountain I've ever had the pleasure of climbing. My release is begging to be let free, to jump, to soar. So when her cue comes a minute later, I'm more than ready. And when we soar, we soar together.

"Look who decided to grace us with his presence."

I roll my eyes at Aaron and walk past him to my spot at the long table where I'm to sign autographs. It's our first signing event since the unveiling. Aaron booked us a gig at Rocco's Tacos in the International Plaza. The handful of guys who were able to make it today are already throwing back shots, getting into the mood.

"Looks like I haven't missed much."

The bartender comes over to ask for my drink order, but I wave my hand, declining. Aaron tilts his head, his forehead furrowed in confusion. "Nothing to drink? You okay?"

I chuckle. "I'm going back to Meadow's after this. Tate requested tacos for dinner. Apparently, they're right up there with pasghetti." I grin at my imitation of little dude.

"Wow," Aaron says with a nod like he's impressed. "I love seeing you like this, man. Happy. Settled." He waggles his brows. "Dare I say... in love?"

I shrug, leaving the playful look on my face. "If I am, you're not going to be the first one I tell."

His smile widens. "Oh my, you are so in love. I can't remember the last time I've seen you this happy."

"It's been a long time since I've felt this happy." I don't expect my tone to become as serious as it does. "But Meadow is perfect, man. And Tate..." I shake my head. "The kid just exudes joy. He's always smiling, even when he's sick."

Aaron claps me on the back. "I can't wait to meet him one day." He squeezes my shoulder and pulls back, his eyes widening. "In fact, why don't you all come over for Thanksgiving dinner? We're having it again on Tuesday this year."

Holidays—Thanksgiving, especially—are guaranteed working days for us, for the most part. We usually enjoy a feast at the station between calls, so we usually have to celebrate with our families on non-traditional days of the week.

"Becca has her heart set on preparing a feast, but only her parents, sisters, and sisters' kids can come. Hey, I think the youngest one is Tate's age. They'll have a blast."

"Sounds fun. We haven't made plans yet, so I'll run it by Meadow. We'll probably bring her mom, if that's cool."

"Of course. Just let me know."

The event kicks off soon afterward. I can't see the end of the line outside the restaurant, but from what I understand, it's still growing. We autograph our photos, pose for photos with those who ask, and give a few sound bites to the radio station crew supporting our event. All in all, it's a fun day, but two hours in, my face and hands already ache.

I take a quick break to go to the restroom and chug some water, then sit down and get at it again. A few minutes after sitting back down, someone slides a calendar in front of me, this one still on the cover page. So I look up to ask where I should sign it. When I see the familiar face staring back at me, my heart sinks straight into my toes, and dread twists my gut.

What the hell is Sheena doing here?

It's beginning to get creepy with her randomly showing up where I happen to be. Between that and her nonstop calls and messages that I had to block, I'm running out of patience.

"What are you doing here?" I ask quietly through gritted teeth, not wanting to attract attention.

Her fake smile falters, and hurt registers in her eyes. I feel like an ass for hurting her, but why? She has no business trying to reenter my life. We had our shot. Multiple shots. Whatever we felt for each other a decade ago is buried six feet deep, and that's where it will undoubtedly stay forever.

"What?" she asks, righting her shoulders. "I can't support your fundraising efforts?"

A tinge of guilt lights my chest. "You absolutely can. Thank you." I put my head down, scribble my name on the cover of the calendar, and hand it back to her. "Thanks for the support."

She frowns, and I can see in her eyes that she wanted more to come from her visit. "You aren't even the least bit happy to see me?"

I look her dead in the eyes then slowly shake my head. "I can't say that I am."

She looks around, appearing embarrassed. "Asher, I've been trying to talk to you. There's something I need to tell you, but…" She looks around again, her face turning an awful shade of red. "I can't tell you here."

My chest flares with anger, and it takes everything in me to contain it. "Sheena, I don't know how to put this, so I'm just going to say it. You need to stay the hell away—from me, from my events. Please stop calling and messaging. You need to move on." I open my mouth to tell her that I already have but decide I've already said enough. "You should go."

Her eyes narrow. "You need to hear what I have to say."

I stand up and lean forward, not wanting to speak too loudly but needing her to hear me without question. "After everything you put me through, I owe you nothing."

Before I even sit back down, a security guard approaches Sheena and demands for her to leave. Aaron is standing a few feet away, a worried look on his face as he traces her exit with his eyes. He approaches me and leans down to whisper. "What the hell was that about?"

I shake my head. "She won't quit. Apparently, blocking her isn't enough."

"She-Devil is stalking you. You need to go to the cops."

I roll my eyes. "Sheena is no threat. She's just… troubled. I don't understand what her problem is."

"What did she say she wanted?"

"To talk."

"About what?"

I shrug. "About us, probably. Look," I say, blowing out a breath, "Sheena is the type of woman who only wants what she can't have. That's the only reason she can't let this go."

Aaron doesn't look so sure. "I hope you're right, man. I'd hate to see you and Meadow get hurt because Sheena suddenly feels remorseful about her infidelity—and for being a shitty person in general."

I let out a laugh. "I don't think Sheena is capable of

remorse. But it doesn't matter. I think I made myself very clear today. She's not coming back around."

Aaron nods and backs away from the table. "Good."

But even with the certainty in my words and the confidence I was able to instill in Aaron, something doesn't feel right. And I'm afraid I haven't seen the last of Sheena. Not by a long shot.

CHAPTER TWENTY-FIVE

MEADOW

Tate wobbles a little on the step stool I set out for him in the kitchen. We're making a few desserts for tonight's Thanksgiving get-together at Becca's, and Tate volunteered to be my sous chef. He's using all his strength to stir the cookie batter—gritting his teeth, growling, and everything.

I place my hands on his waist to steady him while biting down on my lip to stifle my laugh. "There you go. Mix those chocolate chips in real good."

My mom walks into the kitchen, but unlike me, she can't hold back her laughter. She cheers. "Get in there, Tate."

I look over at my shoulder, smirking. "Funny."

Her eyes widen. "I'm not kidding. I love Tate's dedication to everything he does. He won't half-ass his way through life."

Tate gasps, his entire face lit up with shock when he turns to look at me. "Gwamma say *ass*."

Dread swallows me whole. "Tate, that's a naughty word."

He points the silicone spoon at my mom, flinging

cookie dough everywhere. "Gwamma say naughty word, doh."

My mom is still laughing when I grab the spoon that's still in Tate's hand and stick it back in the bowl. "What Grandma meant to say was that you're a very hard worker. And when you work hard in life, there are rewards."

"Wewards?"

His high-pitched excitement almost makes me forget why we're having this conversation. "That's right. For example, now that you've mixed all this batter up, you can have a taste." I hold the spoon to his mouth. "Go ahead, Tater Tot. Give it a lick."

His eyes go wide at the cookie dough with chocolate chips mixed in, then his tongue darts out to lick the spoon. "Yum," he squeals before going in for another lick.

I pull the spoon away and laugh. "One lick's enough, or you'll ruin your perfect batter." I pull him off the stool and pat his butt. "Go play with your toys while I put these cookies in the oven, okay? We're going to leave soon, so I'll come in to get you ready."

Tate zooms out of the room like he's flying a plane, and my mom stands beside me at the counter with a shame-filled smile on her face. "Sorry about that. I'm still getting used to having a kid around, I guess."

I shake my head, smile, and drop the licked spoon in the sink, replacing it with a regular spoon. "It's fine. Hopefully he's already forgotten all about it. Besides, you were on to something. I hope his hard work now carries on throughout life."

"Of course it will, Meadow. He has you for a mother." She folds her arms while leveling me with a serious expression. "You're also far too hard on yourself."

I frown, knowing she's right, but there's still a kick of disappointment deep in my chest. "I thought I was getting better at that."

My mom nods, her expression easing a little. "You are, but I can see how you're tiptoeing around things with Asher, and it just makes me wonder if you've transitioned some of that self-deprecation into self-sabotage."

My jaw drops. I don't quite believe what I'm hearing. Of all people, my mom is the toughest on me, but she's also been the most supportive over the years, especially since Milton died. She came and cared for me while I was pregnant, she visited monthly after I had Tate, and then she opened up her home to me. So it hurts when she calls me out for acting in a way that I don't even realize. How long has she felt this way?

"I'm not self-sabotaging. Asher and I are happy. We've been taking it slow, and I think that's best for Tate."

My mom nods. "Absolutely. I can't argue with that. I'm saying that if there's anyone you can trust with your heart and Tate's heart, it's that man. And I'm not just saying that because he knows CPR, among many other life-saving skills. He's a good man, and he adores you, Meadow."

I grit my teeth, my defenses coming on strong, and I don't even know why. It's like she's triggered feelings that I've been burying deep in my chest. Feelings that I'm not ready to face. "Mom, I know all of those things about Asher. In fact, I'm convinced he's perfect. It's just—"

Her expression transitions into worry. "Uh-oh, here it comes."

I hate that we're even talking about this. I hate that my mom is able to get things out of me that I never planned to mention. But somehow, she's unleashed the fears I've been withholding, and the only way out is through. "It's nothing really. But... I just can't stop thinking about Asher's ex-wife and whatever still lingers between them."

My mom frowns. "And what makes you think there's anything lingering between them? She saw you two together at the haunted house."

I nod. "And at the unveiling event."

My mom twists her head. "Say what? She was at the unveiling?"

I nod again, this time more slowly while searching my mom's expression for her reaction. The way her face quickly transitions from doubt to understanding to worry makes me believe my gut may not be too far off. "I think she was there to talk to Asher, but then after he did that whole dance thing with me, she fled. She looked really upset, Mom. It's not over for her." I can feel myself shake with my words, my fear submerging and completely unavoidable now.

"Okay," she says calmly. "But what does he say about it all?"

I take a deep breath, a sense of calm washing over me. "He says it's over for him. And I do believe him, which is why these fears I have make absolutely no sense, and they're completely unfair to Asher. It's not his fault if Sheena suddenly had a change of heart. He moved on."

My mom grips my hand. "Exactly. He moved on, and he's smitten with you and Tate. I hate that you're worried about this, though. It's only going to interfere with you moving forward with him."

"Right, and I don't want to talk to him about it because then he might think I don't trust him, and that's not it at all. But they were together for over a decade. They were high school sweethearts. I can't compete with that."

"You don't have to, Meadow."

"I know, but... you said it yourself. Asher is an honorable guy. What if he feels like he owes Sheena another chance if she's willing to give him the family he's always wanted?"

My mom squishes up her face. "The family he's always wanted?"

"Sheena didn't want kids, but he did. Ultimately, that's what ended things between them."

She shakes her head. "Okay, but certainly there was more to it than that."

"There was," I confirm, my voice smaller than I intended. "Anyway," I say with a shake of my head, "I really don't want to dwell on this. It's not helping anything."

"No, but maybe you do need to talk to him. If it's bothering you this much, he should know."

"You're probably right." I sigh.

She wraps her arms around me in the warmest hug I've received from her in a long time. It's one of those comforting mom hugs that cocoons me in, making everything appear safe and warm for as long as it lasts.

"Of course, I'm right," she says, her smug tone nearly ruining the moment. "I'm a mother."

Becca gasps at the array of desserts I offer her at the door. "Oh, Meadow, you outdid yourself. Thank you."

I hug her with my free arm and pull back, giving her a big smile. "It was fun. I had a little helper too." I look over my shoulder and grin at Tate, who's holding my mom's hand.

"I help," he says proudly, puffing out his little chest.

Becca's smile widens, and she drops to a crouch. "Well, in that case, I cannot wait to try them." She sticks her hand out. "Hi, Tate. I'm your mommy's friend Becca."

He takes her hand, beaming. "I Tate!"

Becca laughs and stands up, giving me those baby-fever eyes I've come to know well. Tate seems to have that effect on people. "He's adorable."

Becca and my mom hug it out next. It's been years

since they've seen each other, so it's a nice little reunion that makes us all a bit emotional. Luckily, Tate is his showman self, distracting everyone from becoming too serious. He quickly gravitates toward two little kids playing with miniature cars in the living room, and I accompany Becca into the kitchen to set down the desserts.

"Aaron messaged me before you got here," she says, while pulling out a hot dish from the oven. "He and Asher are on their way."

As if on cue, loud voices boom from the entrance of the home. Becca and I walk out of the kitchen to check out the commotion. Lo and behold, it's Aaron and Asher, gracing us with their smiling faces.

Asher finds me instantly and makes a beeline in my direction, swooping me up and burying his face in my neck. "I've missed you."

I'm melting like chocolate right at his feet. That's all it takes. Three simple words, and my chest fills with air, my cheeks burn with an unstoppable smile, and the whole world feels as it should. "I've missed you too. How was work?"

He groans against my neck, causing me to laugh. "Long. Nonstop. But I'm sure it's much better than what Thursday will bring."

I frown. "Really? That bad, huh?"

He nods. "Unfortunately, but I don't have to think about that for thirty-six hours." He lifts his head and kisses me softly. "Where's Tate?"

Before I can even show him, Asher locates him near Becca's nephews and nieces and heads in his direction. Tate's entire face lights up when Asher picks him up off the floor to pull him in for a hug. "Hey, buddy. Good to see you. Did you make some friends?"

Tate and Asher continue their animated conversation while I help Becca hand out appetizers and set the tables for dinner. A movie is playing on the television in the living room, where most of the guests are gathered until Asher, Aaron, Becca's brother-in-law, and all the kids run outside to play football. Asher keeps an eye on Tate, using his body to block him from getting pummeled by a kid or the ball, and all I can think is just how insane I've been for doubting anything when it comes to Asher.

At this moment, I've never felt safer. But I hate that there's still a sliver of a doubt about what will come tomorrow.

CHAPTER TWENTY-SIX

MEADOW

Asher follows my mom and me back to our place and takes over the task of transferring Tate from his car seat to his bed, since he zonked out the minute I strapped him in.

I watch Asher carry Tate into his bedroom as he tries not to jostle him too much. He seems like such a natural by the way he eases Tate onto the mattress and slips his little shoes off. Emotion clogs my throat, and I can feel the prick of tears in the backs of my eyes. I've never let any man get close to Tate the way Asher has over the past two months, and while there's no manual to help me navigate the situation, I can't deny how right being with Asher feels. Like we're a family.

"I don't think you have a single thing to worry about, my dear," my mom whispers as she walks past me to her bedroom.

My smile is small, but I nod to tell her she's right. My freak-out from earlier in the night feels ridiculous at best. "Good night, Mom."

"Good night, sweetheart."

A few minutes later, Asher slides the blanket over

Tate's little body and joins me in the hall. "How'd I do?" he asks with a grin.

My heart feels like it might burst. "Definitely an A-plus, Mr. January. That's what I like to call a successful transfer."

He leans closer, bringing his lips to mine. "Now, it's your turn."

Before I can argue, he scoops me up in his arms and walks me down the hall, but not toward my bedroom as I expected. "Where are we going?" I whisper, laughing.

"The kitchen."

"What? Why?"

His eyes grow wide like an innocent little puppy. "Because I didn't get any dessert at the party. Tate kept eating my apple pie."

I laugh at the memory of poor Asher's face from when Tate snuck bites when Asher wasn't looking. Of course, Asher was completely egging him on by acting oblivious, but it made Tate giggle, so Asher forfeited his entire plate.

"Isn't that why Becca gave you an entire pie?"

He nods. "Yup, and I'm about to eat it. And you, Miss January, are going to watch me."

He carries me the rest of the way into the kitchen and sets me on the counter while he rummages around my mom's fridge for the apple pie she stored as soon as we got home. He pulls it out, a wicked gleam in his eyes. "Please tell me you have vanilla ice cream."

I nod and point at the freezer below the refrigerator. "Help yourself, but don't eat the last bite."

He wrinkles his forehead in amusement. "Why? Will Tate get upset?"

"No," I say, pointing a finger at my chest. "I will. I always get the last bite."

Asher pulls out the tub and opens the lid. "Oh my," he says in mock disappointment. "Looks like there are only a few bites left. I'll do my best to leave some, but..." He shakes his head. "No promises."

I glare at him, too enamored by his existence to actually be upset. But man, I love giving him a hard time. "If you know what's good for you, you'll leave me that last scoop."

Without a word, Asher takes the carton of ice cream and apple pie over to the opposite counter and grabs a plate. He very slowly proceeds to dish out three-quarters of the pie onto his plate before sticking it in the microwave for ten seconds. When he takes it out, he's already got the ice cream scooper in his hand, and he watches me as he plops the last of the vanilla ice cream onto his plate.

"Tell you what," he says while picking up the plate and walking over to me. "You can share my ice cream and my apple pie with me."

I tilt my head, waiting for the punch line. "Why do I feel like there's a negotiation on the horizon?"

His cheeks lift in a cocky smile. "There's no hiding anything from you, is there?"

I shake my head, narrowing my eyes and meeting his flirtatious stare. "Definitely not. You're a pretty easy guy to read."

He takes another bite of pie, this time scooping up some ice cream with it. He waves it in the air between us with a smile "Funny you say that, because I was thinking we could play twenty questions. I ask you a question, then you ask me. Winner gets the last bite of ice cream."

"Wait. How do we know who wins?"

"Easy." He shrugs. "First one to not answer a question. Anything goes."

There's a fluttering in my chest, but it's not from unease. In fact, I like the idea of this little game. "Deal. You first."

"Okay," he says easily. "Tell me your most memorable vacation ever."

A memory immediately springs to mind. "Easy. My parents were obsessed with cruising and took me with them to the Bahamas when I was a teen."

"Nice. I've never been on a cruise."

I tilt my head. "Really? We should go. Nonstop entertainment, an endless supply of food, gourmet dinners, beautiful scenery, and sightseeing... They're so much fun."

He smiles. "Okay, so we're going on a cruise. Now it's your turn to ask me."

"Wait, you answer your own question first."

He purses his lips like he's thinking and then looks back at me. "That's easy. Camping in Yellowstone. My parents were nature lovers. We were always hiking, skiing, or biking somewhere."

"I've always wanted to drive through Yellowstone. We'll have to go there together too."

"I'm loving this game already." He grins. "Now ask me something."

I chew on my bottom lip while I toss around a couple of questions and finally settle on one. "What did you want to be when you were a little kid?"

He shrugs. "A doctor, I guess. I just wanted to help people, but I never thought about becoming an EMT or firefighter until I joined the army."

I tilt my head, impressed. "And look at you now."

He nods. "Only fifty hours away from becoming a paramedic."

"Really?" I didn't realize he was that close, and I can tell by the way his chest puffs out that he's proud of the work he's put in to claim a new title. "That's great, Asher."

"Thanks." He tucks a strand of hair behind my ear. "And what about you? What did young Meadow Matthews want to be when she was growing up?"

"A wedding planner, actually." My cheeks heat, but I

don't know why. Maybe it's the fact that I'm mentioning my little-girl fantasies to Asher. "I think I just loved the idea of everyone getting a happily ever after. Cheesy, I know."

Asher's smile slips slightly as he searches my eyes. "I don't think that's cheesy at all. Everyone should have a happily ever after."

"Even the bad people?" I tease, not thinking about anyone in particular, but by the look in Asher's eyes, I have a feeling he might be.

"I like to think there's someone for everyone. Even the bad ones." His cheeks lift again in a playful smile. "My turn. Time to kick it up a notch."

I laugh, not sure I like the idea of that.

He presses on my thighs and leans in, the gleam in his eyes giving off a devilish vibe. "What's your wildest fantasy?"

My entire body heats. "You did not just go there."

He chuckles. "I did. And you have to answer, or the rest of this ice cream is mine." He smirks and takes another bite of pie.

Sighing, I start to rack my brain. *Wildest fantasy, wildest fantasy.* I think of all the things I've done it and realize how uninventive I've been in my sexual past. Aside from the staff room visits Asher likes to take me on, my sex life has been... boring, to say the least. A thought comes to mind, and another wave of heat rushes to my cheeks. "I've never had sex outside."

He furrows his brows. "Outside as in..."

I shrug. "Outside as in outside of a building with a roof."

"And you fantasize about having sex outside where, exactly?"

I'm aroused and mortified by his questions all at once. "I-I don't know. On a beach, on a boat, on a balcony, on a roof." I bite down on my lip. "In a tent but with the flaps open, facing the water."

His eyes go wide. "Oh my, you've really thought about this."

I laugh and bury my head against his shoulder. "Haven't you?"

"Hell yeah, I have. I don't think there's a surface on this earth that I haven't thought about having sex on."

Bringing my head back up so I can look at him, I tilt my head. "You are such a guy."

He flashes me a grin. "That I am."

"Mm-hmm. So, then, what's yours? Wait, let me guess. An orgy or threesome."

He shakes his head, his eyes darkening. "Hell no. I'm strictly a one-woman guy. I don't like to share. But I might have a little bit of a crush on the Black Widow."

I narrow my eyes. "Crush?"

Now it's his face that's turning red. "Yeah, a crush. It's all that black leather, and I always imagined the front zipper sliding all the way around to the ass." He grins. "You'd look damn hot in that bodysuit. On the balcony of a cruise ship. We really should start booking that trip right away."

I laugh. "Or we could get back to the game. The ice cream is melting."

"True. Okay, go for it."

"How many partners have you had?"

He eyes me warningly. "You realize you're going to have to answer this too. Right?"

I shrug. "I have nothing to hide."

"Neither do I." He sighs. "Four. That includes you."

"Am I your first after Sheena?"

He makes a face like I'd asked him a ludicrous question. "Yes, of course. I thought you knew that."

I shake my head. "I thought so, but I wasn't sure."

"Now you know." He slips his hands up to my waist and slams his lids shut. "I'm bracing myself. What's your number?"

I smile. "Four."

His eyes fly open. "Really?"

I nod. "And you're my first since Milton… so I guess we have that in common."

With Asher's next breath, I swear I can see and feel all the stress that leaves his body. "Well, there you go." He searches my eyes, another serious look crossing his face. "Would you ever consider having another baby?"

My heart triples its beat. "With the right man, yes."

"How many?"

I laugh. "I always said I would have three so that they could all balance each other out."

Asher smiles. "I like that number. That's my answer too."

I bite down on my lip. "Would you ever consider getting married again?"

He nods. "With the right woman, absolutely. And you?"

I mirror his nod. "I believe in happily ever afters, remember?"

Asher takes my chin gently between his two fingers. "Looks like we have a lot in common. We might just be a perfect match after all."

I smile, this time feeling shy under the heat of his gaze. "I already knew that, Asher."

He skims his lips against mine. "So did I. I didn't need a silly game of twenty questions to know the woman I've already fallen head over heels in love with."

My chest thunders at his words. I almost can't believe they're real. "You're in love with me?"

He leans back slightly, a challenge plainly written in his eyes. "Without a shadow of a doubt." He slides his lips to my cheek and kisses me there before continuing on a path to my ear. "To be honest, I'm not sure if I fell in love with you or Tate first, but I'm damn happy that you're a package deal. I don't want to know a life without you two in it."

Tears immediately prick the backs of my eyes as my throat swells and my heart rate quickens. "Every day since I've met you has felt like a dream. I'm so afraid to wake up."

"I'll still be right here when you do."

I release a shaky breath and cup his cheek with my palm. "I'm in love with you, Asher. So much. And I know Tate is too."

He breathes out what sounds like relief and then presses his lips to mine in a deep kiss, one I know I'll never forget for the rest of my life. I'm so lost in it, in him, in us, that I don't realize we're moving until he sets me down on the bed.

"I take it the game's over?" I ask teasingly.

He chuckles before removing his shirt and kneeling in front of me at the edge of the bed. "Fuck yes, the game's over. We have other business to attend to."

"But what about the ice cream?"

"Considering we both won, I think we get to share it." He picks up the plate. I hadn't even seen him bring it into the bedroom with us. "Take your clothes off, Meadow."

From the way he makes the demand, with his tone filled with lust and need, it's like he's been waiting all night to finally fuck me. I know better than to argue with Asher when he uses that tone. I pull off my shirt first then my bra. While he licks his lips, his gaze burning straight through my chest, I slip off my pants, hooking my panties with them.

"Lie down."

As soon as my back goes flush with the comforter, he

bends my knees so my feet are pressed into the edge of the bed. Then he spreads them wide, exposing me to his gaze.

"You're a good listener." He compliments me, amusement in his tone. "Just for that, I'm going to give you the first bite." A cold, wet sensation hits me between my legs. "Shit, I spilled."

I look down to find a creamy line of ice cream running between my slit just as Asher's mouth covers it and begins to slurp it up. He doesn't devour me like I expect. He takes his time, running his thick tongue up and down against my opening and sucking my clit into his mouth with each swipe.

He's trying to torture me. I know he is. The way he watches me, his hooded gaze pinned on my every gasp and moan as his tongue flattens and glides against me. Dear Lord. My fingers clutch the comforter on each side of me, and I swear I'll come if he keeps at this pace. But just like that, his mouth leaves mine, and another dollop of ice cream falls into my belly button.

Everything aches below my waist as he works his way up my body, dripping the sticky cold liquid on every inch of my body he wants to lick. My head is spinning by the time he reaches my mouth to feed me the last scoop.

"What do you think about sharing now?"

I'm too dazed to respond, but he doesn't wait for an answer as he drives his length into my entrance and makes love to me until we both shatter together.

CHAPTER TWENTY-SEVEN

ASHER

It feels strange to step through the entrance of Bayside Regional when I'm not rushing a stretcher through the sliding doors of the emergency room. I'm used to my routine and the urgency that races through my veins every time I transport a patient and hand them off to the best of the best doctors, nurses, and staff. But this visit is nothing like that.

I cross the main lobby, smile at the receptionists, then take a left toward the cafeteria, where I plan to meet some friends. Usually, we try to catch each other at Shipwrecked, but lately we haven't had much luck getting our schedules to align. So I arranged for us to meet for a quick lunch before I have to start my twelve-hour shift at the station.

I'm almost to the cafeteria when I see Lars leaving the side exit of the ER and heading down the corridor that leads to the staff lounge.

"Hey, Lars. You're going the wrong way."

Lars pauses then spins toward me, her entire face lighting up with the most uncharacteristic smile. "Hey, Asher. What are you doing here?"

I laugh. "Lunch, remember? You, me, Beck, Greg. Like old times, except the hospital cafeteria instead of Shipwrecked." I flash her an easy grin.

"Oh shit." She slaps her hand on her forehead. "It totally slipped my mind."

I rock back, surprised. "That's very unlike you."

"I've been swamped more than usual. Nothing serious." Her eyes dart around, as though she's looking for someone, before her full-blown smile returns.

I tilt my head, ready to call my friend out on her weird behavior. She's wearing her hair down too. "What's up with you?"

"Besides the usual?" She gestures around, but she can't pull one over on me.

"You seem very... un-Lars-like."

She huffs out a laugh. "Un-Lars-like? Why? Because I'm happy to see you for once?"

I grin. I think I might have figured it out. "Yeah, exactly. Can I thank Dane's pickled pecker for this, or did you just have a few good rounds with that magic bullet of yours?"

"Why can't it be both?" She pops her hip.

My chuckle comes harder than I intended, but Lars is completely oblivious to just how lovesick she appears. "All right, message received. I'll quit razzing you. Are you free for lunch, or what?"

"Yes, technically." She stalls like she's weighing her options while looking around us again.

"Looking for a certain someone?"

Her gaze settles on me again. "Do you mind if Dane joins us? I was about to check if he's in the lounge."

And there's all the confirmation I need. "Ah, it's all making sense. You're in love."

She rolls her eyes. "Well, yeah."

I sputter on my next exhale. While I fully expected

Lars and Dane to hit it off, I was completely joking about the love comment. "For real? I wasn't expecting you to admit it."

Her smile fades slightly. "I'm not going to deny my feelings for him."

"Of course not," I tell her. "You should shout about it. Cherish the bond. Nurture the emotions and watch them grow. Don't take each other for granted. All that sentimental crap you usually hate."

"Sounds like you're living in your own romance novel."

My lips tilt up at the sides. "Things with Meadow are great. Thanks for asking."

She raises her palms to her chest and sighs. "That makes me so happy. You deserve it, Mr. January."

I scrunch my nose, thoroughly amused by my friend's drastic change. "Okay, you're starting to weird me out. Go find Dane and let him soak it all in."

As if she wasn't acting weirdly enough, Lars launches at me and wraps her arms around my neck in a hug. "Thank you! You're the best."

I pat her back and chuckle. "And it's official. He's really gotten to you. Hold onto that guy."

"I plan to." She straightens and smooths a palm down her lab coat. "Thanks for the rain check."

"Tell my favorite horndog I say hello," I call after her.

She laughs. "I'm totally telling him you said that."

I turn toward the cafeteria and immediately spot Beck sitting in a booth in the corner of the room, the large window to his side overlooking a strip of palm trees and the bay beyond that. I frown when I see his tray is already empty. I head toward him.

"Becky," I scold him, using the nickname I reserve just for him. "You ate lunch without me. That's not how lunch dates work. First Lars bails, and now you ate without me? I'm starting to take this personally."

His mouth pulls up to one side, and that's when I see the sleep lines on his face. "Today got away from me, so I had to grab lunch as soon as I could. I have to discharge a patient in twenty. I promised I wouldn't be late."

"Well, that's nice of you."

Beck has always created his schedule around his patients, not the other way around, which is what makes him the best fucking kind of doctor, in my opinion.

He nods at my brown lunch sack. "What's that? You packed your own lunch?"

I grin. "Meadow packed it for me. She made the meanest teriyaki chicken dish last night. I'm telling you, that woman might just cook better than me."

Beck shakes his head and laughs. "You're not all that, Moore. I'm glad you finally found a woman who could knock your ego down a few pegs."

I lean back in my chair. If Beck only knew exactly how well Meadow manages my many inches of *ego*. I decide to keep those details to myself. "She does all right. In fact, we're already talking about moving in together. It wouldn't be for several months, but we want to ease Tate into it so he's not totally thrown for a loop."

"Wait. Your girlfriend has a kid too? How did I not know this?" Beck's mouth is hanging open.

"Guess it's been a while since we caught up. And text message didn't seem like the appropriate place to give you all the dirty details."

He coughs out a laugh. "Well, shit. I'm happy for you. After what you went through with Sheena, I love seeing things turning around for you."

I smile. "Thanks, man. I appreciate that. How are things with you? You've been awfully quiet since we last talked. You ever get things off your chest with your girl?"

Beck's lips lift on one side. "Let's just say I got more than I bargained for when I went home to *confront the past*.

I'll fill you in, but it's going to take more time than we have right now." He stands. "Let's meet up for drinks tomorrow at Shipwrecked after you get off."

"Anything for you, Becky."

Beck walks off, and I know he would be flipping me off right now if he wasn't at work. On his way out, he knocks fists with Greg, who is strutting into the cafeteria. Maybe *strut* isn't the right word, considering his disheveled appearance. Greg is normally an easygoing, fun guy who always wears a natural smile, but the man walking toward me looks more like a lost puppy. The bags under his eyes tell a story words don't need to—that he hasn't been sleeping—and he could desperately use a shave.

"Where'd Beck run off to?" Greg asks before plopping into the seat across from me. "I thought we were all meeting for lunch."

"He has a discharge he doesn't want to be late for. But we're meeting up tomorrow night at Shipwrecked, if you want to join."

Greg shakes his head. "He dragged me there last week and made me talk about my feelings, so I think I'll pass."

I assess Greg's entire demeanor for another quiet moment. "Is this about that girl I saw you with at the climb back in October?" Since we hadn't gotten much time to chat during the event, I had messaged him afterward, asking for the scoop. He hadn't said much, and I guessed it was because things were still new between them. "Amanda, right?"

Greg nods while toying with a napkin on the table. "Yeah, that's her name."

Man, it's worse than I thought. Greg looks completely beaten down. "I take it things aren't going well."

He cringes and finally looks up to meet my eyes. "Considering my best friend, David, walked in on us in bed together... no, things are shit right now."

I stifle a laugh, not trying to be insensitive, but I can't help but find the visual humorous. "Did David and Amanda date or something? I don't understand."

He levels me with his stare, clearly unappreciative of my amusement. "No, they didn't date, Ash. Amanda is David's *mom*."

My jaw drops so hard I wouldn't be surprised if it smacked the floor. "You're fucking with me."

Greg's eyes roll, and he shakes his head. "I'm definitely not fucking with you. This is the reality I've been living in ever since. I've been a mess."

"You look it."

Greg lets out a disgruntled laugh. "No shit. I haven't slept at all. I've practically been living here."

"And what did David say? Did you talk to him? Maybe he'll understand."

Greg gets a tick in his jaw, and he shakes his head. "I've tried reaching out to him, but he's not answering. Understandably so. I'm sure he's already blocked my number and written me out of his life." He pauses, swallowing a knot in his throat. "She's not answering me either, so I guess she's done the same." He swipes his fingers through his tousled hair. "Let's change the subject or something. This isn't helping."

A pang hits my chest. While I love giving Greg shit every chance I can, I feel for him. I don't know what I would do if an obstacle like that got in the way of Meadow and me, especially after having a taste of what our future could be together. "All right," I tell him. "But I'm here if you ever want to talk."

"Thanks, man. I appreciate it." He clears his throat and forces a smile. "Tell me about the calendar. How's all that coming along?" He cocks a brow. "In fact, if you really want to make me feel better, tell me Samuel got a bad skin rash right before the shoot."

"Even better." I match his cocked eyebrow and raise him a tilted smile. "I kicked him out."

Greg chuckles. "Why am I not surprised?"

I shrug. "I had high hopes, but until he cleans up his act, I can't let him represent us, you know?"

Now that I've seemed to lift Greg's mood a little, we ease into conversation, focusing on the subject of Meadow. I can't shut up about her and Tate, which seems exactly the distraction Greg needs at the moment. We talk about my house renovation, which he again promises to come check out the next spare moment he gets, and we manage to have a nice catch-up despite his terrible mood.

After we say our goodbyes, I have ten minutes until I need to be at work. I quicken my steps toward the lobby, knowing that I can make it to the station in plenty of time. I start to pull out my phone to check in with Meadow when a familiar figure at the front desk catches my eye.

The moment I recognize Sheena, I quicken my steps toward the door, hoping she'll be too consumed by the paperwork she's filling out to see me walk by.

"Thank you, Mrs. Moore," the desk clerk says, and I cringe at the fact that my ex-wife is still using my surname. "If you'll just have a seat, Dr. McLean will be with you shortly."

Just like that, everything freezes—my steps, my breathing, my heart—because there's only one Dr. McLean in this entire hospital. And she's an obstetrician.

Which means...

As if that simple connection doesn't hit me hard enough, the look on Sheena's face when she turns around and spots me certainly does. She mirrors my surprise, save for her widening eyes, and then my gaze falls to Sheena's rounded stomach. I'm not sure the shape of her belly would even be obvious if it weren't for the way her hand wraps it from below, highlighting the small, but entirely real baby bump.

"Sheena, are you—?" I swallow and start again. "I mean, how—?" Everything I plan to say sounds idiotic coming out of my mouth. Of course she's pregnant, and I have no business asking how far along she is. "I guess what I'm trying to say is congratulations."

I bite my tongue when what I really want to ask is why she decided to have a baby now but didn't want to have one with me. None of that matters now.

Sheena's mouth opens and closes, and I can see the fear etched into her eyes. So many thoughts race through my mind. Will she keep the baby? Is that prick she was fighting with at the hardware store the father? If so, why isn't he with her now?

She's silent and stares at me wide-eyed for so long that I almost miss the whispered words when they finally come out of her mouth. "I've been trying to talk to you."

The thundering in my chest becomes louder than my thoughts—so loud I can't make sense of what my brain is trying to tell me. "You have" is all I say. A numbness washes over me as realization hits. "You wanted to tell me about your baby."

It's hard to believe my own words. While I hoped and dreamed and prayed that Sheena would become pregnant with my child when we were married, I never once considered the possibility of her becoming pregnant after we divorced.

Her eyes narrow slightly, and she steps forward until we're only inches apart. "I wanted to tell you about *our* baby, Asher. I'm pregnant. Just like you always wanted." She lets out a shaky smile. "We're going to be a family."

I've never done mental math faster in my life. If what she says is true, then her pregnancy is as old as our divorce certificate—nearly four months old. My eyes lock on the bump she's still wrapping her arms around, and I shake my head, denial hitting me strong. "But you can't be. You've been on birth control for as long as I've known you."

"I had my IUD taken out." She pauses like she's trying to figure out how to tell me something.

"But that night..." I shake my head, knowing I can't be angry at her for not telling me she wasn't still on birth control when we'd been separated for nearly two years at that point. "Sheena, I don't remember..." *Finishing* is what I'm trying to say, but I stop myself before it slips out.

She sighs. "We were drunk, Asher. Of course you don't remember much."

I rack my brain, trying to recall my memories of that night, but the truth is, after one drink at the bar, I don't know what happened next. I just remember waking up naked in her bed.

"You're telling me that in the ten years of marriage, you didn't even want to consider having a baby, but then we divorce, and suddenly you're pregnant?"

She cringes. "I thought you'd be happy. This is what you wanted."

"Yeah," I say angrily. "When we were married. Before you broke our vows and burned them to the ground."

She shifts her stance, her expression quickly turning irritable. "Look, I tried to tell you sooner, but you wouldn't take my calls. You wouldn't talk to me. You must have blocked me, or you would have gotten my voicemails."

"Yeah, because I thought you wanted to talk about *us* getting back together. I didn't know—" I run my fingers through my hair and pace back and forth, trying to make sense of the bombshell she just dropped. "You told me you didn't want kids. You told me you would never get off birth control because the thought of having a baby made you physically ill."

"But I never wanted to divorce you, Asher. If you had

just given me some time, I would have changed my mind on my own about having a baby, but the closer we got to our divorce hearing, I knew I had to do something. So I got off birth control. But then when I learned I was pregnant, I'd already lost you. I was planning to have an abortion. And then I saw you on Halloween with that woman and her kid, and I... "

She falls silent, and I don't even know if I want to hear what she has to say next.

"And then you *what,* Sheena?" I'm boiling inside. In the past ten years, I've put up with so many lies, so many betrayals. I forgave and tried desperately to forget all the pain, but this time, she crossed the line. I don't know what she expects to happen now, but I guarantee things aren't about to go the way she's concocted in her mind.

"And then it made me realize what I could have had. What I could still have." She takes a step toward me while I simultaneously take a step back. "Don't you see, Asher? We can finally have the life you dreamed of for us." She takes my hand and places it on her belly. "Feel that, Asher. You're going to be a dad." She blinks up at me, her eyes wide and hopeful. "We're going to be a family."

CHAPTER TWENTY-EIGHT

MEADOW

It's been quiet. Too quiet. The kind of quiet that turns daytime worries into restless dreams. After what had happened to Milton, I'd sworn to myself I would never date anyone who had a dangerous job ever again. I didn't expect Asher to come into my life at the force that he had. I definitely didn't expect to fall in love with him, which has made the last thirty-six hours harder than I could have ever imagined.

I've learned that there's more downtime at the fire station than emergencies, leaving Asher bored, especially at night. I expect the text messages and phone calls that frequent our time apart. But since he left for his shift two afternoons ago, he's sent only one message—letting me know that he picked up another twelve-hour shift—giving me a feeling deep in my gut that he's not okay.

I sit down on the floor in Tate's bedroom while he makes fake snow angels on the carpet. "What do you want to wear, Tater Tot? You've got a big day at the zoo with Grandma." I lift up three shirts. "Which one?"

He peers over at me while still moving his arms and legs. "Dat wed *T. wex* one."

"Good choice. What about pants?" I set the red shirt aside and grab a selection of plain colored pants, any of which will match his T-shirt selection. "Which one?"

He kicks at a pair of dark jeans. "Dat."

"You are stylin' today. Okay, perfect. Now, you just need to pick out a jacket. It's a little chilly out." I hold up three light sweat jackets. He chooses a black hoodie and then finally stops what he's doing to get dressed.

"He's ready," I call out to my mom, who I can hear walking down the hallway from her bedroom.

She stops in the doorway while fastening a diamond-studded earring. "Perfect timing." Then she gasps when Tate stands up from the floor. "Well, aren't you a handsome little man?" She steps forward, scoops him up, and proceeds to kiss him all over his squishy cheeks. "Are you ready to see the lions and tigers and bears, oh my?" Her eyes widen, making Tate giggle.

"I wanna see gowilla, Gwamma." He rounds his arms on either side, trying to imitate a gorilla, and growls.

I laugh and pluck him from my mom's arms. "Oh, you're going to see gorillas all right. And alligators and birds."

The smile on Tate's face is so infectious, my heart beats a little faster.

"All right, the train's leaving the station. Time to head out," my mom says before making toot-toot sounds.

He hugs me tightly around the neck and plants a wet kiss on my cheek. "Sowwy. We gotta go, Mommy."

Laughing, I set him down and pat his butt. "Go potty first."

My mom and I watch with amusement as Tate crosses the hallway from his bedroom to the bathroom and steps up onto the stool.

"Man, he's growing up fast," Mom says.

My chest squeezes. "Don't remind me. If I didn't have any photo edits today, I would come with you two."

My mom rolls her eyes. "If you feel guilty every time Tate leaves the house without you, you'll get old faster than me. Enjoy your day. Are you seeing Asher?"

I shrug, trying not to come across as agitated, but my mom knows me much too well and narrows her eyes, silently telling me that she expects me to respond.

"I'm not sure. He hasn't reached out since yesterday. Maybe we've been spending too much time together too fast."

My mom frowns. "That doesn't sound right at all. Maybe he's just busy at work. You know people get crazy around the holidays."

I sigh, knowing she's right. "I'm sure that's it. He'll call when he can."

The doorbell rings, and she raises her eyebrows. "Maybe that's him."

My heart thuds hard in my chest, and I take quick steps to the front door. When I swing it open, a disheveled version of Asher stands there, and the fear that has been quickly building up in my mind feels justified.

His eyes are filled with exhaustion, the stubble on his face is longer than normal, and whatever is burdening his heart seems to be weighing down his shoulders too. All I want to do is wrap him in my arms and never let go, but before I can reach him, Tate comes barreling around the corner. He leaps into Asher's arms, and despite whatever mood he brought with him, he laughs and lifts Tate.

"Hey, buddy. You going somewhere?"

My mom comes around the corner next. "Hey, Asher. I'm taking Tate to the zoo today. Long shift?"

Asher plants his hand on top of Tate's head and tousles his hair. "You can say that. The calls just kept coming in, and I'm trying to earn some of the last hours I need before certifying as a paramedic. I've been taking the slow road—about two years now—so I'm looking forward to moving up in the world."

He winks, and for a second, I feel the relief work its way through my veins. I've been paranoid. Clearly, Asher is just a busy, hardworking man. But then he turns to me, his smile slipping some when our eyes meet, and that dark feeling works its way back into my chest. *What the hell is going on?*

We say our goodbyes to my mom, then I wait until they pull out of the driveway to turn to Asher and wrap my arms around him. "Hey," I say softly.

He sighs, his body relaxing against mine, providing another dose of relief to my worry-filled heart and mind. "Hey," he says.

"Why do I feel like you need to talk to me about something?"

Just like I could feel him relaxing a second ago, I feel his body tense up in my arms. "Let's go inside, okay?"

Shit. My chest tightens, and my gut squeezes. Without another word, I turn to walk over the threshold and lock the door behind us. He takes my hand and leads me into the living room, gesturing for me to sit on the couch. I stare at the seat for a second before looking back at him.

"If you're here to break up with me, then just do it, Asher. I don't want to sit down."

His entire face crumbles, and he shakes his head. "I'm not here to break up with you, Meadow. I'm fucking terrified right now."

Why do I feel like my heart is breaking when I have no idea what he's about to say? "Why?"

His eyes roll to the ceiling like he's trying to grasp whatever strength he can. "Because," he says, looking back at me. "I royally fucked up, and I'm still trying to process what I just learned. But you need to know, before I tell you anything—I never cheated on you. Since the moment I met you, it's been only you."

My chest feels like it's about to burst into flames. "Now, it's me who's terrified. Just tell me, please."

He blows out a breath. "So, you know how Sheena and I were separated for two years before our final divorce hearing back in August?"

I nod slowly, clueless as to where this conversation is about to take us.

"Well, after we left the courthouse, we decided to grab a drink as a final farewell of sorts. Emotions were high, and while I had no question the divorce was the right move, it was still hard shutting the door on our past." He looks at me like he desperately wants me to understand.

I grab his hand and squeeze it, despite my every muscle tensing like I'm bracing for the worst storm of my life with no shelter in sight. "Of course. Divorce is a big deal."

He can't even look at me now. "Yeah, well, one drink led to another... I don't even know how we got back to her place. I don't remember much, to be honest, but—"

I think I might be sick. My stomach rolls, and every fear I've had since that night I met Sheena at the haunted house slams into me at once. This is it. This is the moment I realize everything Asher and I have together is, in fact, too good to be true.

I hold my hand up. "Please stop." My voice is trembling. "I really don't want any details, Asher. You slept together. I get it. What does that have to do with what's going on right now?"

"Because," he says slowly, "I was at the hospital meeting some friends before my shift the other day, and I ran into Sheena. She was on her way to an appointment, but I noticed she was..." His eyes scan mine like he's waiting for my reaction, but I don't want him to see the bubbling anger inside of me at the mention of Sheena's name. "Pregnant."

His words hit me like a ton of bricks. Whatever I thought could go wrong—whatever I imagined—this is so much worse. Because why would he even care if his ex-wife was pregnant unless... I look up, trying to find strength from deep within to brace myself for verification of what I suspect is true. "The baby is yours."

I can barely hear the whispered words as they drift from my mouth, but he seems to hear them just fine because he nods.

"She'll be eighteen weeks along on Friday. Her due date is May 13."

Eighteen weeks. That was definitely before Asher and I met, but that doesn't make any of this better. So many emotions are swirling through me right now—shock, fear, sadness, jealousy, hope. But it's not what I'm feeling right now that matters. I scoot closer to him, forcing my own torment aside and pulling his hand into my lap. "That's big news. You're going to be a father, Asher."

He leans back against the couch with a heavy sigh. "I want to be excited. I do. But... I don't know. It just doesn't feel real. Is that awful?"

I frown, not knowing how to answer that. "Why doesn't it feel real?"

"Sheena didn't want kids. You know, at one point after I got discharged, she told me she was getting off birth control so that we could finally try for a baby, and then I found out she got an IUD implanted. She lied to me, Meadow. She hated the idea of having kids and being faithful—but she still wanted me. She would have done anything to keep me, including lying about the one thing I wanted most in the world." Moisture fills his eyes, but he wipes at them before a single tear can spill. "I remember when we got closer to our court hearing, she started to act all weird and panicky—

calling me all the time, telling me we needed more time to figure things out, saying she missed me. My feelings were long gone by then, but that's when she started telling me she changed her mind about kids. I didn't believe her. Apparently, she was serious because she'd taken out her implant before we..." He shakes his head.

"So, what now?" I'm almost terrified of my own question. Because what other logical step is there for Asher to take than to be by Sheena's side throughout her pregnancy? Surely, they'll fall back in love and finally become the family he's always wanted.

"I-I don't know."

My thoughts are in a fast downward spiral that I'm not sure how to stop. Tears spring to my eyes, and Asher leans closer.

"Meadow, I'm so sorry."

In my head, he's telling me he's sorry for our inevitable breakup and all the things we'll never get to experience together. The weight on my chest is crushing, and as much as I want to be strong for him, I can't believe this is fucking happening.

"What are you sorry about, exactly?" I say, blinking past my tears. "Sleeping with your ex-wife or falling in love with me before you found out she was pregnant?"

His face crumbles. "I will never be sorry for falling in love with you. You are the best thing that has ever happened to me. Tate too. Please tell me this doesn't change things for you." He squeezes his eyes shut. "Fuck, I know this is so much to ask, but I can't lose you, Meadow. You and Tate are my whole fucking world."

His desperation only brings more pain to my chest. "In the back of my mind, Sheena has always been a threat to our relationship. And now she's giving you everything you've ever wanted." I don't want to guilt Asher with my words, but if he wants to know the truth, then I need to tell him. If the roles were reversed, then I would want to know too.

He cups my face, his eyes wide and locked on mine. "*You* are everything I've ever wanted."

"But she's giving you a baby. You'll need to be there."

"And I will be." He sits up straighter. "There are plenty of couples who raise children apart. Look at you. You've been raising Tate all by yourself, and he's the greatest kid in the world."

I tilt my head, giving him a small appreciative smile. "But it doesn't have to be that way for you. Sheena isn't dead."

Asher blows out a breath. "No, she isn't, but how good could life be for a child if the parents don't even love each other? Meadow, I get your concern, but I'm not getting back together with Sheena. No matter what."

The certainty in his tone reaches me deep in the chest. I have no reason to doubt Asher. He's proven to be honest, loyal, and so damn supportive. He deserves nothing less than the same in return.

He starts to pace in front of me. "This is total bullshit." His voice cracks. "I'm having a kid. I should be excited right now."

Seeing Asher in pain like this is far worse than the news he just delivered. So I set aside my fears and focus on him. "There's plenty of time for you to be excited." I step in front of him and palm his cheek, almost bursting into tears again when he meets my eyes. "You're allowed to process this. You're allowed to feel whatever you need to feel. The woman lied to you time and time again. She broke your vows. She caused you so much pain. Of course you're having trouble accepting the news. But you know what? You *will* accept it. And you'll do the right thing, not because you have to but because you'll *want* to. You're going to be an amazing dad."

His face crumbles, his forehead lands on mine, and a quiet sob slips past his throat. "I was so scared. I finally found you and Tate. I don't want to lose you."

My heart melts, the flames of anger from earlier doused from the reality of Asher's giant heart and pure intentions. "You're not going to lose us. Never." I press my mouth to his. "I'm going to love your baby just as much as you love Tate. Everything will work out. I promise."

A huge sigh leaves Asher's body, and I swear I can feel the relief pouring from him. "I love you, Meadow." He tugs me onto his lap, my knees on either side of his waist, and pulls me in for a big hug. "So fucking much."

I bury my face between his neck and shoulder, my heart still beating fast. "So, what's next?"

He takes a shaky breath. "She invited me to her next appointment. I guess they're going to tell us if it's a boy or girl."

"That's exciting." I pull back, giving him my best smile. Because no matter how Asher is about to become a father, every step of the next five months is going to be one to treasure. "We should celebrate."

Asher lets out an awkward laugh. "I don't know if I'm in the mood to celebrate."

I smile and stand then tug on him to get up. "Then I guess it's up to me to get you in the mood. Champagne?"

I start to walk away and hear Asher's laughter trailing me. "It's nine in the morning, you crazy woman."

I grin and shrug. "I have some orange juice. I'll make mimosas."

Asher follows me into the kitchen. "Why do I feel like this drink is more for you than it is for me?"

I laugh and rip the foil off the top of the bottle. "I'm just trying to be supportive."

He reaches for me, pulling me to his chest and locking me in with his arms around my waist. "You are supportive. Unquestionably. But you're allowed to have feelings about all of this too. You don't have to pretend with me."

I tilt my head while feeling my love grow for Asher beyond what I ever knew possible. The fact that he's so concerned about my feelings only confirms what I already know. "What do you want me to tell you, Asher? That I'm jealous Sheena gets to be the mother of your first child? Of course I am. I'm human. But I'm also happy that you'll get to experience being a father. I just feel lucky that I get to hold your hand every step of the way."

His eyes gloss over again, and he leans down, touching his lips to mine. "No need to be jealous. I'm going to put a baby inside you one day, Meadow Matthews. More than one, if you let me."

Giddiness erupts in my chest. "Is that so?"

He nods. "Oh yes. We're going to be one big happy family." He kisses me softly, almost timidly, causing a soft moan to vibrate up my throat. He lifts me onto the counter and fits himself between my legs. "Until then..." He kisses my neck before sliding his mouth to my ear. "We should make sure to get in as much practice as possible."

"You're a very ambitious man, I'll give you that."

He leans back and raises his eyebrows like I just handed him a challenge. "You have no idea." With that, he scoops me into his arms, abandoning the celebration drinks, and carries me to my bedroom.

CHAPTER TWENTY-NINE

ASHER

My yawn brings tears to my eyes Friday morning. It's not even five a.m., but I couldn't sleep, even with Meadow wrapped in my arms. Sheena's doctor appointment is in a few hours, and while I'm in a better place emotionally than I was a few days ago, I can't push away the nagging feeling in my gut. Knowing it could mean anything, I try to pass it off as guilt for ignoring Sheena when she had something important to tell me. If I had listened, I wouldn't have missed the first eighteen weeks of her pregnancy.

Willing to try anything to ease my mind and heart, I'd gotten out my computer and started researching pregnancy from bed, being quiet since Meadow was asleep beside me. I'd looked up all the milestones Sheena had probably been going through, starting with conception until now, and found a calendar that related each week of growth to a type of fruit. According to the chart, my baby is the size of a sweet bell pepper and is already developing organs and everything.

My chest squeezes, and I have to close my computer for

a few moments before opening them back up and continuing my reading.

"What are you doing?" Meadow's sleepy voice comes from beside me even though I'd hoped to not wake her.

I sigh and rub her exposed arm. "Just reading up on baby stuff. I have no idea what to expect at the appointment today."

She moans a little and turns to face me completely. "You said it was her eighteen-week appointment, right?"

I nod.

"Well, I learned the gender at my twenty-week appointment, but she can do all that at eighteen weeks. They'll do a full anatomy scan on her, and you'll get to watch on the ultrasound monitor. It's so cool when you can see their little heartbeat. And if the doctor can get a good enough view, then you'll learn if you're having a boy or a girl." Meadow beams, and I know she's thinking about Tate. "I loved being pregnant," she gushes.

I run my hand along her arm. "Except for the morning sickness, I'm sure. That sounds awful."

Meadow shakes her head, her eyes opening a little more. "I didn't get morning sickness, thank goodness. But I did have massive heartburn in the third trimester, thanks to Tate's full head of hair." She laughs. "At least that's what they say caused it." Her eyes soften. "You nervous about today?"

I tilt my head, not sure how to answer that at first. "I'm anxious. Curious. Not really nervous, but..." I look back at my computer. "I hate that I've missed so much of this pregnancy."

Meadow sits up slightly. "I know a lot of moms who didn't even have a clue they were pregnant until they were nearly out of their first trimester. It's more common than you'd think. You haven't missed much, Asher. At least, you haven't missed the important stuff."

I nod, hoping I can feel that way soon too. "Yeah, okay."

She sits up completely, moves my computer off my lap, and straddles me so we're eye to eye. "How much time do we have before you leave?"

I look over at the bedside clock then back at her. "Two hours."

Her lips curl up playfully, and she leans in to plant her mouth on mine. "How about you let me distract you until then?"

My gaze falls to her silky pink midriff top, her pebbled nipples aimed right at me. "I think it's already working."

I bite down on my lip and watch as she slips the fabric over her head, revealing her perfect breasts. I reach out to touch them—already hardening at the thought of having them in my hands, my mouth, around my sliding cock—but she pulls back with a wicked smile and a shake of her head.

She moves down my legs and fits herself between my thighs while pulling my boxer briefs down just enough to watch me spring free. With a firm grip around my hard shaft, she brings her mouth closer and runs her tongue along the bottom from the base to the tip in one clean swipe.

I groan at the tease. "Holy shit. Do that again."

She smiles, never taking her eyes off mine, and she repeats the motion, this time slower, only stopping when she reaches the tip. By the time she takes me in to the back of her throat, I already feel close to coming. The combination of her moans, the sensation of her soaked lips and firm tongue that runs the length of my base as she bobs her head—it's all too much, yet exactly what I need.

I prop myself onto one elbow while palming the back of her head and following her motions. When I feel my pending release, my mouth falls open, and I grip her hair in my fingers, holding her to me while she finishes me off.

"Fuck me," I groan, trying to keep my voice low as to

not disturb the rest of the house. "I didn't know I needed that."

She sits up with a satisfied smile, and I pull her to me, desperate for her lips on mine.

"You're amazing, you know?"

She laughs softly. "I'm glad you think so."

I feel my eyes become hooded as sexual frustration rumbles in my chest. Meadow may be the sweetest and most caring woman I've ever known, but she's also the most tempting little devil I've ever had the pleasure of fucking. Then again, *fucking* is too crude of a word for what we share. I've never felt so connected to anyone in my life, and it's because of times like this. Times when I feel like I'm going through my own personal hell, and she finds a way to make me feel whole.

I reach for her under her arms and pull her up so that she's lying on my chest. "I'm not just talking about the head." I grin, because the head was damn good. "I'm talking about you and how you always know how to make me feel cherished. You deserve so much better than this. Than me."

She tilts her head, her eyes softening and her forehead creasing. "Don't say that, Asher. I never dreamed a man like you existed. I feel *lucky* to be with you."

My chest hammers, like my home isn't the only thing that got renovated recently. My heart did too. "I feel the same way about you."

She smiles and dips down to kiss my lips. "Good, because we have another hour and a half for me to distract you."

By the time I arrive at the hospital, my entire body feels lighter. I know that no matter what happens from here on out, everything is going to be okay. Thanks to Meadow, I have a brand-new perspective on everything. And instead of tormenting myself with guilt from past decisions, I'm looking forward to everything that's to come.

Sheena is sitting in the waiting room of the main lobby when I walk through the main doors, but even after the calmness that washed over me this morning, I still can't bring myself to squeeze out a smile for my ex-wife.

"Hey, Sheena." I lean against the wall beside where she's sitting.

She stares up at me with a hopeful look and a wavering smile. "Hey, Ash. I wasn't sure if you were going to come."

I want to cringe when she uses the nickname she started calling me in high school. It feels like an insult now. "Of course, I came. You're having my baby." I sigh and sit beside her, looking her dead in the eye. "Look, Sheena. I've been processing this the best I can. It hasn't been easy, but there's no doubt that I want to be there for you and this baby."

Her smile grows bright, and I can almost see the happiness bursting from her chest. "You do?"

I nod. "Yes, and Meadow completely understands. Obviously, this situation surprised us all, but we're going to make this work."

Her smile falls. "Meadow understands." It's not a question. "So... you're staying with her." Another non-question.

I frown, trying to read behind Sheena's comments. "Of course I'm staying with her. Why wouldn't I?"

Her mouth falls open. "Because we're having a baby together, Asher. I thought..." Her eyes flash in surprise, and then she blinks a few times before opening her mouth to continue. "I—"

"Mrs. Moore," the receptionist calls. "You can head on up to the second floor."

We stand, and even though I know the way, I let her

lead me on a silent ride up the elevator and down the hall to the OBGYN offices. We don't speak another word as Sheena checks in and we're escorted to a room with a sonogram table and a giant flat-screen television plastered on the wall.

I hold my breath while looking around, the reality of our situation hitting me hard as I take it all in. This is actually happening. Sheena is having my baby. And I'm about to find out if I'm having a boy or a girl. My breath returns, though it's shallow. Everything feels like it's happening in a tunnel.

Dr. McLean comes in and greets us. We've met once or twice before, but we're not as close as I am with Lars, Beck, and Greg so she's not familiar with the history between Sheena and me. Thank goodness. She proceeds to rub a clear jelly-type substance all over Sheena's belly. A black-and-white image pops onto the screen. A beeping noise keeps pace in the background. There's a heartbeat. Everything looks healthy. I blink to get a clearer view of the image on the screen. I honestly can't make out anything until the doctor explains what all the squiggly lines and movements mean.

"Your baby is being a stubborn one today. I can't seem to get a clear view." She continues to slide the contraption around on Sheena's belly. "Oh wait. There you are," she says like she's talking directly to the fruit-sized person inside Sheena. "Well, do you want to know if you're having a boy or a girl?"

Dr. McLean looks expectantly between us, excitement lighting up her eyes. The same excitement that's bubbling up in my chest. "Yes," I say at the same time Sheena says, "No."

We look at each other, confusion filling my every pore. "Isn't that why we're here? You don't want to know?"

Sheena looks back at me, fear in her eyes. "I-I just think

it doesn't matter. We only care that the baby is healthy." She turns to Dr. McLean like she's already made up her mind.

"Well, can you tell me?" I want to know, and I have no shame in demanding to know. I've already missed out on three months of this. I want to be as prepared as possible for the future.

Dr. McLean looks between us, sensing something is wrong, and then she stands. "I'll give you two some time to talk and decide what you want to do. This is a big decision."

She smiles and steps out of the room.

"Look, Sheena, if you don't want to know, that shouldn't stop me from knowing."

I think this is the first time I've truly looked at Sheena since we left the lobby. I have to do a double take because she doesn't look excited or nervous about our appointment. She looks pissed. "Are you fucking kidding me, Asher?"

I step back, feeling like she just slapped me in the face. "Whoa, what?"

She sits up slightly. "What are you even doing here if you have no plans to be with me when this baby comes into the world? Do you know how fucked up that is? That we're about to have a baby together, yet we're not even together?"

I blink through the shade of red blinding my vision. "That's usually how divorce works, Sheena. You don't get to have a redo because you decided to get off your birth control. We're having a baby now, but that doesn't mean we're getting back together. We're no good for each other, and no matter how much we love that baby, it won't fix *us*." When my words are met with a long string of silence, I let out a long, frustrated breath. "I'll be there for you, every step of this pregnancy. And when our baby is born, I'll be there for the baby. You won't go through this alone."

Her lips quiver. "But I won't have you. After everything, I..." She pinches her lips together and shakes her head before looking out the window and staring. "I should have had an abortion when I had the chance."

Her words are so cold. So heartless. So mean. I'm shaking from the conviction in them. The fact that she would have terminated this pregnancy if she'd known then what she knows now is like a fist squeezing my heart. "You don't mean that."

She's silent again, her jaw ticking, but her face is stone-cold and unchanging. "This would have all turned out differently if you hadn't met *her*." Her voice shakes. "She ruined everything."

It takes every source of strength in me to not totally lose my cool. "We were over for two years before I ever met Meadow. She had nothing to do with this, and you know it."

She narrows her eyes. "If you think I'm letting you raise my baby with that woman, then you are dead wrong."

"Our baby," I correct her. "And that isn't up to you, Sheena."

Sheena's chest puffs out as her nostrils flare, and her eyes narrow even more. "It is up to me if this baby isn't yours."

I blink, my senses seeming to all malfunction at once. My head fogs while my vision blurs, and there's a dull knocking on my chest as my heart slows. It's as though I've just been sucked into a vacuum, and my only sense of reality is a sliver of light at the end of the long tunnel. "Tell me you're just trying to fucking hurt me right now, Sheena."

She lifts her chin and looks away.

"You're telling me there's a chance this baby isn't mine?"

She snaps her head back at me, eyes shooting sparks.

"Considering you couldn't even keep it up that night, I'd say the chances are pretty damn good."

My chest constricts, and then I gasp in a breath so deep, I feel the air all the way to my gut. "Funny how you didn't mention this to me until now. Were you ever planning to tell me?"

Her entire body is shaking now. "I wanted it to be you. I wanted us to be a family."

A noise at the entrance of the room startles us both as the doctor walks in and glances between us. "Should I give you more time?"

"No," I snap before Sheena can say a damn word. "We're going to need a paternity test, and we're going to need it now."

CHAPTER THIRTY

MEADOW

Three to five business days. That's how long the DNA testing center says it will be to hear back about the results of the prenatal paternity test. On day five, Asher is restless, to say the least.

"Are you sure you don't want me to call off your party?" I ask. "Everyone will understand."

I'm at Asher's, decorating lightly for a birthday party I had planned before Sheena dropped her major bombshell. It was supposed to be a small get-together with his friends at his house so he could show off all the renovations he'd been tackling on his time off.

He walks out of the bathroom, still wet, with a towel wrapped around his waist. "No way. The results won't change the fact that I'm a day older today." He shoots me a grin. "I've been looking forward to celebrating with my friends." He wraps an arm around me, sliding his palm to cover my ass. "And you've worked so hard putting everything together."

I laugh lightly while letting my hands roam over his wet skin. "You're giving me too much credit. I just made a few phone calls and bought a few decorations."

"And made a cake, along with five thousand appetizers. We're having the party, Meadow."

I shrug. "Okay, just wanted to give you an out if you were looking for one. When do you think you'll get the results?"

"Today. I should go check the mail again."

I take a step back. "I'll go check the mail while you get dressed." I rise to my toes, plant a kiss on Asher's cheek, and step out of the room.

I'm on my way down the driveway when the first car pulls up. It's my mom, who's bringing Tate, so I stop to welcome them with big hugs. "Oh my gosh, is that a tux?" I pick Tate up and beam at him. He will undoubtedly be the best-dressed guest.

"Sure is," my mom says. "We stopped by the mall on the way here. It was either this or his firefighter costume."

"We negoshated." Tate grins.

"You negotiated?"

"Gwamma gimmie *Carnitauwus*!" he squeals.

I laugh, fully certain he's talking about a dinosaur, but I have to look at my mom for help identifying what kind. "A what?"

"*Carnotaurus*," she says with a laugh. "We've been watching Camp Cretaceous all morning."

I stifle a laugh. "Hey, I'm going to keep Tate here with me tonight. Asher finished his mom's new guest suite, so he fixed up her old room to be more kid friendly. He wants us to stay over here more."

My mom raises her eyebrows. "Well, that's a big step. I think that's wonderful, Meadow."

Tate pinches my cheeks. "Mommy, where Ashew?"

I kiss his squishy cheek. "He's inside getting dressed. Walk with Mommy to the mailbox, and then we'll go see him, okay?"

Tate kicks his little feet, and I let him down, grabbing

his hand before he takes off toward the street. My mom walks with us as I catch her up on the fact that we're still awaiting the big news.

"He must be a mess over all of this," she says quietly, for Tate's benefit.

I give her a small smile while feeling an instant swelling in my chest. "He's okay. I mean, he's handling it well. But I think he's had time to brace himself for the results either way."

We get to the end of the drive, and I lift Tate so he can reach into the mailbox. He pulls out a stack of envelopes, I set him down, then he races up the drive to find Asher, but before he takes off, I get a good look at the envelope on top of the stack. It's addressed to Asher from the clinic where we went to get the DNA test. My heart beats faster, and I look up at my mom. "That was it."

Her eyes get wide. "The results?"

I nod and let out a shaky breath. "I guess it's time to face the music."

When my mom and I get inside, several cars are already pulling up to park along the street, so I know our time is running out. Inside, I find the boys in Tate's new bedroom. Kind of. It can still easily convert to a guest room when needed, but it's filled with some of Tate's favorite things—dinosaurs, light-up swords, cardboard bricks, and a basket full of miniature cars.

Tate is so excited to see the toys that he doesn't even notice the fire truck comforter on his new bed. Asher even bought a security bed rail, since the bed is a bit higher off the ground than I would have liked.

"Did Tate give you the mail?" I ask, surprised to not see anything in Asher's hands.

Asher makes a face and shakes his head. "No, he found me and rushed me into the bedroom, and then we came right in here. I didn't see anything." His eyes widen. "Did it come?"

I nod and immediately kneel to get Tate's attention. "Tate, sweetie, where did you put the mail you brought in?"

He looks confused then shrugs his little shoulders. "I dunno."

I stand slowly, biting the inside of my mouth to keep from laughing. "I'm sorry." I face Asher, feeling my cheeks heat. "I'll start looking. I saw him carry it inside, so it's got to be around here somewhere."

I start to walk away to hunt for the missing mail as the doorbell rings. Asher pulls me back. "We can look after the party. Don't worry about it. Like you said, it's got to be here somewhere."

Asher hikes Tate up into his arms, grabs my hand, and leads us all out of the room and to the front door to greet the first pair of smiling guests and then the next and the next. Before I know it, Asher's home is filled with two dozen of his closest friends.

I recognize a handful of them from the station and from the climb we all attended back in October. The original Shipwrecked crew—Beck, Lars, and Greg—are all in attendance. Apparently, that's a pretty big deal, considering they're all doctors at Bayside Regional and have been swept up in the whirlwind that is life, much like Asher.

It's good to see Asher laugh and shoot the breeze when his life could very well be flipped upside down the moment we locate that damn envelope. But I try not to focus on that. Instead, I play my part as hostess, making sure everyone has food and drinks in their hands, while Asher gives tours of his place to show off all the work he's done.

Becca and Aaron show up a bit later, and while Aaron goes off to look for Asher, Becca steers me away to get all the inside secrets. "Well?" she asks. "Please tell me the she-devil isn't having Asher's baby."

I stifle a laugh at Becca's nickname for Sheena. "We don't know yet." I resist telling her that Tate had the answer in his hand not too many hours ago. "Hopefully soon."

Becca chews on her bottom lip as she nods. "So, I want to tell you something so bad, but it feels like such an inappropriate time."

I tilt my head, too curious to care about timing. "Out with it."

Suddenly, I look at my old friend entirely differently. Her skin is glowing, and her eyes are wide and bright. She looks positively radiant, and it seems like she's about to burst with excitement. "I'm pregnant," she gushes. Then she looks around like someone might be listening. "Not pregnant enough to announce yet, but I had to tell you. I'm eight weeks along. We got it confirmed this morning, and I'm so fucking excited I could scream."

I laugh and wrap my arms around my friend. Emotion tightens my throat and swells in my chest. "Oh, Becca. I'm so happy for you and Aaron. He's got to be dying to tell Asher."

Becca nods. "Yeah, but he's going to wait until after Asher gets the results. So don't tell him, okay? Aaron really wants to be the one."

"Of course I won't say anything." I squeeze her again. "Let's get together for lunch next week and make baby plans. You need a registry, and it's never too early to start shopping."

Guests start to leave after cake, including my mom, and by the time they're all gone, Tate is fast asleep in my arms. "Help me put him to bed?" I ask Asher.

He smiles and gently scoops Tate into his arms, another successful transfer. He walks with him into his new bedroom, and I follow, leaving Tate with a kiss on the cheek.

"You still haven't seen it anywhere?" I ask him, completely baffled by the envelope's disappearance.

Asher shakes his head. "Maybe I can just call the office on Monday."

I sigh, refusing to give up. "Where did Tate find you when he ran into the house?"

"I was in my bedroom—wait, no—my closet. I had just finished getting ready. But I didn't see anything in his hands when I turned around."

"Well, I guess we'll start looking in your closet." I laugh, because after being a mom for almost four years, it's not hard to imagine missing items turning up in the most bizarre places.

Lo and behold, the moment we step into Asher's closet, the pile of mail is scattered all over the floor. I bend down and collect it all, rising with a smile on my face as I hand it over to Asher. "Here you go. Right where he left it."

Asher tosses his head back and laughs. "The one room I didn't give a tour of today. Figures."

I can tell Asher doesn't want to wait anymore when he spots the envelope and turns it over. "Go ahead," I say encouragingly.

He gives me a look, like he wants to make absolutely sure it's okay with me, and then tears into the envelope. He pulls out a single white sheet covered with a bunch of numbers. It all looks like gibberish to me, so I focus on Asher's face.

A second later, his eyes close, blood drains from his face, and a loud sigh pushes through his lips. His lids peel open, and he scans the document again, as if he needs to read it a second time to be certain of the results, and then he opens his mouth to speak.

"Probability of paternity. Zero percent."

His eyes flicker to mine and then back down, so I wait to give him my reaction, even though my heart is racing, and tears are already springing to my eyes at the emotional moment.

"The alleged father is excluded as the biological father of the tested child. The conclusion is based on the non-matching alleles observed at the..."

Asher looks back up at me, this time holding my gaze. A film of moisture is in his eyes as he takes in another shaky breath. "Well, there you have it. Not my baby."

I grab his hands and squeeze. "I'm so sorry, Asher." They're the only safe words I can say because I'm cursing Sheena out in my mind.

He sets the letter down on the dresser. "You know, this is all just a fucking poetic end to the relationship Sheena and I had. Her lying, me always hoping for the best, and then the fact that she never wanted a baby until she found out we were over and went and had one with someone else. I'd say it serves her right, but I think about that baby inside her and..." He shakes his head. "It makes me sick to my stomach, Meadow. What if she treats that baby as carelessly as she treated me?"

My stomach squeezes, and I wrap my arms around his waist, looking up into his eyes. "I honestly don't know what will happen, but I can say this. Giving birth has a magical way of putting things into perspective. I can't explain it exactly, and it's something you have to want deep down, but change is possible."

He sighs, and I can almost feel him relax in my arms. Then he surprises me by leaning down and kissing me softly and sweetly, triggering a fluttering near my rib cage. "Thank you for holding my hand through all of this." He kisses me again. "Thank you for trusting me." He lifts me up and wraps my legs around his waist. "Thank you for loving me."

My insides are turning to goo. "Who would have thought a random fender bender on the interstate would have led to finding my happily ever after?"

The smile that appears on Asher's face makes my heart triple its beat. "Happily ever after, huh? I guess that makes me your Prince Charming."

I twist my lips and wrinkle my nose. "Actually, I kind of always had a thing for Thor."

He chuckles while walking me backward into the bedroom. "I love that I'm still learning things about you." He shrugs. "If it's Thor you want, then it's Thor you'll get." He tosses me on the bed and rips off his shirt before climbing on top of me. He settles in between my legs, his rock-hard erection rubbing where I ache the most. He searches my eyes before flicking his tongue out to lick his bottom lip. "But tonight... I think I'll save Thor for another day. All I want to do right now is make love to you nice and slow."

I run my finger along his strong jaw line, feeling nothing but admiration for the man I've fallen hopelessly for. "I'm not going to argue with that."

His lips curl at the corners. "I didn't think you'd put up too much of a fight."

I raise my brow in a challenge. "And if I had, Mr. January?"

He narrows his lids, his gaze darting to my lips. "I think you're forgetting how persistent I can be, especially when you call me that." He nudges his hard shaft between my legs, causing the bottom of my dress to bunch up around my waist. Even with his pants on, I can feel how much he wants me. He groans at the sensation. "I'm going to bury myself deep inside you and never come out, at least not until morning."

"Sounds like we're not going to get any sleep tonight."

He smiles. "Not if I can help it."

CHAPTER THIRTY-ONE

ASHER

"We're home."

I open the front door of my home, which is officially *our* home now. It's Valentine's Day, the official move-in day that we've been prepping for months to ensure Tate would be comfortable with the change. So tonight, we'd taken Farrah and Tate out to dinner and asked Tate if he wanted to make a new home at my place. We'd been met with a resounding, "Yes, yes, yes!"

Tate rushes inside, heading straight for his room to play, but Meadow chases after him to get him into the bath. I take the opportunity to straighten up and crack open a beer out on the back patio.

The past couple of months have been a whirlwind, to say the least. Life has been anything but dull because of Meadow's booming photography business, calendar events, my transition into becoming a licensed paramedic at the station, and Tate's constant thirst for knowledge and adventure.

After I got the paternity results, it felt like the breath of fresh air I'd never known I needed. Sheena had been officially exiled from my life, and while I wished her the best, I was more than ready to jump headfirst into my relationship with Meadow. I'd already known that I loved her, but the way she supported me during that long, hellish two weeks took my love for her to an entirely new realm.

I didn't know love was supposed to feel like this. And I'd never known how much my heart would expand for Tate. Meadow and I have talked about that a lot too—about Tate and what a marriage between us would look like not too far down the road. The possibility of me adopting Tate has come up, and while both of us would like that very much, we agree that ultimately, Tate should be the one to make that decision.

When my beer is empty, I walk back inside and go down the hall to Tate's room. He's already tucked into bed, with Meadow lying beside him. She's reading him a chapter out of *Charlie and the Chocolate Factory*.

"Okay," I say. "New rule."

Meadow and Tate look up at me with curiosity in their eyes.

"No more getting into bed without saying goodnight to me first." I wiggle a finger between them. "Got it?"

Tate giggles, and Meadow smiles. "Got it," they say in unison.

I walk over to the bed and bend over Meadow to plant a kiss on Tat's head. "Night, buddy. Sleep good for fishing tomorrow, okay? I'm going to wake you up super early."

"Okay, Ashew. Night night." He's been working on enunciating his *R*'s a lot lately, but he needs more practice.

Meadow slips her hand into mine and squeezes it before I walk out of the room. "See you soon."

I enter the master bedroom, smiling at the scene before me—a surprise for Meadow that I've been planning all week. The floor is sprinkled with long-stemmed red roses, the bed is covered in petals, and a trail of more petals stretches from the entrance of the room to the bathroom, where I'm about to draw a bath for the love of my life.

Even though I knew today would be a family day, I still wanted to surprise her somehow. I start to run the hot bath water then flip the switches on the bottom of the battery-operated candles I've set up around the room.

The bath is nice and full when I shut off the water and sit on the bed to wait for Meadow. I'm nervous. I don't know why. Maybe because it's our first official night in the house together as a family, and I want everything to be perfect. Meadow deserves that and so much more.

I hear the door to Tate's room shutting then Meadow's footsteps as she pads down the hall. The smile on her face when she steps in the room is one I'll never forget. "Asher," she gushes. "This is so beautiful."

"So are you." I stand and walk toward her, eager to wrap her in my arms after hours of having to behave in front of others. "Happy Valentine's Day, babe."

Her face is full of wonder as she sweeps her gaze around the room. "This is so sweet I think I might cry."

A coat of moisture forms in her eyes, and I hug her to me. "No tears tonight. Tonight, it's my turn to take care of you." Smiling, I pull her into the bathroom so she can see the hideously large display of my affection.

I help her out of her clothes until she's stripped completely bare, her skin breaking out into goose pimples, her nipples hardening despite the warm air. When she reaches for the waistband of my pants, I take her hand and shake my head. "That bath is for you."

Her dramatic pout has me instantly regretting my words. She's so sexy, and she doesn't even have to try. She turns and steps into the bath, one toe at a time, then she sinks into the water like a fucking siren.

"To say my attraction to you has only intensified since we met is a complete understatement." I don't mean for my voice to sound so growly, but I can't help it. Just one look at her, and my body is no longer my own. It belongs to her. Completely.

"Well, then maybe you should come in here with me," she purrs. "Keep me company."

I narrow my eyes. "You're supposed to be relaxing. I think we both know what will happen if I get in there."

She laughs lightly, studying me with her eyes. "So what are you going to do?" She lies her head back and lifts her chest slightly so her tits come above the water. "Just watch me soak here like a queen?"

Until Meadow, I hadn't known it was possible to get hard merely at the sound of someone's voice. But I swear, all she has to do is look at me a certain way, and my cock stands at attention, no foreplay needed.

"I don't mind the view. Is that going to be a problem for you?"

She smirks, her lids falling shut. "No, but I intend to make it really *hard* for you." She spreads her knees as her hand falls between her legs, her lids flutter shut, and then her sweet pink lips part on a gasp.

Shock and arousal spread like wildfire through my system, until I strip down to nothing and step up to the tub. "You win."

Her lids fly open, she smiles, and she scoots forward so I can climb in behind her. "Much better." She sighs. "Thank you for this. You seem to always know exactly what I need, even when I don't know it myself."

I run my fingers along her arm. "I feel the same way about you."

"Really?"

I nod. "Knowing each day is one closer to the moment I ask you to marry me makes me the happiest man in the world. You and Tate, you're all I need."

"Until you put that baby inside me, right?"

I groan into her ear. "Fuck yes. This is only the beginning."

She turns her head to rest it against my chest and sighs. "Thank you for putting Tate first."

I slide my hand to her cheek and smile. "You don't have to thank me for that, Meadow. You two make me the happiest I've ever been. I get how important this transition is for him."

She bites down on her lip and flips around so that she's peering up at me. "Tate asked me tonight if you're going to be his new daddy."

At first, I think I can hear exactly how fast her heart pounds, but then I realize my heart is beating faster. "And what did you say?"

"I asked him if that's what he wanted and why." She smiles. "He told me that he loves you and that he'll never forget his first daddy, but he really wants you to be his second."

Shit, I think my throat just clogged up so much that I can't breathe. "Really?" Tears fill my eyes, and one slips out before I can stop it. "That's..." I shake my head, completely surprised. "That's incredible. What did you say?"

"I told him that I wanted that very much too." Her eyes flicker to mine. "I hope that was okay."

If only she could feel the fireworks lighting my chest. "I'd say that was pretty fucking okay." I slide her body up my chest enough to kiss her hard on the mouth while concocting an epic plan in my mind. One none of us could have expected.

CHAPTER THIRTY-TWO

ASHER

It's still dark out when I wake Tate to go fishing. I get him dressed, we both kiss Meadow goodbye on the cheek, and then we're off to the marina to borrow Dane's boat for the day.

I already stopped by the store last night for tackle and bait, so all Tate and I have to do today is head over to one of my favorite coves where we're guaranteed to catch some fish and cast away.

I secure Tate in a bright-orange life vest that looks funny on his little body, and then I situate him on the seat beside me, where I can keep my eyes on him, and we cruise slowly away from the dock.

Even in the early morning, I can tell it's going to be a perfect day. A slight winter chill lingers in the air, and the few clouds in the sky are already parting to the soon-to-be-rising sun.

"Hey, Tate, wanna steer?"

His wide eyes look much bigger because of his bulky life jacket and windswept hair. A giant smile takes over his face as he nods. I hold out my hand to him, and then I pull him over to me while I sit down. Once he's situated on my lap, I help him take control of the wheel.

"Good job. We're going way over to that group of trees." I point in the direction I want him to steer. "Can you take us there?"

He nods and adopts a serious expression, taking his mission seriously.

Once we're anchored at the cove, I set up our lines and help him cast one into the water.

"Nice job, buddy. Now, let's lock your line like this." I help him reel it in slowly until it clicks. "And now you wait."

He looks up at me with a funny expression. "Wait fo' what?"

I chuckle. "For a fish to tug on your line. You'll feel something tug at your pole like this." I pull on the line slightly until his mouth forms an O, which tells me he understands.

"Okay, Ashew. I wait."

It's silent for a few minutes while we watch the sunrise over the water. Even with the perfect setting and knowing what Meadow had told me last night, I'm still a bundle of nerves over the conversation I'm about to have with Tate.

"No fish coming," Tate says with a cute shrug, like he's tried his best for the day.

Before I can give him my big speech about patience, he squeals. I jump to attention, instantly reaching for one of the straps of his life vest to keep him from falling overboard because that's where my mind goes first. But he's not about to fall over. He is, however, about to lose his grip on his fishing pool.

"A tug! A tug!" He squeals again. This time, I understand and reach for where his hands grip the pole.

"You've got something, all right. Reel him in slowly. You don't want to lose him."

His line jerks another time, making Tate's face light up like it did on Christmas morning. I never thought I would ever see anything cuter, but this might just take the cake. I help him reel in the line until we can see the faint view of two beady fish eyes staring back at us.

"Look at that. We've only been out here for ten minutes, and you caught a fish." I chuckle and help him reel the line in more until an eight-inch bass comes flapping out of the water. I lift the fish, position it in front of Tate, snap a few pictures, and then pull the hook from the fish's mouth.

"What now, Ashew?"

"Well, unless you want to eat him, we'll toss him back into the water."

"Eat him. Eww." Tate claps one hand over his mouth and points at the fish. "Put fiss back." He motions toward the water.

With another chuckle, I successfully unhook the fish and toss it over the edge of the boat to live another day. "Wanna try that again?"

Tate makes another face. "I dunno. I no like hurt da fish."

"Okay," I say gently. "How about we hang out here for a bit and talk a little?" I sit down on a bench seat that faces the front of the boat, and Tate sits across from me.

"What we talk about?" His genuine interest in having a conversation with me is the cutest thing ever.

"I don't know. Anything we want, I suppose. Ask me anything?" I hold my breath, hoping Tate will take the bait and broach the subject himself because that would be so much easier than me bringing it up.

"Anyting?" he asks, cocking his head.

I shrug. "Yeah, is there anything you want to ask me or talk to me about?"

Tate twists his lips. "No, I no tink so."

Darn. "Hmm, okay." I take a few seconds to think about my next question. "We can talk about something we have in common, like how much we love your mommy."

Tate tilts his head. "You lub Mommy?"

I nod. "Very much. I love you, too, buddy."

"Den why you no mawwy her?"

I bite down on my lip so I don't laugh. "I hope to marry her one day. Would you like that?"

Tate nods. "Den you be my daddy?"

"Well," I start, wanting to approach this as carefully as possible, "if your mommy and I got married, then I would be your daddy, but you know I can never replace your first daddy, right? He made you with your mommy, and that's a very special bond that I can never replace."

Tate appears to be thinking. "So den I have two daddies."

"Exactly." I smile.

"Den when you mawwy Mommy?"

I chuckle and lift Tate off his seat to place him in my lap. "Well, I need to ask your mommy to marry me first. Then she would have to say yes."

Tate gives a big nod. "She say yes!"

"You think so?"

"Mommy lub you. She say yes." The certainty in his high-pitched tone completely melts my heart.

"Thank you for the vote of confidence, buddy. If she does say yes, then we can get married."

Tate gasps and claps his hands together. "Ask Mommy doday."

"You want me to ask your mommy to marry me today?"

He nods so eagerly I'm afraid he might give himself whiplash. "Yes, doday. You lub her. She lub you. Why not?"

Oh, the simplicity of it all in the mind of an almost-four-year-old. “Well,” I tell him. “I can’t just walk up to your mommy and ask her to marry me. I need to ask her in a very special way. And there are a few things you’ll need to help me with first.”

CHAPTER THIRTY-THREE

MEADOW

Shipwrecked is packed on a Tuesday afternoon with Davis Islands lunch-goers. Decorations from Valentine's Day are still strung up all over the walls, and tables are filled with guests in everything from suits, white jackets, and scrubs to workout attire, like I'm wearing. I can see why Asher loves this place so much. The atmosphere is so inviting that my friends and I finished eating more than an hour ago but can't bring ourselves to leave.

Lars and Becca sit on either side of me in a booth, while our new friends Carly and Amanda sit across from us. Apparently, Carly and Beck have been rekindling an old romance that someone could write a book about. And Amanda is the woman Greg has fallen head over heels for. Both women are gorgeous, sweet, and badass in their own rights. I'm hoping we can make these lunches a recurring thing.

Right now, they're deep into conversation about someone's upcoming wedding, and I begin to zone out, thinking about how much things have turned around for me since Tate and I moved to Tampa.

I look over at the bar where our favorite British

bartender, Harry, is helping a customer, while a memory of Asher approaching me at the bar months ago flickers through my mind. It's incredible what can happen when your life is falling to pieces all around you, and you finally make that decision to move forward.

While my first week in Tampa may have been bumpy, to say the least, it was a necessary evil that led me to fall straight into Asher's arms. I haven't stopped falling since.

I look over at the digital clock above the bar and sigh. "Sorry, babes. I need to take off. Asher and Tate should be home soon, and I still need to start dinner."

Becca's hand grips mine, and she pouts. "No, please. Let's get dessert." She perks up.

I balk. "Since when do you order dessert?"

She widens her eyes and looks down.

My hand moves to her belly, which isn't even showing a bump yet, especially not in the baggy blouse she's wearing. "You can have mine. This right here is the best excuse in the world to eat two desserts." I wink. "But seriously, I should go."

"C'mon, Meadow, stay," Lars pleads. "It's not every day we can all get together."

Lars and I have become extremely close lately, and she's not one to beg unless she absolutely means it. I start to crack.

"Yeah," Amanda adds. "You still need to give me your availability so I can book a session too."

Carly gets in on the action by leaning in and covering my hand with hers. "And we're finally getting to know each other."

I'm getting it from all ends at this point, so I hold my hands up and laugh. "Fine, I'll stay a little bit longer. Just enough time for this one over here to eat her dessert."

Becca weaves her fingers through mine. "Good. You

won't regret it. Promise." She winks, and a strange feeling flits through my chest, like she knows something I don't.

In a quick subject change, we all start comparing Valentine's Day stories, and I can't keep the smile off my face thinking about what Tate said to me before bed last night and then Asher's surprise. It had been the perfect day, and when the ladies hear my story, they gush along with me.

"You think he's going to put a ring on it?" Amanda asks.

"He'd be so lucky," Lars jokes, winking in my direction.

I cover my face with my hands in embarrassment, drop them, and laugh. "We've talked about it, but we both want Tate to be ready for that huge leap, you know?"

"From what you said, it sounds like Tate is more than ready." Becca wraps her arm around my shoulder and kisses my cheek. "I still think about the night we met up after you moved back. I remember worrying about you then. You were always putting everyone before yourself, sacrificing your own happiness. I'm so damn happy you and Asher found each other."

I want to cry from her touching words. "Thank you, Becca. It's funny how life has a way of working out, isn't it?"

"That it is."

We raise our waters in a toast, and I'm about to attempt an escape when the music makes a drastic transition from the Backstreet Boys' "I Want It That Way" to Chase Rice's "Eyes on You."

My heart flips in my chest the instant I recognize the tune. It was one of the many songs Asher and I danced to at Becca's wedding, but it's one of my stronger memories of that night. In fact, it's so strong, I vividly remember thinking Asher was going to kiss me while the song played. Instead, he proceeded to tell me about his *inflated* ego.

"Mommy, can we haf dis dance?"

I jerk my head around to find Tate standing beside me. He's wearing a suit with black pants, a button-down shirt, and a red bow tie. And he isn't the only one standing there. I look up to find Asher, wearing his same suit I recognize from the wedding. That's when I make the connection. Asher requested the song playing over the speakers.

"Well," Asher says with a smile, "may we have this dance?"

Still in complete shock, I stand, picking Tate up as I rise. "How could I say no to that?"

"You can't." Asher smirks. "It's kind of why I had Tate come over here with me. He's irresistible."

I look at Tate and smile. "That he is." I narrow my eyes at Asher. "You're pretty irresistible too."

He winks and guides us forward. Shipwrecked doesn't have an actual dance floor, but a few tables magically get pushed aside, giving the three of us room to move. Not that we're going far. We're just kind of swaying there while I try to make my head stop spinning.

"So, how was fishing?" I ask, amused by the turn of events.

Asher winks at Tate, causing Tate to giggle. "Tate caught his first fish, and then we decided to call it quits."

"What?" I look between them. "Why?"

"Because we wanted to ask you something."

My heart is pounding so fast, I cling to Asher a little tighter for support. "O-Okay."

Asher smiles. "Do you remember the first time we danced to this song?"

I bite down on my bottom lip and nod. "I remember it quite well."

"Good, because it was during our dance to this song that I knew you were the one for me. It hit me like lightning on that dance floor. The way you smiled so effortlessly from the inside out. The way you laughed at my jokes and shot back with even better ones. The way you fired me up by challenging me at every turn. I couldn't get enough of you that night, and even though we'd just met, I could see my future with you right then. The only thing missing that day was Tate."

My heart is pounding, and tears are already sliding down my cheeks. I try to look at Tate, but he's clinging to my neck. "So you left your fishing trip to dance with me at Shipwrecked?"

"Not exactly," Asher says with a smile then sinks down on one knee.

"Oh my—" I clap a hand over my mouth, still holding Tate to me. Asher and I talked about marriage and becoming a family, and while I've always known a proposal was inevitable, I never anticipated just how much I wanted that proposal to come today.

"Meadow Matthews, you are the love of my life. My forever. And I can't wait to spend the rest of my life with you and Tate. Will you marry me?"

The proposal has obviously caught the attention of everyone inside Shipwrecked—it's so silent I could hear a pin drop if one fell. I suck in a quick breath, desperate to answer his question but also wanting my words to actually come out when I do.

Tate grabs my face, brings his mouth to my ear, then whispers, "Say yes, Mommy, so Ashew can be my daddy."

I'm not even sure how I can see straight with tears flooding my eyes, but somehow, I make out the love of my life still kneeling. His smile is so bright, so certain, and there are tears in his eyes too.

"Yes," I burst out, not caring how imperfect the word may sound in my emotional state. "Yes, Asher. I will marry you."

Thunderous cheers and applause break out throughout the room as Asher lunges to his feet. He plants his mouth on mine, whispering, "I love you," on each parting breath.

I don't know how long we stand in that embrace, with Tate giggling between us, but it's long enough to feel Asher's heartbeat and mine fall into time together.

"Wait, Ashew. You fogotted da wing."

Asher laughs and looks at Tate, who pulls a blue velvet ring box out of his pocket.

"Look, Mommy. Open."

I swallow against the thick lump of emotion in my throat and take the ring box from Tate's little hands. I open it, gasping at the gorgeous cushion-cut diamond set in a rose gold band. My absolute dream ring.

My gaze floats up to Asher, my body shaking from the inside out. "Asher, it's beautiful. How did you know?"

His throat bobs, and he takes the ring out of the box. "I might have found your dream wedding Pinterest board when I was googling you months ago."

I burst out with a laugh, but it dies quickly when he holds the ring against my finger and kisses me again. "What do you say, *Miss* January? You ready to become my Mrs.?"

I smile. "I guess that means I'll need to make a new Halloween costume."

He chuckles and slips the ring on my finger. "Apologies for the inconvenience."

With a quirk of my lips, I slip my arm around his waist. "I'm sure you'll find a way to make it up to me."

He gives me a teasing glare. "You can count on that."

EPILOGUE

ASHER

One year later

Utter and complete bliss envelopes me as I stare out over the glittery surface of the ocean. Waves dance in the form of peaks below, cresting and crashing against the side of the massive vessel. I lean my elbows against the balcony nine stories above and breathe in the warm, salty air.

A vacuum of wind grows loud behind me, and I turn to find Meadow struggling to open the tightly sealed door. I chuckle and reach for it, tugging the door open with one hand while offering my free hand for her to grab. She does and squeezes it tightly, accepting the leverage as she steps over the steel doorframe to join me at the balcony's edge.

Her eyes close as she inhales a lungful of fresh air, and I know she's feeling exactly what I am. It's our first night on the cruise ship, our first vacation with just the two of us since our honeymoon in the Florida Keys. While it was hard to leave Tate behind for an entire week, a vacation was just what the doctor ordered.

"You clean up nicely, Mrs. January."

Her smile comes easily. "Thank you, Mr. January."

Five months ago, Meadow had made me the happiest man in the universe by saying, "I do." We had a small, beautiful ceremony at a lush garden overlooking the lake, in front of a few dozen of our family and closest friends. Everything was perfect, Meadow was a stunning bride, and Tate made a spectacular ring bearer.

Tonight, she's wearing a short red wrap dress that accentuates her full breasts and silky smooth legs while also showcasing five months of the most beautiful miracle of life I've ever witnessed. In four months, Meadow will give birth to our baby girl. By then, my adoption of Tate should be finalized, and he'll officially be a Moore. Together with his little sister, we'll be one big ridiculously happy family.

I position myself behind her, my lips falling to her neck while my palms rest on her stomach. Arousal swirls through me at the feel of her. I thought Meadow was the sexiest woman alive before, but seeing her cocoon and grow our little nugget is by far the hottest look on her yet.

A groan slips out, catching on a breath that floats against her skin. "Have I told you lately how goddamn gorgeous you are?"

Her laugh is light. "Only a million times today, but you really need to stop lying to me. I'm just going to keep getting bigger, you know? I won't even be able to see my toes."

"Why do you need to see your toes? I can put your shoes on for you."

"That's sweet."

"I'm sweet for you." I breathe her in. She smells fresh from a recent shower, with a hint of coconut from her after-shower spray. Her hair is already blow-dried and hanging in natural waves around her shoulders. I push a section of dark-brown tendrils away so that I have better access to that spot between her neck and shoulder. A simple kiss in that sensitive place always makes her toes curl with delight.

She sighs at the sensation. "You are so good to me. I just wish we had taken this trip when I wasn't bursting out of my clothes."

"Stop it. You look beautiful."

"You're the best. I swear I wasn't this big at five months when I was pregnant with Tate. You could barely tell I was pregnant then. It's a good thing our doctor ruled out twins, or I would swear we were having a pair of these suckers."

I bite down on my lip to keep my laughter at bay. "What's wrong with two? I thought we wanted to have two more."

"Yeah." Meadow hitches her brows. "But not at the same time. Sleep will be hard enough with one."

Shrugging, I place a kiss on her temple. "Whatever you want. I'm here for the ride."

"Mm-hmm." She swivels to face me, looping her arms around my neck. "We both know you're more than ready for a good ride."

I nod, not even trying to hide my very large show of attraction for my wife. "Damn straight." I press my lips to hers. "Speaking of," I murmur against her mouth, "lucky for you, you got dressed with time to spare."

Her mouth curls up on the sides. "But you haven't even changed into your suit yet."

I peer down at my black boxer briefs and shrug. "Exactly. Why waste time getting dressed when we're about to get naked?"

My mouth finds hers again as I slip my fingers through hers. Every kiss shared with Meadow is like a little slice of heaven I just want more of every single time. Desperation licks through me at the thought of stripping her totally bare. Before our cruise, I was out of town for EMT training. The week before that, Meadow took a long trip with Tate and her mom to California. We might have boned like rabbits the second we got into our cabin if not for muster drills and Meadow's eagerness to join the sail-away party on the Lido deck. I don't want to wait another second to be inside my wife.

I nearly cry when I pull my lips from hers. "Remember that night we played twenty questions, and you were telling me about your wild fantasies?"

A blush heats up her face. "You don't happen to be referring to my wild outdoor sex fantasy, do you?"

A visual plays cruelly across my mind. "We are on a cruise ship balcony." I waggle my eyebrows. "This week is about making dreams come true, isn't it?"

She tilts her head. "I thought it was about spending some quality time together before this baby is born."

I shrug. "I mean, yeah, but quality time is code for nonstop sexcapades. I thought you were well aware."

"I'm afraid I missed the memo."

"Well," I say, leaning into her neck, "let me fill you in." My fingers slip out from hers, find her leg, and slide up her smooth skin beneath her dress. "Oh, Meadow," I scold when I find her slick center. "You're not wearing any underwear."

Meadow's wicked gaze meets mine, revealing a ploy I never saw coming. "Plot twist," she teases. Then she pushes me back into the lounge chair behind me.

I lean back, my unbelieving eyes glued to her as she unwraps her red dress and exposes her naked body. The fabric hangs to her sides like she's wearing a robe.

"Well, fuck." I blow out a breath as my wife takes a step toward me. I was not expecting that. With the way Meadow's been talking about her body lately, I thought for sure

I'd have to rev her engine a little before she even considered touching me.

Her dress hangs to her sides as she steps around my legs. She bends down and grabs the waistband of my underwear. "I've missed you," she whispers while dipping her knees into the plush blue cushion on either side of me.

"You have no idea how much I've missed you." A growl is in my voice that I couldn't help if I tried. Meadow is a vision of dark hair and silky, olive skin, awash with a moonlit glow. When she slips the dress off and tosses it to the side, I nearly choke on my next breath. "You're killing me, babe."

She looks down at my fully ready and waiting shaft and lifts it into her small hand. "Not as much as it killed me when you were gone." She strokes me slowly, twisting me in her grip. "It's just not the same without you."

I groan when she removes her hand to reposition herself on top of me. "How many orgasms did you give yourself while I was gone?"

"Hmm." She makes a sound, like she's replaying them all in her head. "At least one a night."

I cup her neck and pull her down onto my mouth, kissing her hard before pulling back just enough for her to see my lust-filled gaze. "That is so hot."

Her eyes widen. "It's good for the baby."

"It is?"

She nods. "Orgasms release my body's oxytocin, which is like a natural pain and stress reliever. The more sex the better, my doctor says. Just don't blow my back out."

I chuckle. "Got it. No rough sex. I'm too afraid my dick is going to hurt you, anyway."

"That's impossible. No dick is that big. Not even yours, babe. Sorry."

I balk. "You wound me."

"Calm down. If you were any bigger, it would be

impossible to do this." She aligns my cock to her center and begins to squeeze around me, her movements slow but unrelenting.

My next breath comes out as a wheeze as she shudders at my base. She's right. I can't imagine a tighter squeeze. We fit like a glove, with me stretching her just enough to give that added friction that sets us both off. And after being without her for this long, I'm afraid it won't take much to detonate inside her.

My hands find her breasts and squeeze them in my palms while she starts to rock against me, her clit rubbing against me as she moves. Her eyes close, and her lips fall apart like she's already on the verge of orgasmic bliss. Maybe she is.

Before we'd even found out that Meadow was pregnant, we both noticed the subtle changes in her. Everything became more sensitive. Her breasts tingled, and her orgasms came faster, harder. And while she's had the occasional nausea, her sex drive is still the same beast it's always been. If anything, it's stronger.

"Asher, I need to..." A high-pitched cry leaves her throat, and by the speed of her friction against me and by the way she's digging her nails into my chest, I can't wait to see her completely lose herself around me.

"Come for me." I'm getting close now, the sight of her too intense to ignore. She's got me so fired up that my own buildup is strengthening with the force of a deadly storm.

She's a melody of moans and sighs as she pulses around me, weakening the second her release shakes through her. And I'm right there with her, draining my release into her until there isn't a single ounce left.

She collapses beside me, and my arms envelop her, spooning her with my palm resting back on her belly. I rub it gently, in awe of how a soul-deep love like ours is forming right before my very eyes.

Meadow and I share a connection that was born in the aftermath of our own pasts. Our worlds had burnt down around us, forcing us to get up and start anew. Somehow, in all of the rubble and debris, at a time when neither of us was looking, we'd found each other.

For once, it's not me being the hero, because it was Meadow who saved me.

WANT MORE BAYSIDE HEROES?

What to read next? How about the next steamy Bayside Heroes romance—*Tangled Up* by Tia Louise? Keep reading, because I have the first couple of chapters just for you!

SURPRISE. Want to meet the men and women of the Firefighters Calendar mentioned in *Fired Up*? Each month, you will get FREE chapters of my upcoming romance, *Calendar Boy*. This book will be exclusive to my newsletter subscribers for now. Use the link or QR code below to sign up now and get the first set of chapters in January!

www.smarturl.it/firedupbonus

Do not miss all the Bayside Heroes books:

Washed Up (Greg and Amanda) ➜ smarturl.it/washedupbook

Screwed Up (Dane and Larsen) ➜ smarturl.it/screwedupbook

Tangled Up (Beck and Carly) ➜ smarturl.it/tangledupbook

Fired Up (Asher and Meadow) ➜ smarturl.it/firedupbook

Check out the series ➜ www.smarturl.it/baysideheroes

Now, enjoy your sneak peek of Tangled Up!

TANGLED UP SNEAK PEEK

6:30 a.m., Bayside Regional

BECK

"A car wreck." The skin at the back of my neck tightens, and I rub my hand over it. "Why does it have to be a car wreck?"

"Not just any car wreck, a twenty-nine-car pileup at the I-4 split." Rick the orderly balances a phone on his shoulder. "Dense fog, Code T. They're asking for anybody we can spare to head down to trauma."

"Which would include me." Picking up my stethoscope, I loop it around my neck as I head for the elevator.

When the metal doors open on the large, first-floor facility, it's already chaotic, with EMS workers wheeling bloody patients through the double doors, doctors in green and nurses in light blue or pink moving fast and shouting directions.

A rainbow of emergency lights blasts through the gray morning, and a gurney transporting an injured patient flies past me, along with an intake nurse doing her best to get a name, address, and next of kin, while tapping on an iPad.

The next patient is unconscious. I can't tell if it's a man or a woman, but blood covers their forehead, and a bone is protruding from the lower leg.

"Open fracture, left lower leg, good pulses." Asher Moore, our best EMT and a close friend of mine is at the head of the gurney. "I've administered two milligrams of Dilaudid."

Dr. Mains quickly steps up to take over guiding the bed. "I've got him. Take him to trauma room two."

Like clockwork, the next bed slams through the double doors, and Tessa, the ER head nurse takes over for the EMS worker. "Beck, we have a seventy-five-year-old male here!"

I join her at the side of the metal bed, moving fast down the hall as she takes the info from EMS. "Trauma room five is open."

The older man's eyes are squeezed shut, and a plastic oxygen mask is over his nose and mouth. He clutches his chest, and his face is pale and distorted with pain.

"Jeb Callahan, trapped in his car, complaining of chest pains, could be a fractured rib or two." Tessa's all business as she reads the notes. "He's had baby aspirin and nitro. EKG readings elevated."

"Jeb Callahan?" My brow lowers, and I take a step back as if I've been shocked.

"You okay?" The nurse studies me.

We don't have time to waste.

"Yes, let's go." Grasping the side of the bed again, I guide us into the treatment room. "Start him on 500 cc's saline. His numbers are in the good range. I'm going with ribs."

The ER nurses quickly set an IV, and I get closer to the man's face. "Mr. Callahan? Do you know where you are?"

Pale blue eyes flutter open briefly, and his head rocks side to side. "Colby General?"

"You're at Bayside Regional. You're in Tampa. Do you remember being in Tampa?"

"Yes..." His voice is papery. "I was on my way to my nephew's house."

Placing my hands carefully on his side, I hold my palm against his ribcage. "Can you take a deep breath for me, please?"

His eyes flutter, and he takes a shallow breath as the nurse attaches monitors to his chest. Fast beeping fills the room as I slowly move my hands in a circular motion.

"Any pain here?"

He shakes his head no.

"Good. How about here?" My hands move closer to the center and he jerks, crying out sharply.

"Okay, that's good." I turn away, grabbing the iPad and speaking to Tessa. "We need to cue up some pain medication, and—"

I glance up in time to see Tessa's eyes widen. "Dr. Munroe—"

She charges forward, and I turn fast.

His head has fallen to the side, and his eyes stare blankly at the corner where the ceiling meets the wall. The room tilts and a knot twists my throat. *No. This isn't happening. This can't happen again...*

"He's in arrest!" Tessa's shout propels me into action.

"Get the paddles." My voice is calm, but I can't fully inhale. "Someone call the time. This isn't a drill, people."

A nurse shouts out, "Six fifty-eight!"

Rubbing the paddles together as the charge builds, my mind screams *not again, not again...*

Closing my eyes briefly, I allow it to happen, allow the panic to fill my veins for the three seconds it takes the defibrillator to reach go time.

Three...

Two...

One...

Another nurse places an oxygen pump over Mr. C's nose and mouth, and I step forward, holding the silver paddles over his bare chest.

My palms are clammy. "Clear."

I press down, and as the energy fires through the metal, his body rises off the bed. We all step back, eyes fixed on the monitor, waiting for that blip, barely breathing. Seconds drag by like frozen water over a dam.

"Come on, Mr. C." My voice is a quiet plea. "Come on..."

Nothing changes. I say a mental prayer as we wait, transfixed.

"It didn't take." Tessa breaks the silence.

"Chest compressions." Clasping my hands, I place them on his chest and begin to pump up and down as the new nurse continues with the ventilation. We count in time.

All eyes are on the monitor, waiting for it to blip again.

"Come on..." My voice is a low growl this time.

Every muscle in my body is tight, and I'm right back in that place reliving it. Another life in my hands, slipping through my fingers, and I'm powerless to stop it.

Fuck that. I'm not fucking powerless.

My jaw is tight, and I grind out a NO as my fists clench. I'm about to beat them against his chest, fractured ribs be damned, when a blip stops me. My lips part, and I hesitate, waiting.

We all hold our collective breaths as we stare, waiting for one more...

One more...

Blip! It comes.

Then another... another... steady, regular.

"We've got him!" Tessa cries, and my shoulders drop.

I step back, adrenaline flooding my veins so hard, I have to touch my eyes. No time for emotion. My fists unfurl, and I return to treatment mode.

"What happened?" The old man's voice is hoarse. He blinks at me first then Tessa and back to me.

That's when it happens—recognition breaks across his face, and his brow lowers. "Beckham Munroe. You've been stealing my watermelons again."

A laugh escapes my lips, and I shake my head. "Not today, Mr. C." Reaching out, I gently place my palm on his forehead. "Not today."

"You and that little girl... Edward's kids. Carly and Henry."

I'm still grinning, relief flooding my bloodstream as I glance up.

Tessa's brow is arched, and a half-grin curls her lips. "Stealing watermelons, Dr. Munroe?"

"I think we can rule out brain damage." Placing my hand on his chest again, I lean closer. "Fractured ribs, not so much."

His vitals are strong, and a heavyset young man steps up at the foot of the bed. "Uncle Jeb?"

I move away, allowing the nephew access to his uncle. The nurses can take it from here.

Stepping into the empty hallway, the commotion has cleared, and calm is momentarily restored. It won't last long, but I've got to get back up to twelve.

CARLY

"I can't believe you're exiling me to Eden." I'm speeding down Interstate 75 in my ancient, light-blue Ford F-150 to the small island community between Saint Petersburg and Fort Myers, where I spent the first twenty-one years of my life. "It's so unprofessional."

"It's not exile." My police chief Ronnie's voice carries through the portable Bluetooth speaker attached to my dash.

He sounds like he's smoked a pack a day for the full sixty years he's been alive. The truth is, he quit about ten years ago.

In my mind, I can see his black brow lowered over his creviced face, his white hair a mess from constantly shoving his hands in it. "Consider it witness protection."

"I'm not afraid of my patients, Ronnie."

"You should be afraid of this one, Carls. Those messages, that note... It's *Silence of the Lambs*-level shit. She wants to hurt you, and until we find her, you're on leave."

He's referencing an aggressive email and a poorly worded, hand-written letter from a female prisoner who recently went MIA while out on a limited-visitation furlough—which I recommended.

"Alize Willis is an impulsive young woman with bipolar disorder and mild paranoid delusions." My logical, therapist-brain calmly places her behavior in the appropriate boxes and makes the appropriate diagnosis. "She needs behavioral therapy and possibly a low dose of lithium."

"She needs to be behind bars. I was against letting her out from the start."

"It's rehabilitative for her to be in the community,

around people. The worst thing you can do for someone in her condition is lock her up."

"She's crazy."

"Calling women crazy is a cop-out, and you know it."

Using that term is also what makes them scary, makes them monsters. It's what leads to situations we all want to avoid.

"Have I told you you're a pain in the ass?"

I squint an eye, even though he can't see me. "Pretty much every day since I joined your unit."

His gravelly chuckle makes me grin. "How about you give that bleeding heart a rest and follow orders. You can't save them all, Miss Dennison."

"I am well aware of my limitations, Major Wilcox. How about you give that cave-man vibe a rest and start throwing a little trust my way?"

"I trust you. I also don't want to lose the best criminal psychologist on the force."

"Best... criminal..." I pretend to choke, but it breaks into a chuckle. "You must really be worried if you're giving me compliments."

"Shut up and let me know if you get a single crank call, text, email, letter. If a squirrel sits still too long, I want to hear about it."

"I will. I haven't worked in law enforcement this long not to have learned anything."

"Just do it. I'll be in touch."

We disconnect, and I chew the inside of my lip, thinking. I've known Ronnie Wilcox since I moved to Pensacola to join the police force right out of college. I completed my master's degree at night while getting my on-the-job training under the previous female psychologist, who retired once she pronounced me ready to take her place.

Ronnie's the closest thing I've had to a dad since my own passed when I was a kid, followed quickly thereafter by my mom, leaving my older brother Henry and me in the care of our aunt Vivienne in the tiny coastal community of Eden by the Sea.

I've never seen him so worried about a case before, and I'm trying to decide if he's right, and I'm being naïve or if I'm right, and he's watched too many movies.

I take a lot of shit from the old guys. They call me soft, bleeding-heart, and all those other labels that basically mean I'm weak and out of touch.

Only, I'm not weak, and Ronnie knows it. I'm kind to people when they need it most, and kindness is *not* weakness. It'd be great if more people internalized that message.

Still, I'm following orders and heading home for who knows how long.

Eden by the Sea. If you close your eyes and imagine white, sandy paths, picket fences, and canned lights, where people eschew driving cars for riding bicycles and leave their screen doors open at night, you're in the right place. I wonder if anything has changed since I left.

Tapping my phone face, I call my aunt. Her deadpan tone fills the cab after one ring, same as always, no greeting or formalities.

"Where you at?" Aunt Viv cuts straight to the point.

"Hey!" I make my voice light and upbeat. "Just crossing the Bridge. Should be there in a half-hour."

"Is there a fog?"

"Not a bit."

"Well, keep your eyes open. Jeb Callahan was in a wreck last week and had to stay in the hospital in Tampa for a few days."

My stomach plunges. "Is he okay?"

"Twenty-nine-car pileup—"

"Holy crap! Twenty-nine cars?"

"I keep saying these traffic engineers are trying to kill

us, bringing four lanes of busy highway together like that over the bay. It's thinning the herd."

"Is he back home now?"

"He got home a few days ago. Doesn't seem too different, but time will tell."

Aunt Viv is the original Debbie Downer. I've occasionally wondered if my stubborn optimism is my way of rebelling against her persistent pessimism.

"If they sent him home, I'm sure he's fine."

"I'm not so sure." Her tone drips with skepticism. "It only takes a few seconds of oxygen deprivation for dementia to take hold."

"Aunt Viv! He is not demented."

"I hope you're right." She exhales dramatically. "Well, I'd better let you go. Distracted driving is the number one cause of car accidents."

My eyes roll, but I don't groan, *Oh my God!* Or make any of my other, former teenage epithets.

Instead, I hold my smile firmly in place. "I'll be there soon."

Ending the call, I shake my head. *Damn*, being a mature adult is hard, but I guess if I can be patient with mentally ill strangers, I can be patient with my somewhat sane aunt.

She's getting older, and with the way I've been working for the last several years, I've had zero time to drive home and check on her. This exile is probably a good thing. When older people are alone too much, they tend to get more suspicious and paranoid.

Only... she's always been this way, so that's no excuse.

Shaking my head, I gaze out the window at the stunning, blood-orange sunset over the bay. The truck windows are down, and my old radio plays classic rock. I let the cool, fall air sweep away my tension.

The bridge rises, and I catch a glimpse of the crystal-blue water stretching as far as the eye can see.

I lift my chin and belt out the chorus, "You're going to make me lonesome when you go!"

It's hard to resist the pull of my hometown. It awakens a familiarity deep in my soul, like it's imprinted on my consciousness. Being in Eden is effortless, intuitive. I know what to say and what to do. I know how people think. I know what to expect.

It's October. Halloween is coming, and a surge of warmth rises in my chest. I decide to reframe my "exile" into a sort of unplanned, paid vacation.

A toll booth is at the entrance to the bridge leading out to the island, and I smile at the young woman inside as I slow to a stop.

"Well, hey, there! That'll be one dollar or..." She leans out, studying my windshield. "You don't have a resident sticker, so—"

She leaves the statement hanging, and I briefly consider telling her I grew up here. What's left of my little family still lives here. Instead, I flip down the sun visor and a five-dollar-bill falls into my lap.

"Here you go." I pass it over, and she gives me my change.

"Finally got a break from the heat. Looks like it's going to be a great week at the beach." Her pale blue eyes sparkle, and her stringy blonde hair is tied up in a high ponytail with whisps swirling around her face.

"I'll have to get out there, then."

"You're not a tourist?"

Nobody is behind me, and I take a minute to chat. Socializing is a way of life along the coast. "I'm actually visiting my aunt. Vivienne Dennison? She lives over on Pine Run."

"Miss Viv?" The girl's brow rises, and she almost looks horrified. She recovers fast. "She's an interesting lady."

I swallow a laugh. My aunt is a grumpy old crone, especially when it comes to anyone under twenty. "She's newsy, I guess." *Bad* newsy.

Her face brightens. "Are you from Eden?"

"I was for about twenty-one years. I'm up in Pensacola now."

"Well, welcome home! I'm Sadie Frost. If you need anything, just let me know!" She's a sweet teenager, and I nod.

"Thank you, Sadie. I'm Carly Dennison. Maybe I'll see you around."

A truck pulls up behind me and honks, and I shift into drive, giving him a wave.

"Oh, keep your shirt on!" Sadie grouses. "Nice to meet you, Carly!"

I wave as I pull away, and I'm officially home.

It takes less than two minutes to cross the pass connecting the two miles of island to the mainland. The southern half of the island is pristine Eden by the Sea, while the northern half is Pleasure Island, where most of the worker bees live. It's a bit spicier, less expensive.

The tourists are all segregated to the middle of the island, closest to the bridge, while the permanent residents are farther apart on each end.

I take a left, heading south, and when my tires hit the red-brick road, I drop my speed to a crawl. Ancient palm trees stretch over the median, and white picket fences line the yards.

A group of bikers are in front of me, and I slow even more. A family walks from the beach, and I pause to let them cross the street.

The first house to greet me when I reach the residential portion of Eden is an enormous mansion. It's dark and closed, and "Ocean Pearl" is painted in pale blue script on the white, wooden sign attached to the white picket fence surrounding the yard.

My stomach tightens at the sight of it. Memories rush back, hitting me so hard, it's like the storm surge ahead of a hurricane. Ocean Pearl is the old Munroe place, the most expensive estate in Eden and property of the family who used to own the whole island.

They're all in Tampa now, and only one member of that family ever came here—a boy with brilliant blue eyes and wavy dark hair. A boy whose smile lit up my insides before I even knew what that meant.

Every summer he came here with an entourage of staff and caretakers, and I pause in the street to lean forward and stare at the dark windows. I half-expect to see his face gazing back at me. My chest tightens, and heat floods my stomach.

I shake it away. Beck Munroe is long gone, and those days are far behind me in the rearview mirror. Still, touching them aches like a bruise. *Is this why I haven't returned since the day I left?*

"Ridiculous," I grumble.

I've worked hard to categorize Beck Munroe and everything that happened between us as a learning experience and nothing more. I won't allow this time at home to upend all the progress I've made.

"Go away, ghosts," I whisper, shoving my dark hair behind my ears and steering the truck towards my aunt's house. "You're in my past, and that's where you'll stay."

DEAR READER

I hope you enjoyed Meadow and Asher's story! If you have a few minutes to spare, please consider leaving a review on Amazon, Goodreads, and BookBub. Reviews and sharing your love for our stories mean the world to an author. Just a few lines goes a long way!

You can also connect with me on social media to be sure and never miss a new release, event, or sale!

Subscribe: smarturl.it/KK_MailList
Instagram: Instagram.com/KKAllen_Author
Facebook: Facebook.com/AuthorKKAllen
TikTok: Tiktok.com/@k.k.allen
Website: www.KKAllen.com

Join Forever Young
Enjoy special sneak peeks, participate in exclusive giveaways, enter to win ARCs, and chat it up with K.K. and special guests ;)

➜ Facebook.com/groups/foreveryoungwithkk

CENTER OF GRAVITY

If you loved Fired Up *then you'll love this steamy forbidden romance! Here's a peek...*

Chapter One

"I got an audition," Shane announced when he walked into the apartment, slamming the door behind him. A grand flourish if I'd ever seen one. Not even I would walk ten blocks in four-inch stilettos. But that was Shane, my six foot two inches of a man-friend whom I'd known since our very first dance class back in Seattle at age five.

His jersey bag landed at his feet, and his hands pumped the air as they often did when he was overly excited about something. "Sorry. Not *just* an audition. I got an *invite*."

My eyes grew wide, excitement flourished quickly, then anxiety ripped through me at the speed of a freight train. So many emotions all at once. Up until that point, everything had been good. We'd been living off our savings, spending as little money as possible, and taking a variety of classes at Gravity Dance Complex, the premiere studio of the commercial dance world. No pressure. Just fun.

"An *invite*? For the Janet gig?" my voice squeaked. I scrambled to my knees. "But we've only been here three months. Is that even possible?"

He winked. "When your name's Shane Masterson, anything is possible, honey."

I fought back a groan. Shane had always been innocently cocky, aware of what his charm did to the human race. He was devilishly handsome, too, with raven-black hair cut short on the sides and always spiked in one direction or the other, rarely in the middle. But it was his personality that won everyone over. And yes, for Shane, *anything* definitely seemed possible.

Refusing to respond to his joke, I crossed my arms. "I thought we decided to wait. We're finally getting into a rhythm here. You can't—"

"Lex." He pursed his lips as if he were about to scold me. "I got an *invite*. I'm not going to turn it down. That would be career suicide, and you know it."

I was speechless. Professional gigs for music videos and stage shows came through Gravity all the time. It was the mecca of dance talent where A-list celebrities and casting directors nationwide frequently recruited, primarily for stage, television, and film bookings. Shane and I had talked about attending an open audition *one day* after getting our feet wet. The plan was always to take the plunge together. But getting an *invite* to audition was rare. He couldn't turn it down, not even if he wanted to.

My mind was still reeling as Shane started to raid the cabinets, though I wasn't sure what for. The only food remaining was the jar of peanut butter that sat half empty on the counter. He must have realized it almost as fast as I thought it, and he slammed the door shut. "We're ordering a pizza."

"Shane," I warned. We'd set aside money for one year of dance classes and rent. He knew we didn't have money to indulge.

"Lex," he warned back. "We dance eight to ten hours a day. You've still got that ass, but I will not be held responsible for you turning into a pile of bones. It's time to indulge in a big ole pie of heaven."

I let out a laugh despite the residual shock from the bomb he'd just dropped. Leave it to Shane to mask any tense situation with the topic of food.

"Look," he said, his sweet smile telling me he knew he'd won. "Just think. If I get this gig, we'll be better off. We can't take classes and live off Skippy and ramen while we wait for something to happen. Aren't you tired of waiting, baby girl?"

"Yes, but—"

He popped his hip and pursed his lips. "But what?"

"You'll get the job." I didn't mean for my voice to come out so whiny, but we'd just moved to LA.

"You don't know that."

"Maybe not this job, but it won't take you long. And then what? You might have to leave LA ... and leave me here ... alone."

He tilted his head and quirked his lip. "So dramatic."

I bit back my smile. The exaggerated pout was a little much.

"You could start auditioning too."

"Ha," I said on a sarcastic breath.

"C'mon, Lex. It's just like dating. You have to put yourself out there. Let them know you're interested. Check out your options." His eyes lit up, and he smacked the counter before leaning forward. "Speaking of dating options."

Oh no, here we go. My entire body cringed.

"There is this gorgeous hunk of man who teaches some of my classes. Do you know Reggie Maynor?" He fanned himself with his hand as his lids fluttered dramatically. "Dear Lord." But when he looked up and my expression hadn't changed, he threw his hand down while rolling his eyes. "Doesn't matter. You'd know who he was if you saw him. Anyway. He was trying to be sly, but he was asking about you today."

I knew exactly who he was talking about, but I didn't come to LA to find a man. So I chose to ignore his second attempt at changing the conversation.

"You know I'm not ready to audition yet. I thought we *both* wanted to get some training first and—"

"We've been training our whole lives. This is why we're here. Besides, what better training than to audition and check out the competition?"

I snapped my mouth shut. He was right, but I wasn't ready to pay the ultimate price of my dream—losing my best friend. Not yet. Frustration shook through me. "Who gave you the invite?"

"Her name's Janelle. She scouts for a bunch of artists. Heard she's friends with that dreamy choreographer you love too. Theodore Noska." When his eyebrows wiggled suggestively, I picked up the nearest object and chucked it at him. My black-and-pink tennis shoe smacked him in the chest, causing him to shoot me a glare and stab a finger in the air. "I'm dragging your freckled ass to the next open audition just for that."

I wanted to scream. He didn't get it. In this industry, it wasn't enough to be the best dancer in the room. It was about friendships, connections, timing, and a little bit of luck. I saw the way the veteran dancers had looked at Shane and me when we first arrived, some with their side-eye glances or, worse, those who didn't see us at all. We were blips on their radars, passersby there for the experience, and immediately dismissed as contenders. I wanted that to change—I wanted to earn my spot.

And maybe somewhere deep down there was fear of failure too. Of getting rejected for the one thing I loved most in the world. I'd only ever had a plan A, despite my parents' wishes. And taking class was fun. Taking class didn't lead to the inevitable disappointment that came with this industry.

I was comfortable, but maybe that was a bad place to be. Still, the insecurities swarmed my chest, and I couldn't let them go.

"Do you know how many times I've been told I won't make it as a professional dancer? I'm not ready to hear it from the people who matter. This studio ... those dancers ... the choreographers. I need this community to accept me. If I ever get a job, I want them to know I earned it."

Shane's expression changed drastically from the happy-go-lucky man who walked through the door minutes ago to someone with only my best interests at heart. I cringed at the ass kicking to come.

"Don't let your father's words hold you back, Lex. That's all they are. *Words*. You're here because you belong here, and you'll see in time, it was the right decision."

His comment hit me in the gut.

"I will?"

"Yes." He leveled me with his eyes. "You're the biggest fucking rock star on that dance floor, Alexandra Lorraine Quinn, and I'm not just saying that because you bought me my first pair of stilettos."

I giggled, but his eyes remained serious.

"You think those dancers are going to respect you if they see you taking a million classes before you ever audition?" He shook his head emphatically. "Wrong, sweetheart. They won't even know your name until you slap a numbered sticker on those tight abs of yours, strut onto that dance floor like you think you're Beyoncé, and then fail—and then fail again. And third"—his eyes narrowed on mine, silencing my giggles—"the only person holding you back from your dream is you."

My eyes filled with tears as he made his way over to my air mattress, plopped down, then pulled me into his arms. I loved the closeness we'd maintained all these years. I loved how Shane had always been the one to push me toward my dreams and comfort me when things didn't go as planned. So yeah, I was terrified for all of that to go away. And I could feel it in the air; the time was coming.

Shane lived life full out. Nothing scared him. Nothing was worth backing down for. That might have been what I loved most about him. He'd faced all kinds of adversity, from his sexual orientation to surviving a toxic home life to always being considered freakishly tall compared to the rest of our peers. And all that was mixed with the ridicule he'd received for being a male dancer among our adolescent peers. He never let anything stop him from reaching what he wanted.

Shane and I were opposites.

Doer versus dreamer. Life of the party versus wallflower. And for some reason, we loved each other more for it all. We balanced each other. Or rather, *he* balanced *me*.

When Shane spoke next, my head was tucked safely under his chin.

"You might never feel ready, Lex. You just have to take a leap at some point. It might as well be now. It's time to fly, baby girl."

Chapter Two

The next audition didn't appear on the bulletin board in Gravity's community area until a couple weeks later. "You're coming with me to this one," Shane had demanded that night over a homemade platter of meats and cheeses.

I hadn't put up an argument since the Janet audition was a sore subject. Shane hadn't even made it past the first round of cuts, but at least he had tried, which was a hell of a lot more than I had done since venturing with him to LA. Maybe he was right about auditioning for the experience. When I thought about it like that, the outcome didn't seem so intimidating.

We were lined up in the hall, waiting to register for a music video for up-and-coming urban pop artist, Dominic Rivas, when a couple of girls in front of us started to whisper.

"Oh my God. He's here."

"Who?"

"Theodore Noska."

A gasp.

"Where?"

"He just walked in the front door."

As soon as the words left the girl's mouth, the world around me began to spin in slow motion. Voices played through a vacuum, muffled and quiet, conveniently drowning out their gushing. And my movements decelerated, as if I were being dragged through quicksand.

"Ho-ly shit." Shane's voice pulled me to the surface. He'd spotted Theo too.

Refusing to turn toward the rising commotion, I looked up at Shane just as he peered down at me. The sight of his whiskey eyes and jaw agape was enough to warn me that Theo Noska was every bit as delectable as he appeared in the media.

My body began to quake, a ridiculous reaction to a celebrity, but Theo wasn't just a celebrity. He was everything. He was all that I aspired to be and the one person whose opinion would mean the most, if I was ever lucky enough to have it.

Shane's warm fingers landed on my shoulders and swiveled me to face front. He turned my head toward the dance god himself.

The first thing I noticed was wild sandy blond hair—a perfect display of controlled chaos that one could happily sink fingers into in the throes of passion. Because clearly, there was only one good reason to have hair that sexy. Paired with the dark shades that masked his eyes, a leather jacket wrapped around his upper body, and ankle-length black jeans, he was every bit as intimidating as his choreography.

"Absurd." Shane groaned, and I could have sworn drool was pooling in his mouth.

Sure, Theo was all kinds of gorgeous, but it wasn't his looks that had made me fall in love with him from afar. I'd obsessed over his YouTube channel since its inception and had perfected every single one of his routines that I could lay eyes on.

He was hip-hop and contemporary fused with elements of ballet, jazz, tap, Bollywood, and every other dance style I could think of. His choreography could be epically dark and twisted or immensely beautiful and romantic, sending an audience to the edge of their seats while tears streamed down their faces.

All of America had watched the episode of *Dance Idol* where he came on as a guest choreographer and taught a contemporary partner routine to the finalists. The dancers executed the number flawlessly, but it was the emotionally charged choreography that made the video clip go viral. I remembered watching the routine and knowing that if

Theo Noska wasn't a household name before that day, he would be after.

My heart beat like crazy just thinking about it.

Theo had put Gravity Dance Complex on the map, so it wasn't a complete surprise he'd shown up. I even hoped he would offer a class or two so I could mark that one off my bucket list. But I studied the weekly schedules as if that were my job, and Theo's name never appeared on any of them. *So, what is he doing here now?*

My eyes followed as he inched his way down the corridor in my direction then stopped briefly and collected a few fist bumps and one-armed hugs. He didn't stop for long or smile for anyone as he drew closer.

"Yo, Theo. What's up, buddy?" someone behind me called.

Theo was only a few feet away when he did a quick sweep of the line before giving an uptick of his chin to whoever had greeted him.

Then his head dropped slightly, his gaze connecting with mine—I thought. Theo's glasses hid everything, so I couldn't be entirely sure. It was just a second, a flash, but I felt it—a connection I don't think I could have made up despite my fierce crush on a man I knew only from his interviews. I wanted to stretch time to stay a little longer in the moment because the instant it was gone, I knew I would never get it back again.

I was lost in my thoughts when I felt fingers splay across my back. A shove thrust me onto my toes, tipping me off balance.

What the—?

I shot forward, my hands reaching in front of me, ready to catch my fall, when I realized only one thing was there. Or one man, rather.

Theo's arms reached out, his expression unchanged, as if catching me were the most natural thing in the world.

My palms slammed against his chest just as his arms wrapped around me. Then he stood me up, his grip firm as I stared into his glasses, desperate to see past the reflection of myself.

All I could think about was the sturdiness of his form, the strength of his hold, and how absolutely consuming his rough, calloused hands were as they skimmed the bare skin of my shoulders and arms.

"Think you can be more careful next time?" He grumbled the words over my shoulder, snapping me back to the present.

Shane. A snare shot off in my chest. *He pushed me.* It had to have been him. But I didn't want to pull away from Theo long enough to confirm my suspicions.

"This is a dance studio, not a mosh pit." Theo's accusing tone was filled with raspy disapproval. He shifted me slightly, scenting the air with fresh apple cinnamon and leather, an intoxicating mixture that left me dizzy. "You don't want to be responsible for shortening this young girl's career. Apologize."

I turned then, ready with my glare as I caught the eyes of my best friend.

I'm going to kill him.

"I'm sorry, Lex." Shane's tone was sincere, but there was no denying the hint of amusement it carried. Theo's arms left me, forcing me to stand on my own. I turned around, ignoring Shane and offering my savior a polite smile.

"Thank you for catching me."

He didn't smile. In fact, his brows stayed dented in the center. "Glad you're okay." He didn't ask whether I was, and he didn't wait for me to reply. Instead, he aimed one final look at Shane, the crease lines in his forehead expressing his annoyance.

"It was just an accident," Shane pressed, pulling me

into his arms in what I'm sure was meant to be an apologetic hug.

But as Theo backed away and continued down the corridor without another pause, I was certain it wasn't an accident at all.

❤❤❤

"I should murder you."

I was patient enough, waiting until we'd left the dance studio later that day to let Shane have it. We had just started our ten-block walk to our place, and I felt as if I would burst if I didn't say something.

His laughter started, and I threw an arm out, knocking him in the stomach. He cringed and swooped me up cradle-style, despite my flailing limbs.

"Put me down, you big, giant asshole."

His laughter never ceased and only grew louder. "You should be thanking me. And I'm not letting you down until you promise to keep your hands to yourself. You heard what Theodore said about being careful. Oh, and what else? Shortening the life of this young girl's career." He burst into another fit of laughter. "He thinks you're twelve."

I was mortified and completely furious at my best friend.

"Let me down, or I'm moving back to Seattle."

"Oh, stop it. You would never."

"You have no idea what I'm capable of doing right now, Shane Masterson. And right now, you are not my best friend. You're this evil *thing* of a person sent to earth to destroy me. Right now, I hate you. I can't believe you did that to me. Why? I just want to know why you felt the need to embarrass me in front of the one person—*the one person*—I care about impressing."

Shane put me down, leaving a hand on my shoulder. I shook myself away, and his laughter finally silenced. "Oh, Lex. I'm sorry. If it makes you feel better, I think I'm officially on Theo's shit list. He was mad at me, not you."

"No," I squealed. "That does not make me feel better. We're in this together, remember? Don't make me regret signing up for tomorrow's audition."

"Okay, okay. But at least you got to touch him. How did he feel? Please tell me his skin is as soft and velvety as it looks." His head snapped toward me. "Oh my God. How did he smell? Like sunshine and roses? No. I bet it was more like dandelions after a warm rain shower."

It was Shane's heavy, dreamlike sigh that broke the spell. I laughed, because laughter was so much easier than staying mad at my best friend.

"Thank God," Shane said, clearly noting my amusement. "I cannot handle angry Alexandra. You remind me of your mother, all spun up and spewy, like a whacked-out sprinkler system." He shook his head as if disturbed by whatever visual had played in his mind. "Hey, let's go out to eat."

The change of subject happened so fast my brain did a complete three sixty.

"No. Not until you explain to me what the fuck you were thinking back there. You thought that was how to get Theo to notice me? Really?"

He gasped and held up a finger, tsk-tsking me. "Cussing sounds dirty coming from your mouth. Don't do it."

"Shane," I shot out. It was my final warning.

"Fine. He was standing right there in front of you, and I could practically see the little Theo and Lex babies running around in the background. It was this sixth sense. I pictured the entire epic love connection. You know, the ones you see all the time in movies, where the couple makes eye contact for the first time and these little stars and hearts start fluttering around the air."

"Yeah, pretty sure I've never seen a movie like that."

He stomped his foot and placed his fists on his hip. "Whatever. You've only been in love with the guy for the past decade. I was trying to help you out."

"How'd that go for you?"

He pursed his lips, as if deep in thought. "At least you can count on the guy if you ever decide to play 'Trust Fall.' He caught you, didn't he? And then he asked if you were okay."

I rolled my eyes as hard as I could. "Wow. Yeah. I think it's love. Maybe he'll fly me to his summer house in Spain and propose to me there."

Shane's eyes grew wide. "He has a summer house in Spain? Is it nice? I'm sure it's—"

"Shut up!" I growled.

Keep reading for FREE with Kindle Unlimited: www.smarturl.it/centerofgravity

MORE K.K. ALLEN BOOKS

Up in the Treehouse

Haunted by the past, Chloe and Gavin are forced to come to terms with all that has transpired to find the peace they deserve. Except they can't seem to get near each other without combatting an intense emotional connection that brings them right back to where it all started... their childhood treehouse.

Under the Bleachers

Fun and flirty Monica Stevens lives for food, fashion, and boys... in that order. The last thing she wants to take seriously is dating. When a night of flirty banter with Seattle's hottest NFL quarterback turns passionate, her care-free life could be at risk.

Through the Lens

When Maggie moves to Seattle for a fresh start, she's presented with an unavoidable obstacle—namely, the cocky chef with a talent for photography and getting under her skin. Can they learn to get along for the sake of the ones they love?

Over the Moon

Silver Livingston has spent the past eight years hiding from her past when the NFL God, Kingston Scott, steps off the bus to mentor a football camp for kids. Kingston wants to be anywhere but at Camp Dakota... until he sees her. The intoxicating woman with the silver moon eyes, the reserved smile, and the past she's determined to keep hidden.

Dangerous Hearts (A Stolen Melody, #1)

Lyric Cassidy knows a thing or two about bad boy rock

stars with raspy vocals. In fact, her heart was just played by one. So when she takes an assignment as road manager for the world famous rock star, Wolf, she's prepared to take him on, full suit of heart-armor intact.

Destined Hearts (A Stolen Melody, #2)
With stolen dreams, betrayals, and terrifying threats--no one's heart is safe. Not even the ones that may be destined to be together.

British Bachelor
Runaway British Bachelor contestant, Liam Colborn, is on the run from the media. When he gets to Providence to stay with his late brother's best friend, all he wants is a little time to regroup from his time on a failed reality show. That is, until he meets the redheaded bombshell nanny who lives in the pool house.

Waterfall Effect
Lost in the shadows of a tragedy that stripped Aurora of everything she once loved, she's back in the small town of Balsam Grove, ready to face all she's kept locked away for seven years. Or so she thinks.

A Bridge Between Us
With a century-old feud between neighboring families with only a bridge to separate them, Camila and Ridge find themselves wanting to rewrite the future. It all starts with an innocent friendship and quickly builds to so much more in this epic second chance coming of age romance.

Center of Gravity (Gravity, #1)
Lex was athleticism and grace, precision and passion, and she had a stage presence Theo couldn't tear my eyes

from. He wanted her...on his team, in his bed. There was only one problem... He couldn't have both.

Falling From Gravity (Gravity, #1.5)
Amelia was nothing like Tobias had expected. Even after all the years—of living so close to her, of listening to her giggle with his sister in the bedroom next to his—he hadn't given much thought to his sister's best friend, until a secret spring break trip to Big Sur changed everything.

Defying Gravity (Gravity, #2)
The ball is in Amelia's court, but Tobias isn't below stealing —her power, her resolve, her heart. When he wants a second chance to reignite their connection, the answer is simple. They can't. Not unless they defy the rules their dreams were built on and risk everything.

The Trouble With Gravity (Gravity #3)
When Sebastian makes Kai an offer she can't afford to refuse, she learns taking the job will mean facing the tragedy she's worked so hard to shut out. He says she can trust him to keep her safe, but is her heart safe too?

Enchanted Gods
As powerful forces threaten the lives in Apollo Beach, Katrina can't escape the evocative world of mythological enchantment and evil prophecies that lurk around every corner. If only she wasn't cursed.

Find them all FREE in Kindle Unlimited

ACKNOWLEDGMENTS

WE DID IT! To my Bayside Babes—Tia Louise, Kandi Steiner, and Harloe Rae—I've had so much fun working with you, collaborating, and creating our fun world. I feel so lucky to be part of something so special.

To first responders everywhere who put their lives at risk every day to help others. Your heroism inspired Asher's character. Thank you for all that you do.

Along with that note, a special thanks to my betas who helped me through some of the tougher parts of this novel. Erin and Jenna, I'm so thankful for all the medical expertise you were able to share and hunt down for me. I couldn't have done this without you!

To Sammie, Cyndi, Patricia, Emily, and Renee—thank you for always reading my books early and sharing your thoughts. Your honest feedback and enthusiasm always play a huge role in making my stories the best they can be.

To my son, Jagger, who gave me all the ideas for little Tate, pumpkin guts and all. You have the biggest heart, the best smile, the warmest hugs, an exciting love for football (go Seahawks), and I love you to infinity times infinity. Thank you for making me the happiest momma.

To my bestie Heather. I just love you so much. Thank you for always being there with your undying support (and mad brainstorming skills). You're an incredible human and an even better friend. BESOS!

A special shoutout to the inspiration behind the Firefighters Calendar—the WSCFF Burn Foundation and all the wonderful people I was able to work with during those years! What a fun and rewarding experience that was.

Now, for that cover. Let me take a moment to raise the roof for Kandi Steiner and her cover expertise, along with Lauren Perry Watson for her photography skills. Y'all are such a dreamy combination.

I want to thank my editors at Red Adept Editing. I really can't say enough about your professionalism and your sharp eyes when it comes to reviewing my manuscripts. I can always trust that I'm in the right hands. So thank you, Lynn and Darlene!

Aside from creating the story, I am blessed to have a team of loyal supporters who are always willing to shout me out. Angsters and Booksters. I love you all so so much.

Thank you to Forever Young for giving me the happiest place to hang out on the internet. It really does feel like we're all good friends. Best group ever!

Thanks to my beautiful assistant Lindsey who is days away from having her first baby! To Renee, again, for being far more than a beta reader to me. I love you both so much. And to Dani and the Wildfire team for all the support!

I truly do not know how anyone would ever know to read my books if it weren't for the wonderful bloggers who put in so much time and heart in recommending our books. Thank you for taking the time to read *Fired Up* and for sharing your love of this story with your friends and following. It means the world!

That's right, I'm saving the best for last. To you, the reader, for taking a chance on my words. I am beyond grateful for your support. I hope you loved Asher and Meadow's story!

Much Love XOXO,
K.K.

ABOUT K.K. ALLEN

K.K. Allen is a *USA Today* bestselling and award-winning author who writes heartfelt and inspirational contemporary romance stories. K.K. is a native Hawaiian who graduated from the University of Washington with an Interdisciplinary Arts and Sciences degree and currently resides in central Florida with her ridiculously handsome little dude who owns her heart.

K.K.'s publishing journey began in June 2014 with a young adult contemporary fantasy trilogy. In 2016, she published her first contemporary romance, *Up in the Treehouse*, which went on to win the Romantic Times 2016 Reviewers' Choice Award for Best New Adult Book of the Year.

With K.K.'s love for inspirational and coming of age stories involving heartfelt narratives and honest emotions, you can be assured to always be surprised by what K.K. releases next.

Printed by Amazon Italia Logistica S.r.l.
Torrazza Piemonte (TO), Italy

30500437R00187